Secret of the Rose

By

Ellen Dugan

Secret of the Rose

Edited by Katherine Pace

Cover art designed by Kyle Hallemeier

"Legacy of Magick" logo designed by Kyle Hallemeier

Copy Editing and Formatting by Libris in CAPS

ACKNOWLEDGMENTS

Thanks to the friends and family who have enthusiastically supported me.

A very special thank you to the folks who provided me with new and improved editing, for both content and copy.

Finally to the fans who gobbled up *Legacy of Magick* and demanded to know how soon the second book in the series would appear.

Here you go. Enjoy, and Blessed be.

CHAPTER ONE

The last thing I expected when I came home from the university that afternoon was to walk into the kitchen and trip over the body of a cheerleader.

My heart stopped in my chest as I saw bright red spilling out across the hardwood. Horrified, I grabbed for the counter to keep from falling on top of the body on the floor. My backpack fell off my shoulder, hit my bent elbow hard, and yanked me down. My long hair spilled in front of my face obscuring my vision, and for a couple of hideously long seconds, my mind raced as I imagined the worst.

The "body" that had been sprawled on her belly moved, and the heart that I swore had stopped in my chest began to beat again.

"Oh no, the paint!" someone squealed.

Paint. The spreading red pool was *paint.* I rapped my fist against my chest and tried to breathe while I waited for my heart rate to ratchet down from critical. Meanwhile, the girl I'd tripped over, who apparently was painting a large banner while lying on the floor, hopped up.

A half dozen other girls wearing cheerleading uniforms jumped up from various spots on the floor and scrambled to clean up the mess. *Oh god.* I flinched. *There are six uniformed high school cheerleaders in my Aunt's kitchen.*

I, Autumn Bishop, grad student, Seer, and the clumsiest Witch in town, had literally tripped over a football banner painting session.

Having The Sight, or being a clairvoyant, was a mixed blessing. Sure, the heightened instincts and accurate hunches helped in my everyday life. But I'd had to suppress my witchy talents for most of my life, and because of that, I was only now learning to embrace my psychic abilities. And as for my magick... it was still hit or miss.

Resigned, I shoved my hair out of my face, slung my stuff on the counter and reached for the garbage can under the sink. The least I could do was to offer to help clean up the mess I had caused.

Somebody tossed me a roll of paper towels while the rest of the girls bopped around the kitchen all perky, cute and energetic. Which was only *slightly* less disturbing than thinking that I had tripped over a dead body.

"Sorry…" I quickly searched the spot where I knew the name for the latest victim of my clumsiness would be embroidered. "Cypress. I didn't see you down lying down there," I said to the pretty girl with the caramel colored skin that I had fallen over.

"No worries," Cypress smiled at me, and started gingerly tucking paint-soaked paper towels in the garbage can that I held carefully away from my jeans.

Seeing the red smeared paper towels made my stomach roll. As I stared down at them, the noise of the cheer squad bopping around the kitchen faded away. I could hear my blood pounding in my ears, while my physical vision disappeared, replaced by a new scene all together.

Blood was splattered on a white paneled door, thick and deep crimson, it dripped slowly down. The blood was smeared and it spelled out a word. There were letters written in that blood. The vision started to fade away... so I focused my intention and reminded myself to reconnect to the earth. The vision returned, along with a feeling of dread, but I made myself look again. *Letters, scrawled across a white door. A red letter 'H'.* The mundane noises in the kitchen resumed, and the vision faded away.

Slowly, I came back to myself. It had been a quick precognitive vision, just a flash into the future. *And damn it, I ought to be used to these visions by now!*

I reminded myself that these witchy talents were a part of my family's legacy, and I really needed to learn to roll with them whenever they occurred. (Even when I saw and felt things that were less than pleasant.) Suppressing the shudder that was trying to take over my body, I began to focus on the present.

"You're not going to get sick are you?" Cypress said.

"Ah, no. I'm okay," I lied, and tried *not* to be creeped out by the disturbing images I'd seen.

"You look like you're gonna throw up," Cypress frowned at me.

I felt like I might throw up, but I tried to smile instead. "Nope. I'm good." I sat the garbage can down and purposefully looked anywhere else but at those red, dripping paper towels. Goose bumps ran down my arms as if I'd been hit by a cold breeze.

While the other girls rescued any other banners in the vicinity, Holly, my spirited cousin, grabbed a mop and a bucket from the garage and was competently filling it with water and soap. She turned from the sink and began to mop up any remaining paint.

"Let me do that," I offered. *There, that sounded almost normal.* I silently congratulated myself for keeping my cool around my empathic cousin. There was no reason for her to worry about the vision too.

"I've got this," Holly said waving me off, her strawberry-blonde curls bouncing as she turned to the other teenagers in the room. "Hey girls, this is my cousin, Autumn."

I was greeted with a chorus of hellos. I waved to the group and tried to settle down. Which was not as easy as people would think. After what we'd been through three weeks ago when my perfectly gothic cousin, Ivy — Holly's polar opposite twin sister— had been abducted, my nerves were stretched a little thin.

My musings were cut short as the girls all took their banners out to the garage to dry. The topic of their cheery discussion centered on their upcoming Homecoming parade, game and dance.

"Sorry, again," I said as a trio of cheerleaders carried a banner past me.

"It's not the first time paint has been knocked over," one of the girls said.

"I'm looking forward to the big Homecoming parade." I moved to hold open the door to the garage for them, and the comment about the parade earned me smiles all around.

My new home of William's Ford, Missouri was a pretty little college town with a strong love of high school football. It was also, as I'd recently come to learn, a town with plenty of secrets as well as magick. So, I was admittedly curious to see the ordinary side of things. After everything that had happened since I had moved here for grad school, *normal* would be a nice change of pace.

I walked over to Holly. "Where's Ivy?" I didn't want to hover, but I felt better when I knew where she was. I couldn't even imagine how my aunt let her daughter out of her sight these days. But Aunt Gwen was a very capable Witch. I imagined she was keeping tabs on her daughter through some type of sophisticated locator spell... or something along those lines.

"She's upstairs in the turret room." Holly neatly

dumped the mop water down the drain. "Go on up, so you can stop worrying about her."

"I will." I nodded at Holly's accurate perception. Turning to pick up my bags, I said to the group, "Bye girls, it was nice meeting you."

"Bye Autumn," responded each girl in a terrifyingly cheerful kind of unison.

Gathering my stuff, I headed upstairs. I tossed my purse and backpack on the padded bench at the foot of my bed and kicked off my neon green running shoes. My mismatched, ankle length socks clashed violently, but they made me smile. The right sock had purple and yellow stars while the left featured pink and green stripes.

I studied my reflection in the mirror over the dresser and discovered that my face was slightly pale, and my green eyes were a little too wide. I scowled at the mirror. "Some Witch you are. Pull it together." I told myself, and tucked my long brown hair behind my ears.

I stood there and made an effort to ground and center myself before I went to check on my cousin Ivy. After a few moments of concentrating on my breathing, I pulled my magickal energy towards my center, I felt steadier.

I checked my reflection again. *There, I don't appear quite so frazzled.* I pulled the chain on the Tiger's eye pendant I wore to the center of the scoop neck of my navy t-shirt. The golden striped stone was thought to be protective against dark magick, and I'll admit it did seem to make me feel less vulnerable these days. I psyched myself up, thinking to project self-confidence instead of anxiety, and moved to poke my head in Aunt Gwen's sitting room.

Ivy sat in the window seat of the turret, her back lit by the afternoon sun, with a half dozen modern books on magick spread around her. Ivy's hair was currently dyed a more natural color. And the soft brown shade still caught me off guard, I had gotten used to the coal black color. She sat in a full lotus position on the curved seat, and Celtic music played softly while she studied.

As soon as I saw her, any of the stress that I still carried from tripping over the "dead" girl downstairs and then the blood-spattered vision, slid away. I attempted casual and strolled into the turret room. "Hey Shorty."

"I'm five foot six. I am *not* short," Ivy said, not even glancing up from her book.

"You're still three inches shorter than me," I told her, hoping for a reaction. When I got nothing in response, I tried again. "What are you studying?" I asked, and scooped up a few books so I could sit next to her.

Ivy lifted her head. Her black eye and bruises were fading, but still visible. "I'm okay. Don't worry so much."

"I wasn't worried," I lied and drew my hair over one shoulder.

"Cousin, I could *feel* your worry as you walked up the stairs a little bit ago."

I frowned at her. "I didn't know you were empathic. I thought only Holly could read a person's emotions."

"Well, I don't consider myself especially empathic. But you tend to psychically broadcast your emotions. *Loudly*," she said.

"I do?"

"Yeah. You are going to want to work on that," Ivy said, and returned to her books.

"What do you suggest, Yoda?" I picked up a book as if the answers to her recommendation were to be found within.

Instead of answering me, she pulled her gray hoodie closer around herself. She flipped a page in her book, and tried to change the subject. "How's your contractor boyfriend doing?"

"He's been busy. He started gutting a house today." I smiled, thinking about him. A month and half ago Duncan Quinn and I had ran into each other, literally. Our attraction and magickal connection had been instant. At first, my family had been strongly against me having anything to do with a member of the Drake family. But they'd come around when it became clear that Duncan walked his own magickal path and was not a part of his family's tradition of darker practices.

We'd started working together when he wanted someone with landscaping experience to fix up the yard of one of the homes he was rehabbing. Now Duncan and I were officially dating. And after everything we had been through, it seemed really strange to do 'normal' things like other couples. It was fun and beautifully *ordinary* to go to the movies, get coffee, and go jogging together these days. I was looking forward to us attending the town's annual Halloween Ball, most of all.

I watched Ivy carefully as she sat there, pretending to read her books. She was withdrawn and much quieter since her ordeal. I didn't have to read her using The Sight to know that she wasn't okay. Call me psychic, but between the radical alteration to her appearance and the marked difference in her behavior, I was really worried about her.

I peered down at the books and ran my hands across the pages, searching for the topic of her study. I had made a promise to myself not to use my psychic or magickal abilities to riffle through anyone's head ever again after it had been done to me a few weeks ago. But scanning the books for a clue as to what she was studying? Sure, I'd do that and not feel guilty at all. So, I focused my growing witchy abilities on the pages, and then I *knew*.

She was searching for spells that would stop nightmares.

"You're having nightmares," I said. It wasn't a question.

Ivy flinched at that, but stubbornly kept her face turned down to the books. I slung an arm around her stiff shoulders and gave her a one-armed hug. Finally, she relented with a sigh and leaned her head on my shoulder. I waited a few seconds, tipped my head over on top of hers, and gave her shoulders a supportive squeeze.

"You're not the only one who is having trouble dealing with everything that has happened," I admitted. "I'm pretty jumpy myself, these days." I left out the part about having a bloody vision, and wanting to make her smile, I told her instead how I'd gotten a good scare tripping over the cheerleaders in the kitchen.

Ivy let out a snort of laughter, covered her mouth and laughed even harder.

"Don't laugh at me. I think I'm traumatized," I said, deadpan.

"Well, those damn cheerleaders can be pretty scary." Ivy shook back her hair, with a trace of her usual verve.

"I know, right?" I shuddered dramatically. "They were like *color coordinated*!" I whispered in mock-horror.

"Dear gods, no!" Ivy played along, knowing full well my aversion to anything that matched or coordinated.

"Even their big hair ribbons matched," I whispered to her. "They *must* be stopped."

Ivy shook her head at that and became very quiet again. The silence was so unusual for my fabulously dramatic, goth-girl cousin. Well, former goth-girl. I missed her crazy slogan t-shirts, dramatic hair color and makeup, and I really missed seeing her solid black, witchy outfits.

"Do you want to tell me what you're having nightmares about?" I asked her as carefully as possible.

"I re-live when I was taken," Ivy whispered. "And then I dream about the Blood Moon Grimoire."

The Blood Moon Grimoire was an antique book of dark and powerful magick. Linked to the energy of the current cycle of four successive lunar eclipses, it was a dangerous and deadly item that my family, and half of the Drake family, were at odds over. Take one missing, potent book of spells and add in a couple hundred years of bad blood between the Bishops and the Drakes that first began in Colonial era America, and what you have is an explosion looking for a place to go off. The first salvo in the recent conflict had been an ultimatum from Thomas Drake, to me: find the book and return it, or else. The second had been Ivy's abduction by his son, Julian.

"Do you dream about finding the rest of the grimoire?" I asked, and tucked her farther under my arm. Two other sections of the grimoire were still lost. And the segment we did have safely in our possession was not of much use to us. Bran, my older, annoying cousin, had concluded that the antique pages had been torn out of the *middle* of the old grimoire.

Ivy sighed. "No, I don't see the other pages."

"I understand that it's hard, but if you tell me exactly what images are in your dreams, I might be able to help."

"I dream about someone coming out of an arched red

door. They are carrying a big red leather book tucked under their arm like a football," Ivy said.

"You know..." I said to her, "that makes me wonder if you are seeing the past in the second part of your dream."

Ivy shifted her gaze to mine. "I never thought about that. I suppose I could be."

"The person carrying the book, do you recognize them?" I pressed her for an answer.

"I don't know." Ivy seemed to slump in defeat. "I can't see the person's face. I'm not even sure if it's a woman or a man holding the grimoire."

"When you think about the second half of the dream, are the images sharp and crisp?" I asked.

"Well, no." Ivy sat up straighter, and her green eyes cleared. "When I relive getting abducted it's crystal clear. It's like I'm there all over again... but the rest of the dream seems misty, and like the colors are faded."

"I bet you are dreaming about the distant past. When my dreams are out of focus and the colors seem washed-out, it generally means I'm *seeing* the past."

"I get that the book was stolen and hidden to protect the future generations..." Ivy leaned against me again. "But I'm afraid of what will happen while we search for the rest of the grimoire. An awful lot of people suffered the last time that book was around."

The price for stealing the Blood Moon Grimoire had been very high indeed. It was the reason my father and mother had packed up and relocated back east with a two-year-old me. So I had grown up in New Hampshire, completely unaware of my family's legacy of magick or the shared history of the two families. That is, until a couple of months ago when I had reconnected with my dad's side of the family.

"Do you think any of this would have happened if I hadn't moved here to go to grad school?" I asked her as we continued to sit there with Ivy's head on my shoulder.

"None of this was your fault. Besides, you can't run away from your destiny," Ivy said. I tried not to flinch at her statement, as she'd sounded eerily like her mother.

No you can't. I silently agreed.

I saw movement in the doorway and spotted Duncan standing in the entrance of the turret room with a big smile on his face. *But sometimes you could run literally smack right into it.* I smiled in return.

Duncan's dark blond hair had grown out over the collar of his shirt. He wore dark jeans and a clean button down chambray shirt that made his eyes seem a brighter shade of blue. "It's two of my favorite girls."

I didn't get up and go to him as I normally would have. He met my eyes, and I saw that he understood.

With a nod, he crossed the room and crouched down in front of Ivy and me. "How're you doing, Shorty?"

"I'm not short," Ivy sighed tiredly.

Duncan tipped her chin up with a finger and studied her healing bruises. "Yeah, you do look better. The hair color's new, isn't it?" he asked.

"I thought I'd try something different," she said, still too quietly.

Duncan rubbed a hand over his chin. "You think you would be up to going through a kitchen catalog with me?" he asked Ivy.

I watched Ivy brighten up a bit. She had a real interest in home repair and rehab, and so far, she hadn't had the chance to help out his crew on the weekends. "For the new project you started today?" she asked.

"The kitchen in the main house had to be gutted, and I thought you might have a thought or two on how I should rework the layout." Duncan stood, and hooked his thumbs in his front pockets. "I wanted to do something different this time and thought I'd ask you what your opinions were on color."

I stayed silent. I knew damn good and well he had an excellent eye for interiors, color schemes and layouts. I also had a hunch he was trying to find a way to distract and to cheer up Ivy. Since that night a few weeks ago, he'd become very protective of her.

"You have the catalogues with you?" Ivy asked and sat up straighter.

"And the dimensions and rough sketches of the kitchen," Duncan told her. "They're all downstairs on your dining room table."

"I'd really like to see them," Ivy said.

"Go ahead," I invited gesturing to the scattered books. "I'll put these away for you."

"I'll be right down," Duncan said as Ivy scrambled out of the room and headed for the stairs.

Once she was gone, he scooped me up right off the window seat and into a big kiss. I kissed him back, and for a few moments there wasn't anything else on my mind— not disturbing visions, or the search for the grimoire— nothing except the two of us and the energy we seemed to create every time we touched. When we finally came up for air, I threaded my hands through the hair that spilled over his collar. "That was really sweet, what you did for Ivy," I told him.

"I've been worried about her too."

"Well, I think you made her day. That kiss certainly made mine," I said.

He linked his hands around my waist and rested his forehead against mine for a few moments. "The guest cottage is all cleaned up now," he said carefully, as if testing his ground. "Maybe you could come over and see it, and we could actually spend some time alone."

I smiled up at him. The house he was rehabbing boasted a little guest house in the backyard. Duncan had moved out of the Drake family's mansion and into it a few weeks ago. "So, you got the painting all finished?"

"It's nothing fancy— but it will do me, for now."

Here it was. The next step in our relationship. I met his eyes. "Yes. I would like to come over and see your new place."

Duncan's eyes twinkled a bit and he pulled me close again. I let out a sigh and felt everything smooth out, simply by being in his arms. “Are you nervous?” he asked.

I grinned up at him. “Of being with you? No. It’s been a stressful couple of weeks. I feel like I’m waiting for the other shoe to drop,” I admitted.

“Well, try and relax. The second lunar eclipse has passed and *nothing* happened,” Duncan pointed out.

“I half expected your uncle to come bursting into the house the other night shooting lightning bolts out of his fingers and demanding the grimoire back.”

“That’s never going to happen.” Duncan ran his hands down my arms, as if to soothe me.

I stepped back and crossed my arms. “Your uncle doing *nothing* on that night has made me jumpier than if he would have simply come after us. You gotta admit, it was weirdly anti-climatic.”

And what a nerve-wracking night that second eclipse had been. We had gathered with my family and my aunt’s coven in the backyard of the manor house to watch the lunar eclipse— what they called a *blood moon*, back in the day. All had been calm and quiet as we’d watched the moon fall under the earth’s rusty colored shadow.

The coven had held a discreet full moon ritual in the back yard, and afterwards they’d gathered around the fire pit. They’d even drank wine and cider, roasted marshmallows and made S’mores! I still wasn’t sure if celebrating like that had been brave, or foolish. Not with waiting to hear what Julian’s fate would be, and

Thomas Drake lurking.

"Did you find out what happened with Julian's preliminary hearing?' I said. "What did the judge decide?"

"My uncle and his lawyers managed to convince the judge to drop the criminal charges against Julian," Duncan said.

"Seriously, after what he did to Ivy?" I was shocked at that. "*No* criminal charges?"

"I found out today, that in lieu of criminal charges, the judge ordered a drug rehab program and three months worth of inpatient psychological counseling for my cousin."

"So he's locked up good and tight." I turned away and went to look out the turret window. *Well, I suppose that was something.*

"A room in a locked psych ward is as good as a jail cell in my opinion. Maybe even better," Duncan said.

"What's going to happen when Julian gets out? What about the other eclipses?" I asked.

Duncan came over, tipped my chin up, and made me look at him. "Autumn, the third lunar eclipse won't be until April the fourth. So we have almost six months. The final lunar eclipse in the tetrad cycle won't occur until September twenty-eighth." Duncan managed to sound upbeat despite the seriousness of the situation we found ourselves in.

"I know, I memorized all the dates of the tetrad, too." I tried to smile at him, but it still felt like an axe was hanging over all our heads.

"Maybe we should let the search for the Blood Moon Grimoire rest for a while," he said.

"Ignoring the magickal threat won't make it go away," I argued.

"No, but we can recoup, prepare, and gather up our strength." Duncan moved his hands up to the back of my head and tangled his fingers in my long hair. I was about to argue another point, but he kissed me, effectively shutting me up.

"No more talk of my cousin and uncle. Not today," Duncan whispered. Gently tugging my hair back— a move that always made my knees go weak, Duncan lowered his lips to mine.

I tried to lose myself in the kiss. But part of my mind would not stop thinking about Thomas Drake and the grimoire.

We *had* to locate the remaining two thirds of that old spell book. Only then would we gain the knowledge needed to understand what Thomas Drake was really after. When we had the grimoire back and reassembled — we could stop him.

Once and for all.

CHAPTER TWO

The next few days passed quietly. Well, as quiet as it can be with cheerleaders bopping around the manor. I had retreated to my room to work on a paper for class as Holly and her cheer squad seemed to be underfoot more and more the closer it came to the big Homecoming Parade. A float was being built in the garage, which was also storing the colorful banners. Those terrifyingly perky girls had actually conned me into helping with the float a few times. It wasn't a horrible experience, but I never wanted to see yellow and royal blue tissue paper again.

Merlin always seemed to be dragging a tissue paper flower or a bit of crepe paper around the house lately. He was in kitty heaven being cooed over by the girls on the squad. At the moment, he was crashed out on the foot of my bed, one white tipped paw wrapped protectively around a chewed up tissue paper flower he had probably liberated from the homecoming float.

I took a break and set my laptop aside to charge it. A

soft breeze blew in my room and set the prisms that hung on clear line spinning. Rainbows from the refracted light of the prisms danced across the walls. I stood up to stretch, glanced out the window and noticed a woman kneeling in the rose garden along the side of the manor.

She was working on the plants and appeared to be trimming them back. I pulled the curtains back farther so I could study her. I knew Gwen was at the shop until five, so I was curious about what the woman was doing there. Was she a friend of Gwen's, maybe? I sincerely doubted she'd be a minion of Thomas Drake's, as she was out there in broad daylight. But still... it worried me. A few moments later, I had shrugged on my denim jacket and was walking around the side of the manor to confront her.

"Hello?" I called out. As I strolled closer, I saw that she was an older woman. She wore well used denim overalls. A thin pink sweater was buttoned over them. As she turned to face me, I saw that silly, hot pink flowers decorated the brim of her gardening hat. Hardly the outfit of a person bent on evil, or searching clandestinely for the grimoire.

"Well," she said with a nod. "I wondered when you'd finally come and see me."

"Ma'am, can I help you?" I asked as politely as possible in case she was lost or confused. It's not everyday you discover an older stranger gardening in your own rose garden.

She studied me for a long moment. “You look like Arthur.”

The comment had me reconsidering her. *Must be a neighbor or a friend of the family,* I guessed. “I know, thank you.” I ignored the little pang her comment about my resemblance to my father had caused.

She gave a nod and started to prune a tall hybrid tea rose bush. “If you keep these bushes pruned, they’ll continue to bloom through November,” she said.

“Does Gwen know you’re here?” I asked, thinking that might be the most polite way to find out if she was supposed to be in our gardens.

“Of course.” She seemed to find that hilarious and let loose a cackle of laughter in reply.

Oh. Maybe she was swapping plants with Gwen or helping out with the gardening. I watched her prune back the roses, and, whoever she was, she knew her way around plants. She moved from bush to bush clearing away deadwood and old spent blossoms. She stopped and tilted her head to look at me. Almost as if she knew I was sizing her up for up any possible hostile intentions.

As she met my eyes, I felt a wave of warmth and affection. Those blue eyes weren’t confused or malevolent. Whoever she was, I had a hunch this older lady was harmless, and sharp as a tack. *Aw, the hell with it.* I followed my gut hunch, walked over, and knelt down beside her.

“Since you know who I am, why don’t you tell me

your name?" I asked.

"You can call me Ro." She tucked a long strand of gray hair under her hat, then kept right on pruning.

I watched her chuck a stem over her shoulder and towards the bucket at her side. *Two points.* I settled in and prepared to be entertained. "Hello Ro. It's nice to meet you."

"We've met before." Another stem dropped into the bucket. "I used to change your diapers, young lady." She seemed to be chastising me.

"Oh," I smiled at her tone, "close friend of the family, are you?"

Ro pushed her silly straw hat back, revealing shiny silver hair and looked me square in the eye. "You need to study the family tree girl. Discover your roots."

Her comment wiped away my smile. I was starting to get a weird feeling in the pit of my stomach.

"So you're settling in now. Embracing your power and stretching your wings a bit." She neatly cut a long stemmed purple rose from a bush and set it at the base of a statue of the goddess Diana. "It's been hard waiting for you to notice me."

Notice her? "I don't understand." I felt the hair rise up on the back of my neck.

"Just remember, my girl— I'll be right here if you need any help."

"Okay. That's good to..." I sputtered to a halt as Ro began to fade away.

"Shit!" I squeaked. *Another freaking ghost!* I

scrambled up and backed up from the apparition a few feet. The scent of roses hit me, intense and sweet, and I froze.

"You can always find me by the roses." Ro's voice was still strong, even as her image became transparent. The aroma of roses in the air faded. I blinked— and she was gone.

A breeze came through and a few bright orange maple leaves tumbled down to land between where I stood and the now empty area of the rose garden. I walked carefully forward to double check and discovered the purple colored rose that Ro had cut was still lying neatly at the base of the goddess statue. My mind raced as I stood in the October sunlight, and trembled.

Was that rose real or not? Quickly, before I could change my mind, I bent over and tried to grab the flower. "Ouch!" I swore as I pricked my thumb on the thorns. The flower was definitely real. I lifted it up to study it carefully. "How could a ghost have affected physical reality like that?" I said to myself.

It was a damn good thing I had enjoyed the last couple of weeks of almost-normalcy. Because apparently those nice, average days were over for the time being. I walked back to the manor, shoulders slumped, and I resisted the urge to look back. I made it without incident. Once I was safely back in my own room, I sat the rose on my nightstand, grabbed a notebook and tried to write down everything I could recall about what I had experienced. Gwen had suggested journaling as a part of my magickal studies, and this seemed like the perfect time to begin.

When I'd seen and communicated with David Quinn's ghost last month, I had dearly hoped that it had been an isolated incident. My cousin, Bran, had even commented about me having mediumship skills. I had sincerely hoped he was wrong, but now I had to wonder. I began to doodle on my notepad, reflecting on my latest ghostly encounter.

Yes, I was a Seer or clairvoyant— and had what they used to call in the old days "The Sight." I'd hidden or pushed aside my ability as best I could my whole life. Well, I *had* hidden it up until I moved here with my father's family. Living with Witches granted me the freedom to let my abilities, both psychic and magick, all come out. But letting my powers out to play had allowed other talents I'd never even known about rise to the surface as well. And while these had been exciting, I'll be damned if they weren't troublesome and sometimes a little spooky.

According to my own research, being a clairvoyant did *not* mean I was destined to communicate with the spirit world. Mediumship and clairvoyance were two totally separate things. Maybe this was happening because Halloween, or what Witches called Samhain, was right around the corner.

The veil between the physical world and the world of spirits was supposed to be at its thinnest. Maybe that's why I was seeing ghosts? *With all of the other witchy talents that run in the Bishop family tree, has anyone else ever had to deal with this? And if so, would they be able to teach me how to control it?*

I made another note in the margin, *Who is Ro?* I needed to find out— like yesterday. Was she a Bishop? I glanced down at the notepad and noticed that I had drawn a tree. I stared at it and recalled what the ghost had said to me. "Look at the family tree. Discover your roots," I said to myself.

I jumped up and went directly to Gwen's bedroom suite. I searched through the books on the shelf in her turret room and found nothing on our recent family history. Merlin padded into the room and sat by my feet.

"Hey Merlin," I said as he leaned into me. "Don't suppose you'd know where I could find a copy of the family tree, would you?"

Merlin *meowed,* and pawed at my leg.

I deliberated as he sat and stared at me with wise golden eyes. Well, he was a Witch's cat after all. "Can you show me?" I asked and felt a little silly.

Merlin trotted to the doorway, paused and looked over a feline shoulder as if to say, *You coming or not?*

I followed.

Merlin went down the hall and stopped at a door on the second floor landing. When he pawed at the door, I slowly opened it. As I did, the door gave a loud squeak. "Very haunted house-like," I muttered to the cat as I studied the entry to the attic.

Merlin went in immediately and scampered up the steep stairs. I spotted a light switch inside the door and checked over my shoulder to make sure all of the girls were downstairs. With the coast clear, I stepped in and closed the door behind me.

I'd never been up in the attic area before. The family used it for storage as far as I knew, and I'd seen them bring big containers out when they had decorated the house for Halloween. But I had only helped to haul the boxes from the second floor to the main floor.

I found Merlin waiting at the top of the stairs in front of a white painted door. I smiled at the clear glass door knob and pushed it open. Not sure what I would find, my breath caught on a delighted gasp.

Light filtered in through a few fancy stained glass windows that featured an art nouveau rose pattern. Colored patterns of light lay scattered across the wide planked floor. The ceiling was high, so I went in and searched for another light switch. I didn't see any, but there was a tall floor lamp with a ratty tasseled shade sitting nearby on a threadbare rug. I stepped over and clicked the lamp on.

What I found made me sigh in appreciation. The space was large and, despite the old pieces of furniture, clean. The walls were unfinished, and the wooden slats were stained in a pretty color. Along one slanted wall a short, deep storage shelf was arranged. I saw color coordinated plastic storage bins for the different holidays. Beyond that was a crib, a wooden rocking chair, and the frame for an old wrought iron bed. While some of the walls were at funny angles due to the Victorian architecture, I thought it only made the attic more intriguing.

I turned around and took in the whole space. I noticed that at some point someone had framed in a bathroom— the two by fours appeared newer, and I could see that plumbing had been roughed in. A few old chairs that needed reupholstering sat by the rough-in, as if waiting to be made pretty again. I noticed that Merlin waited for me in a colored beam of light from the windows. His tail flipped once.

"Coming, kitty." As I walked over to him, I ran my hand over the arm of the old rocker and along the exposed bricks from one of the fireplace flues. Merlin trotted over and leapt up on top of one of a few old trunks that were lined up along the bricks. He started pawing at the lid.

"Okay. I get it," I said. I knelt down in front of the trunk and waited for Merlin to hop down. The trunk opened easily and Merlin stretched up and started to sniff at the contents. I reached in and found a few pieces of vintage clothing and baby books. There were three of them. Pink ones for Holly and Ivy and a faded blue book. I opened the blue, out of curiosity, and discovered pictures of a young, smiling Gwen and a somber faced, toddler-aged Bran.

"So you've always been serious," I murmured to his

picture.

Merlin meowed at me again and jumped inside of the trunk. He was digging, not unlike a dog, at another old faded book. I reached in and pulled out the hardback book. It had words "Our Family" stamped in gold on the brown leather cover.

It only took a couple of seconds to realize what I was looking at. Births, deaths, and weddings were all recorded over the last one hundred years or so. I was in history-nerd heaven looking at the old book. The family tree had been carefully filled in, and the pages had been beautifully embellished with drawings of herbs and flowers. Delighted, I rested my back against the brick fireplace flue and started to read. The history began with the marriage of my great-grandmother Esther.

Esther Catherine Morgan, born in 1905, had married Walter Christopher Bishop in 1925. She and Walter had three children— Irene, Morgan (my grandfather), and Faye. Esther, I recalled, was the artist who had drawn and water colored a series of botanical subjects. I had three of the drawings that I had 'inherited' from my father framed and hanging in my room.

The trio of drawings may have very well been stolen from the family collection— a collection that dated between 1925 and 1926. The botanical drawings/paintings had originally numbered thirteen, and Gwen had the remaining ten. No one knew for sure how or why my father had 'acquired' those particular three prints. Running my fingertips close to the roses drawn so carefully around the family tree, I figured that this enhancement was also Esther's work.

"Why isn't this book included with the other family journals and grimoires?" I asked Merlin. He popped his head over the edge of the trunk and narrowed his eyes at me. No matter what his magickal talents, I didn't think Merlin was going to be able to answer that question, so I went back to the book.

Further along the family tree, I discovered the writing changed, and now Rose Bishop, Esther's daughter-in-law, appeared to have taken over the family history. I searched for Rose's maiden name and found it in a section that listed the dates of her marriage. Rose was born Rose Olivia Jacobs in 1937, and had married Esther's only son, Morgan Brandon Bishop, in 1960. My grandparents, Morgan and Rose, had two children — Gwen, my aunt, who'd been born in 1962, and my father, Arthur, who'd been born in 1964.

I didn't remember my grandparents, as I'd been around two years old when they'd died. As far as we knew, Morgan and Rose Bishop had been the victims of the curse Thomas Drake unleashed when he'd discovered the Blood Moon Grimoire was missing. Even though it had been my father and Duncan's father who had been the ones to take and hide the book, we were never sure why the curse had targeted my grandparents. *How had my father ducked that curse anyway?*

I returned my gaze to the neat family tree graph and

noted that Aunt Gwen didn't appear to have ever been legally married even though she'd had three children. My lips twitched at that, but it really didn't surprise me. She was too much of a free spirit to settle down. However, she did seem to keep a friendly relationship with the twin's dad.

My gaze traveled farther along the family tree, and I saw my father's name and birth date listed. But there was extra writing around my dad's name. Beneath the date of his birth in 1964, I read in smaller lettering the name: W. Sutherland Born:1967.

Right below that, his marriage was noted to my mother Susan, and the year of the wedding was listed as 1988. I ran my finger along to the right of my father's line on the tree and saw that there were two prongs for children filled out.

Shocked, I promptly bobbled the book.

"What?" I gasped. Merlin hopped out of the trunk and came to sit next to me. "*Two* children?" I whispered and tried to steady the book on the edge of the open trunk.

I sat there in that beam of sunlight with my heart pounding and made myself look carefully again. There was my name entered: Autumn Rose Bishop. Born: September 23, 1990. And on the line above was an entry marked as: Son. Born: 1985.

"No. They would have told me *this*," I said, and felt tears rise to my throat. I double checked the date written for my parent's marriage. It was clearly listed

June 3, 1988. That was right as far as I knew.

Thinking fast, I did the math. If there had been a child born to my father in 1985, my dad would have been around twenty-one years old. And that child had been born three years *before* he'd married my mother.

The proof of it was right in front of my eyes. 'Son. Born: 1985'. That meant that I'd had a brother. I continued to focus on my father's branch of the family tree and realized that with the positioning of the entries, *W. Sutherland* was probably the mother of my father's son. So, technically, that baby would have been my half-brother.

"But what had happened to the baby?" I said, letting Merlin climb into my lap. The entry only said 'Son. Born: 1985'. There was no name listed. Did that mean he'd been stillborn or died shortly after his birth? An overwhelming sadness hit me.

"More secrets," I hissed. *God damn it! There were more secrets!* I had almost gotten to the point that I was beginning to forgive my father for hiding his family's legacy of magick from me. I tried to understand why he'd bound my powers when I was little. I had almost convinced myself that he'd been noble and tried to protect me by stealing that damned grimoire we were now desperate to find.

I really hadn't thought anything else would ever shock me again. But seeing this entry about a brother who had died at birth was devastating. A tear rolled down my face as I mourned for the brother I'd never even known existed until today.

I'd always wanted a big brother. When I was little, I'd been so lonely for a sibling— that I had actually created an imaginary brother. My breath hitched as I recalled how I used to blame *him* whenever I got into trouble.

I set the old book aside very carefully. I folded my arms on the open edge of the trunk, and let the tears come.

***

I wasn't sure how long I sat there with tears running down my face, but eventually they ran their course. I hiccupped a little, and wiped my runny nose on my jacket sleeve. I belatedly searched my jacket pockets for a tissue, found a slightly used one, and put it to use. As I mopped up my face, Merlin began head-butting my belly insistently. I reached blindly for his head to pet him when, suddenly, I smelled roses. I swung around half expecting to see the gardening ghost, but nothing was there. I saw that the old rocking chair was moving slightly, but I wasn't sure if that was because I had touched it earlier.

I pulled my phone out of my jeans pocket and checked the time. It was close to supper now, and I'd spent more time than I had realized up in the attic uncovering old family tragedies. Resigned, I put the baby albums and vintage clothing back in the trunk. I kept the family tree book. I closed the trunk and tried to pull myself together. My phone rang, and I saw that it was Duncan calling.

"Hello?"

"What's wrong?" Duncan asked without preamble.

"How'd you know I was upset?"

"I've told you before— you broadcast your emotions very loudly."

"I guess we should add broadcast my emotions *far* to that," I sniffled.

"Whose ass do I get to kick?" he demanded.

"I am crazy about you," I said to him. "I hope that 'broadcasts' clearly through the cell phone."

"I'm coming to get you. Wanna go get dinner?"

"Yeah, I want out of here tonight," I admitted. Tucking the cell between my ear and shoulder, I got up and went to turn off the floor lamp. Merlin raced to the open attic door and waited for me.

"Can you be ready in ten minutes?" he asked.

"Sure." I closed the attic door behind me and went down the stairs with Merlin at my side.

"You can tell me what's bothering you over dinner."

"See you soon," I told him just before hanging up. I paused inside the door to the hall, eased it open, and saw no one. I let myself out and went straight to my room. I tucked the book into my backpack and grabbed my cosmetics bag off my dresser. I had ten minutes to make myself presentable.

***

Duncan surprised me by taking me to the park with a bucket of chicken for supper. We settled side-by-side under the willow tree where Ivy and I had broken the spell my father had used to bind my powers, and dug into the food. I thought I might feel uncomfortable there, but I felt right at home.

I filled Duncan in on my ghostly visit, and my discovery of the trunk in the attic. After we finished eating, he wiped his hands carefully and studied the book.

"Oh damn, babe." Duncan studied the family tree page, and pressed a kiss to my head. "I'm so sorry."

I wrapped my arms around my knees for comfort. "I guess it's silly to mourn a baby that I never knew."

"No," Duncan said, and his expression was serious. "No, it's not silly at all."

"I hate secrets. I mean, really, I'm learning to *despise* them."

"I know what you mean. Secrets have caused both of us a lot of heartache."

"I swear," I said getting riled up. "The next person who lies to me is getting punched right in the nose!"

"Duly noted." Duncan grinned at me.

I took the book back and tucked it away in the backpack. "Let's take a walk," I suggested. "It's going to be a pretty night."

We threw away our trash in a nearby garbage can

and took a walk along the river to watch the sun set. We talked about his progress on the house rehab, my improvement with spell casting, working with Marie on our costumes for the upcoming Halloween Ball, and my classes at the museum. Finally we discussed possible places to search for clues as to where to find the rest of the Blood Moon Grimoire.

You know... normal things. Well, normal for us.

CHAPTER THREE

I had exactly fifteen minutes to submit my paper on the history of Natural History Museums via email to my professor. I'd been slaving away at my desk in my room for most of the day, and it was a damn fine paper if I did say so myself. Happy with the results of my hard work, I saved my file. Feeling giddy, I typed in the email address, attached the file and sent the paper in. All done, I sat back in my chair with a sigh and rolled my shoulders. I took off the headphones I'd had on to drown out any noise from the cheer squad who were, once again, in the manor finishing up the Homecoming float.

I stood up and worked the kinks out of my neck. As I rolled my head around on my shoulders, my stomach began to growl. What I wanted more than anything was a shot of some kind of caffeine and a snack. I caught my reflection in the oval mirror above my dresser as I started out of my room and backed up. *Yikes!* I appeared slightly insane with my hair sticking up all over the place. My nose was shiny, and my face was pale.

The door to my room clicked open, and Merlin made the leap from the floor to the top of the dresser. He sat on the dresser top and meowed at me.

"I'd really like to know how you open and shut doors," I told him.

Merlin simply meowed and tucked his tail around himself.

"No comment?" I said to him and pulled my hair out of the messy clip I'd twisted it in. I brushed out my hair and tossed the clip and brush in a basket on my dresser. Merlin made a chirping sound and put his paw on my cosmetics bag. "Fine, fine," I grumbled applying a little powder, some blush, and slicked on lip gloss.

"Let's go," I said to Merlin, scooping him up. I set him down once we got to the top of the stairs. I fully and freely admitted to being a klutz, and I wanted to have one hand securely on the wooden banister. Merlin took off down the stairs with me following him.

I trailed my hand along the decorated banister as I went downstairs. The family really went all out for Halloween. A pretty black feathered garland was wound with orange lights from the second floor all the way down to the main landing. Black silk roses were worked into the garland. It was gothic, and festive all at the same time. Merlin seemed to leave the feathers alone for the most part. Gwen had informed me that they had an agreement in which Merlin will leave the garlands and decorations be.

As I swung down the last step into the main foyer, I almost smacked into a dark haired girl. She was standing still and staring at a black, artificial holiday tree that sat in the foyer— tucked behind the end of the curving banister.

"Oops!" I managed to stop a few inches from her.

"Oh!" she jumped back at the same time.

I didn't recognize her, but it was obvious she was part of one of the cheerleading squads. The cheerleading t-shirt was a dead give-away. "Hi, I'm Autumn." I smiled to try and put her at ease.

"I'm Leilah. I was hunting for the bathroom." She fiddled with her hair that was cut into a cute pixie style.

"The powder room is off the family room and kitchen." I pointed back in the general direction.

She didn't turn and go towards it; instead, she stood and continued to stare at the decorated Halloween tree. "I've never seen one of these— not this big before," she said reaching out to one of the artificial black pine branches.

"Yeah," I gestured to the slim, six foot tall tree. "It is pretty amazing." The midnight tree was strung with orange lights. Pumpkin orange and frosted white glass ornaments popped against the black pine branches while artificial sprays of autumn leaves and bittersweet were tucked in for texture. Finally, there was an assortment of clever glass ornaments all in a witchy or classic Halloween theme hanging from the branches.

She ran a fingertip over a glass ornament shaped like

a crescent moon. "I didn't mean to be nosy, but I couldn't resist looking around at all of the Halloween decorations."

"That's okay." I smiled and gave her an 'after you' gesture. She took the hint and went back towards the kitchen.

I really didn't blame her for wanting to nose around. The rest of the downstairs also had whimsical seasonal touches. From the huge decorated grapevine wreath on the front door to the orange and black floral centerpiece on the dining room table— no surface had escaped the bewitching décor. Even the mantle in the family room had taken a dramatic shift, from the rustic fall leaves and a scarecrow for the autumn equinox to its current gothic and spooky display.

Leilah went over to the mantle and studied it. "Now this is really great."

"Thanks. I helped decorate the mantle. So I'm partial to it," I said. Sphagnum moss dripped from the mantle. Black branches and midnight colored eucalyptus were tucked into that moss and were used as a frame for moon white pumpkins and orange and white striped gourds and mini pumpkins. A silk crow perched on the top of a vintage birdcage at the far end of the mantle while candle holders of mercury glass held an assortment of black and white candles ranging from tapers to pillars to votives.

"This is like something out of a magazine." Leilah ran her hand over a bit of the draping moss. "Well, I better go help out the girls." She waved at me, ignored the bathroom entirely, and let herself back out to the garage.

I followed her, stopping in the kitchen. I grabbed an apple, some cheese and a soda out of the fridge. I immediately took a swig of the soda and prayed for the caffeine to hit my system. I sliced up the apple and cheese, arranged it on a plate and hopped up on a barstool at the kitchen counter. I sat there enjoying my apple and cheese slices as Holly and the girls bounced back and forth from the garage to the potting room while they worked on the finishing touches for the Homecoming float.

Ivy came in through the potting room and silently pulled up a stool next to me. A second later, my little plate slid— all on its own— across the counter. Ivy snatched up one of my apple slices.

"Hey!" I grabbed my plate back.

Raising an eyebrow at me, Ivy crunched on the apple slice. "Resistance is futile..." she said in a deep, dramatic voice.

The plate came right out of my hand and glided over to hers, *again.*

"Tricky Witch," I grumbled and yanked the plate back. I popped another slice of apple and cheese in my mouth, waiting to see what she'd do next.

Ivy drummed her fingers on the countertop, and my soda can slid across the counter— straight into her outstretched hand.

“Don’t make me get tough,” I said.

Ivy batted her eyelashes at me and deliberately raised the can to take a drink.

Waiting until she was about to swallow the soda, I shot my hand out and dug my fingers into her side. She coughed and squealed at the same time, and I snatched the can back again.

“Your telekinesis bows before my ninja-like reflexes,” I said.

“You are the klutziest Ninja I know.”

“Yet, I hold the soda can, Grasshopper.”

“I am defeated.” Ivy bowed her head.

I laughed at that, then gave in. “Here,” I passed what was left of my snack over to her.

“Thanks,” she said, polishing off the last of the apple.

It was nice to sec her starting to act like her old self. While her dramatic goth-girl look was long gone, her flair for drama and humor was returning. I was still getting used to her more natural hair color, though.

“You all done working on that paper?” Ivy asked me.

“I am.” I swiveled on the barstool and noticed for the first time that her purple t-shirt said, *I’m not antisocial. I just don’t like you.* My lips twitched. Yeah, our girl was coming back. Funny how seeing someone wearing snarky slogan t-shirts could lift your mood.

“What’s up?” I asked her as she pushed my now empty plate aside.

“Hey, you’re wearing the shirt I gave you for your

birthday." Ivy noticed and smiled a little.

I glanced down at my own ivory colored graphic tee. It featured a vintage looking Ouija board printed in black. "Well, Halloween is only a couple weeks away." I grinned at her. "It seemed pretty appropriate to me."

"We call it Samhain," Ivy corrected me.

"Right. I've been studying the sabbats. Samhain is the Witches' New Year. It's the night of the year when the veil between the physical and the world of spirit is at its thinnest."

"You know, I got that shirt for you before I realized you were a Medium," Ivy said, referring to my ability of being able to communicate with the spirit world—not my actual shirt size.

"Your mom already told me that Ouija boards are tools, not toys. No worries, I'll leave them alone." Especially since according to the Witches, this was a hot time of the year for ghost and spirit activity. I didn't say so to Ivy, but the *last* thing I wanted was more ghostly company. I still hadn't worked up to talking to Gwen about Ro, the ghost yet. Or my discovery of the baby brother who had passed away all those years ago.

While I sat there trying to figure out the best time to approach my aunt about the subject, I got a strong gut hunch that Ivy was working up to something herself. "What did you really want to talk to me about?" I tossed the empty soda can towards the recycle bin. *Two points.*

"Have you noticed anything unusual about the girls

on the cheer squad?" she said carefully.

"Besides their baffling habit of color coordinating everything?" I grinned at her. "One of the girls even had a royal blue wrist brace on!" Talk about devotion to the school colors...

Ivy didn't laugh as I'd expected. And I felt a little uneasy at her silent appraisal of me. "What's wrong?" I asked.

"Do you remember when I challenged you to figure out which pebble was spelled and which was not?"

I nodded. "Yeah. You had me scan the pebbles, and I improvised that charm..."

"Okay, keeping that idea in mind... think you could tell which of the girls has had a spell cast on them?" Ivy's expression was very serious, and her gaze was intense.

"Why would anyone cast on the cheer squad?" I asked my cousin.

"Do you remember Holly and me talking about a girl, Kellie, who was hurt and unable to cheer for a few months?"

"The one with the broken leg?" I tried to recall.

"Yeah. Now Kate has sprained her wrist. And *another* girl got hurt in practice only yesterday."

"Wow, they do sound a little accident prone. But, Ivy, maybe it's simply a coincidence." I tried to placate her. "I remember reading somewhere that the sport with the most serious injuries was, in fact, cheerleading."

Ivy drew herself up, clearly offended. "You think I would bring this up if I wasn't sure something hinky was going on?"

"Okay, okay." I held up my hands. "Don't get angry." I considered it for a moment and wondered about how I would go about discreetly scanning a bunch of teenage girls. "What if I went out in the garage and looked at them using The Sight? I wouldn't scan their private thoughts, but I bet I could see their energy and their auras," I said to Ivy.

"That's exactly what I was hoping you'd do." Ivy nodded.

"So we'll hang around for a few moments and see if I notice anything unusual." I stood up.

"Cool. And if I took a picture of the group I'll tell them it's for the yearbook, and we printed it out here at home; you could try and read the photo too," Ivy said. Clearly she had put some thought into this.

I had never read a photo using my abilities before. That did pique my interest. Honestly, I thought Ivy was overreacting a bit, but I didn't want to upset her after what she'd been though recently. So, I agreed to her plan.

Ivy left the room to collect her digital camera out of Gwen's home office on the main floor, and we went out into the potting room. The door to the garage was open, and from there we could stay out of the way watching as the girls put the finishing touches on the float.

Trying to act casual, I stopped and stood in the

doorway right underneath one of the wards Aunt Gwen had made to protect the house from negative energy or dark magick. I leaned against the doorframe. I could admit now that I had been working with my ability more and more, it wasn't so much 'opening up" to it- as it was allowing it to come out and play. So, I relaxed into it, and let myself *see* the girls and their energy.

There were eight of them today. They bustled around all in matching shorts and homecoming shirts. I let my eyes go unfocused and ignored the overabundance of Central High royal blue and yellow, hoping to see other colors around the girls.

I considered a trio of cheerleaders that were carefully attaching a banner to the front of the float. Their energetic fields, or auras, were nice and bright; an intellectual golden-yellow, a vibrant orange, and a rosy-romantic pink. I focused on the girl with the pink aura, Megan, and sure enough, she was talking about her boyfriend. I saw some bright spring green and warm blue mixed with green colored auras on the other girls. Holly seemed to sparkle in a combination of white and bright aqua blue. In my magickal studies, I had learned that empathic abilities were often aligned with the element of water. So, Holly's watery blue colored aura made sense.

Cypress, the 'body' I had tripped over earlier in the week, had an aura that was bright and vibrant. It was a glowing violet color- which meant she was probably psychic herself. Or maybe a Witch. No sooner did I think that, Cypress lifted her head and met my eyes. Her hazel eyes sparkled, and she tossed me a wink.

Well shit. I jolted a bit and nodded to her in a sort of silent acknowledgment. I hadn't expected to find another Witch on the cheer squad. However, I reminded myself there were lots of families here in William's Ford with a magickal heritage. *Note to self: find out who Cypress was connected to.*

I scanned the rest of the girls and discovered to my surprise that the brunette with the wrist brace had a muddier colored aura than the other girls. I wondered what I'd see when I focused on the girl who'd been admiring the Halloween decorations.

But I didn't see Leilah. "Where's Leilah?" I asked Ivy.

"She left a little while ago," Ivy said and adjusted her camera lens.

"Leilah's new isn't she? I met her today. She was in the house checking out all the decorations."

"She's a sub from the JV squad," Ivy explained.

A blonde girl shuffled awkwardly around the back of the float on crutches wearing a brace on her right ankle. My breath caught in my throat. Her aura appeared dark, almost as if whatever color would have been there was cloaked over in a charcoal gray. "Who's the blonde girl on the crutches?" I asked Ivy out of the corner of my mouth.

"That's Viviane," Ivy whispered.

Holly must have felt the scan. She walked over to

where I stood in the doorway. "What are you doing?"

"Viviane has a dark, shadowy aura," I told Holly very softly.

Cypress appeared, and I managed not to jump in reaction since I hadn't seen her walk over. "Viviane was hurt in practice yesterday," Cypress pointed out.

"I think it's more than that," I murmured as Holly and Cypress turned to inspect Viviane themselves.

Ivy called out to the girls to all gather together and pose for a picture with the homecoming float. As the eight girls lined up, half sitting up higher on the float the other four standing below them. Ivy snapped several pictures with her fancy digital camera. As it ended up, Kate with the wrist brace and Viviane with the ankle brace were posed right next to each other.

I tried to read the energy of the group, but it was a kaleidoscope of colors with them standing so close together. However, at the end where the two injured girls posed, there *were* darker and muddier colors. I blinked, pulled The Sight back and realized my shoulders were tight and that I'd been holding my breath. I let it out in a slow steady stream, telling myself to relax.

"Thanks, girls," Ivy called out. As she walked back in the house, she whispered to me, "I'll go load these up on my computer and print out the best one for us to work with. Be right back."

Cypress strolled over to me. "You gonna ask me who my people are?"

"Huh?" *Yeah, that's me. The ever articulate grad student.*

"Anybody ever tell you that you psychically project your emotions very loudly?" Cypress smiled.

Damn it! "Yeah, I get that a lot."

"You were wondering which of the founding families I'm from?"

I stared at Cypress. I had a moment to realize that she was referring to the four magickal families from the Colonial era who had first gone up against the Drakes. "Umm..." I hesitated, not sure what to say to that. Finally, I stepped down into the garage so I could speak to her without being overheard.

"Actually, I'd been thinking of the current families that I knew from Aunt Gwen's coven," I admitted.

Cypress grinned at me. "You know my aunt, Marie. Marie Rousseau."

"Marie with the tattoo shop. That's your aunt?" I tried to put the pieces together. They did have similar coloring. The gorgeous caramel toned skin and thick, dark hair, but other than that I didn't see much of a family resemblance. Marie had dark brown eyes, was curvy, and vivacious. She also sported dozens of tattoos all over her arms, hands and upper chest.

Cypress' hazel eyes sparkled as I studied her. She was softer spoken, willowy, almost elegant. Also, Marie was a Hoodoo practitioner, a root worker. I tried to imagine Cypress conjuring up some Hoodoo with her Creole aunt. As we stood there and she grinned at me, it suddenly didn't seem like much of a stretch after all.

"How is Marie?" I asked since I couldn't think of a single thing to say that wouldn't make me sound like an idiot.

"She's busy now that the tattoo shop is open," Cypress explained. "You should come by soon and see. I bet you would like it."

To be polite, I agreed to stop by the shop, all the while noticing the squad had called it quits for the day and was starting to clean up and gather their belongings. One of the girls picked up Kate's bag for her since she had the wrist brace, and Holly was hovering over the blonde Viviane who was a little wobbly on the crutches.

I had to give it to Viviane. She was trying to figure out how to sling her backpack over one shoulder, keep her balance and still move forward with the new crutches all at the same time. If that would have been me, I would have probably fallen on my face. Holly tried to help out her friend as she went to navigate the step up into the house, but before she could step through the doorway to the potting room, the contents of Viviane's backpack hit the garage floor with a splat.

"These crutches are harder to use than I thought they would be." Viviane stopped and shrugged off the backpack. She blew out a frustrated breath, tossed her long ponytail out of the way and frowned at her crutches.

"The squad sure has had a run of bad luck lately."

Kate grimaced and held up her arm that was in the brace.

Cypress and I automatically bent down to pick up the notebooks and papers. I picked up the backpack and scooped up a three ring binder. As I went to tuck the binder away, I saw what appeared to be a fashion doll tucked inside of the bottom of Viviane's backpack. Caught off guard, I pulled the backpack open a tad wider. And as soon as I did, I got a good look at what had to be the ugliest doll I had *ever* seen.

Every sense I had developed since first learning about my father's family legacy of magick went on full alert. My stomach dropped and my mouth went dry. I felt my heart speed up, and it took everything I had to not throw the backpack as far away from me as possible. I centered myself and carefully studied that doll. It seemed to be wearing a miniature version of a cheer uniform, but it was a little hard to tell since it was all wrapped up in strips of fabric and twine. The doll's blonde hair was in a ponytail; its face was scratched up and dented in. Its right leg was missing.

"Viviane," I tried for a neutral matter of fact tone of voice. "Did you know there is a creepy doll in your backpack?"

"What?" her eyes went wide as she balanced on her crutches.

I raised my eyebrows at Holly and Cypress. They caught my hint and moved forward to see for themselves.

"Let me see," Cypress said and calmly reached in, pulling the doll out of the backpack. As she did, the other girls gasped in reaction. "That is one ugly-ass doll." Cypress carefully held onto it with her fingertips.

A few of the girls laughed nervously at Cypress' comment. Holly had recoiled from the doll when it was removed from the backpack. She recovered and put her hand on Viviane's shoulder, standing with her.

Viviane frowned at the doll. "That nasty thing was in my backpack? I've never seen it before!"

"You know..." Kate spoke up, "That's sort of like the creepy doll someone stuffed in my locker last week."

Cypress frowned down at the doll. "Was that before or after you hurt your wrist?" she asked Kate.

"The day before," Kate said. "I remember because it spooked me a little. It had on a cheer uniform like this one, and its hair was brown and cut in a style that was like mine."

Cypress took a piece of newspaper out of the garage's recycle bin and wrapped the doll up in it. She set the doll on the workbench. "Do you still have that doll?" she asked Kate sounding very calm.

"No. I threw it away in the garbage can at school." Kate shuddered.

"Why don't we all go into the kitchen?" Holly suggested. "I'll get some bottled water for everyone."

Viviane hopped up the step and swung through the potting room without further incident. I couldn't help but focus on that dried floral swag- the herbal ward that hung above the door. It hadn't escaped my notice that she had not been able to take the backpack *inside* the house.

Holly came in behind her friend. "The ward," she whispered to me.

"I know," I mouthed back as Viviane went past me on her crutches.

Cypress walked over to Holly. "Go keep the girls busy for a while. I want to stop any more bad mojo from affecting them."

"Was that a Voodoo doll?" Holly asked Cypress as she pointed to where the doll lay wrapped in newspaper out in the garage.

"No, it's more like a poppet. Leave it to me," Cypress assured her.

Holly went to join the rest of the girls, and I said to Cypress. "I'd like to help if I can."

Cypress nodded and went straight to the work sink in the potting room. "I should be able to lessen the negative effects the poppet is having on Viviane," Cypress said as she washed her hands.

Even though I had not touched the doll, washing my hands seemed like a smart move, so I joined her at the sink. I reached up for the paper towels and tore a couple off. "What do you need?" I handed her a towel.

Cypress scanned the potting room. Green plants grew in abundance, a few orchids and African violets were blooming in pots, and dried herbs hung from the ceiling. She went over to the large apothecary chest with its neatly labeled drawers. She scanned the names written on the labels. “I don’t see bay leaves here. Do you have any in with your kitchen spices?” Cypress asked.

“I’ll go check.” I went directly into the kitchen and hit the spice rack.

Bless my aunt’s organized little heart. She kept her kitchen spices in alphabetical order. Remembering that Aunt Gwen had used salt before to stop evil, I took a container of salt too. I stepped around the girls who were all gathered at the kitchen counter chatting away, and for good measure, plucked a pair of tongs out of a drawer. I left them to it and went into the potting room, closing the kitchen door gently behind me.

“Here you go.” I set the jar down on the butcher block work table. “I brought these because I don’t think we should touch that doll again. And I figured the salt couldn’t hurt.”

“Good thinking,” Cypress replied.

“What else do you need?”

Cypress seemed to consider her options. “Do you have any angelica?”

I knew that we did because I had helped harvest it from the gardens a couple weeks ago. It was hanging up and drying from a hook in the ceiling. I reached up-sometimes being tall comes in handy, and broke off a large round seed head and handed it to Cypress. Competently, she stripped the seeds from the flower head and brushed them into a neat pile on the work counter.

"This will hold things until our aunts can get together and take a look at this." Cypress frowned at me. "It worries me that Viviane also found a doll right before she was hurt."

"She said that it had a similar hair style. The doll that was in Viviane's backpack had blonde hair in a ponytail — the same way she wears her hair."

Cypress scooped up the angelica seeds. "Its right leg was missing, and Viv severely sprained her right ankle yesterday."

"So, we can guess that Kate's doll probably had a messed up arm." I tried to think about it calmly, but it was hard to stay dispassionate. When Cypress tipped her head towards the door, I grabbed the salt and bay leaves, and we headed out to the garage.

Cypress stopped and took another section of newspaper from the recycle bin, setting the paper flat on the garage workbench. She carefully un-wrapped the poppet using the tongs. "Bay leaves break jinxes," Cypress explained as she took four dried leaves and arranged them in a circle on the empty piece of newspaper. Using the tongs, she set the poppet in the center, then poured the dried angelica over the doll.

"Angelica is used to protect women and children, isn't it?" I asked as she neatly re-wrapped the doll in newsprint.

"It is," Cypress agreed, looking serious as she added a single bay leaf to the top of the wrapped poppet.

Proud of my actually remembering some of the magickal lessons, I held up the salt, and Cypress gave me the go ahead. I carefully poured a circle of salt around the wrapped up doll where it sat on the workbench.

As I finished the circle, Cypress held up her hands over the doll. "By blessed herbs and salt poured in a circle round; All evil and negativity will now be bound." She turned to me, "As we will it..."

"So shall it be," I chanted with her to help finish up the spell.

We left the garage and headed back into the potting room to wash up again before joining the gang in the kitchen. "So what do we do now?" I asked Cypress. "It would be a little awkward to tell the other girls to check their lockers and backpacks for dolls. I mean poppets."

"I'm not sure," Cypress said. "I'm going to send a text to Marie. Why don't you contact your aunt?"

"I think I'll make that phone call in my room where I don't have to worry about being overheard." I blew out a frustrated breath thinking of the ghost I'd seen a couple days ago and now the poppets. "So much for things being nice and normal."

"Being normal is hugely overrated," Cypress replied completely straight faced.

I tried not to laugh at that and went up to my room wondering how to fill in my aunt on the day's events.

Hi Aunt Gwen, hope you're not too busy at the shop, but somebody is making nasty poppets to take out the cheerleading squad. Oh, and when you have the time, could you fill me in on my father's other child, and, by the way... did you know we have a ghost in the rose garden?

I rolled my eyes at my own inner monologue and picked up my phone to make the call.

CHAPTER FOUR

Well, I had learned something new: Never piss off a Witch. I had only heard my aunt raise her voice one time since I had moved to William's Ford. That was the day Bran and I had a little magickal showdown in the turret room. Even when Ivy had been abducted, she had kept her composure— pretty much. I mean, obviously she was upset and frightened, but she never got angry.

Apparently, her tolerance for bullshit was at an all time low because my ears were still ringing from our phone conversation. And I hadn't even brought up my discovery of a half brother or the ghost in the rose garden.

My aunt had closed the magick shop early. She was home and on a tear. She'd slammed the front door and, before I could even say hello, she said, "Show me." Her voice low, and her tone very controlled, Gwen stood in the foyer practically vibrating with anger, which seemed to confirm for me that I had been correct not to bring up the other subjects. Not right now, anyway.

"I'm sorry that I had to call you away from the shop..." I began. I didn't think she was angry at me, but when I caught her expression— my first instinct was to step back. "This way." I said and led her out to the kitchen.

We gathered around the kitchen table, and Holly and Cypress were retelling how they had found the poppet.

"...and there it was," Cypress said. "That ugly doll didn't even come with a dream house or hot pink car— Just a whole lot of bad juju."

Ivy chuckled at her friend's statement, and I noticed Gwen didn't find that particularly humorous. I sat with them waiting for the opportunity to share what I'd *seen* when I had used clairvoyance to look over the squad's auras.

Come to think of it, I wasn't sure if that was exactly ethical behavior or not. I sipped from a bottle of water, mulling it over. I was torn. On one hand, using The Sight was a bit of an unfair advantage, but on the other hand, it was a way to confirm there was, indeed, some type of dark magick at work.

I heard the front door open, and Marie Rousseau called out as she let herself in. As I twisted to look, Marie stalked into the kitchen wearing distressed jeans and a denim jacket. Her dark hair was knotted up in a casual bun. She went directly to her niece and dropped a kiss on the top of Cypress' head. "How you doing, baby?"

"I worked the magick how you taught me, Aunt

Marie. I think it should minimize the effects of the poppet," Cypress said. Quickly, she explained what she and I had done with our counter spell.

"What I want to know..." Marie said. "Is why anyone would be petty enough to target the girls on the cheer squad?"

Petty was a good way to describe it, I realized, and spoke up. "It does seem a little juvenile. And besides that, what were they hoping to gain by injuring cheerleaders?" Everyone swung their gaze to me.

"Excellent point," Gwen stated.

"I want to see this poppet," Marie said.

"It's in the garage," Holly, Cypress and I answered together.

After the aunts left the room, Holly drummed her fingers on the tabletop. "We need to see that doll that Kate found in her locker."

"That was a week ago," Ivy pointed out. "Kate said that she'd thrown it away."

"What if we used a locator spell?" Holly suggested.

Cypress seemed to consider that. "We could... but we'd need something personal of Kate's to link the missing item to the spell."

Holly reached into her pocket and pulled out a folded tissue. "I imagine her hair would work." She unfolded the tissue and revealed a tangle of brown hair.

Cypress let loose a cackle, Ivy beamed at her twin, and I almost spit water on the table at Holly's sly maneuver.

"Where did you get that?" I asked after I managed to swallow the water.

"I took her brush out of her backpack and removed her hair from it." Holly shrugged. "I figured our resident Seer could use a little postcognition and look back to see where the doll ended up.

"Damn Blondie, that's impressively sneaky... especially for you." I smiled at her.

Holly set the tissue down. "This is *my* squad being attacked. *My* friends who are getting hurt. That makes it *my* responsibility to find out who is doing this, and to stop them."

"*Our* responsibility," Cypress corrected.

"Our responsibility," Holly agreed, and squeezed Cypress' hand.

"I assume you want to get started right away?" I asked. Standing up, I was met with three very determined faces. "Alright, let's do it. Ivy, go tell your mom and Marie what we're going to try."

We decided to do the postcognition attempt/ locator spell in the twin's room. The twin's room was located in the back of the house, and it also boasted a turret. When I had first moved here, I had half expected a room that was divided down the center with pink ruffles and sparkles for Holly and black gothic opulence for Ivy.

"You know, this room still throws me off." I said as I was struck again by the décor as I entered. The left was Holly's side which had a romantic shabby-chic vibe. An old red and ivory patchwork quilt was spread over a white iron double bed. The bed was mounded with pillows in red and white toile pattern, and art prints of various goddesses hung on the ivory wall next to her bed.

"It *is* sort of a sweet and sassy Witch décor." Cypress agreed as she went over and sat on Ivy's vampire-like red and black, brocade bedspread. As art for her side of the room, Ivy had black and white nature photography that she had taken herself. Plus, a huge framed poster of the comic book character, Harley Quinn.

Ivy draped her camera strap over the dark stained wood of her bed knob. "It works for us," Ivy said as she clicked on a crimson tasseled lamp. It cast a circle of light on a round skirted table that served as a nightstand between the beds.

I chosc a spot on the area rug in front of the turret. Cypress came over and took a seat directly across from me. The twins gathered a few things and joined us, creating a circle.

"Let's all sit cross-legged and scoot in closer so our knees touch," Ivy suggested. As soon as my knees bumped into Holly and Ivy's, I felt a current pass around the circle we had created.

"Wow," Cypress breathed, her hazel eyes large. "I see what Marie was talking about. Y'all pack a punch when you link together." She did a happy little butt wiggle. "This is going to be awesome!"

"Are we ready?" Ivy held up her hands, and we fell

silent. "By the powers of earth, air, fire and water, Lord and lady bless your daughters," she chanted.

"The circle is cast. Blessed be," Holly added.

I had a moment to wonder at the much simpler circle casting than I had seen the coven perform a few weeks ago. Ivy set the photo of the cheer squad that she had printed in the center of the circle that we'd created. Next, Holly produced a clear quartz crystal point that she had wrapped several strands of Kate's hair around.

"The hair is the link to Kate, and the crystal point works as an amplifier." She handed the crystal to me. "Look at the picture of Kate and let your mind travel back to last week when she found the doll."

I was careful to take the crystal in my receptive hand— the better to receive impressions. I tried not to feel nervous, nodded at my cousins, and thought that this was very similar to when I had scryed trying to find Ivy a few weeks ago.

Maybe it was that I had seen the past in a circle before. Or maybe I was more relaxed without the urgency I had felt when Ivy had been abducted. But as soon as I closed my fingers around the hair wrapped crystal, I started to see.

Kate stood at a row of brightly painted lockers. She worked the combination and popped open the door and tucked a few books inside. She pulled her backpack out, and a doll tumbled to the floor. Kate frowned down at the doll and picked it up. She glanced around as if to see who had played a prank on her.

Kate shuddered as she stared down at the doll. She ran her fingers over the doll's brown hair and fiddled with the crude fabric that was wrapped around it. The she hitched her backpack over her shoulder and closed her locker. She walked quickly down the hall and out the door where she seemed to debate as to whether or not to keep the doll. As she looked down at it, she shivered and pushed the doll in an outdoor garbage can that was painted in vertical blue and yellow stripes.

I came back to the present and told the girls what I had seen.

"Look again," Holly urged. "Where is the doll now?"

I nodded and thought back to 'seeing' Kate toss the doll in the outdoor garbage can. But all I could see was the striped garbage can. I frowned and concentrated. Nope. All I saw was that can sitting right outside the door of the school building. I opened my eyes. "I think it's still in the striped garbage can."

I carefully set the crystal point down on the photo. I took a deep breath and grounded, centering my energy. Ivy opened the circle, and I sat there wondering what the girls would do next.

"We need to go right now to see if that doll is still in that can," Cypress said.

"I'll drive," I volunteered.

"Okay," Holly agreed, and the girls rose.

I went to my room for my purse and truck keys. "I can only fit two other people in the truck," I reminded the girls as they all stood, waiting at the top landing.

"I'll stay here; let Mom and Marie know what's happening," Ivy said.

I felt like something was pushing me to hurry, so I nodded to her and jogged down the decorated manor stairs with Holly and Cypress on my heels.

We grabbed a garbage bag, a carton of salt, then hopped in the truck. I backed up and drove out the conveniently open gates. So far as I knew, there wasn't a remote control for them, and I still hadn't figured out how the manor's gates always seemed to be open or closed whenever I needed to come or go.

Shrugging that off, I drove to the girl's high school as fast as the law allowed with two cheerleaders riding shotgun. The parking lot was deserted when we got there. I followed Holly's directions and pulled around the far side of the building.

"This is the closest exit to Kate's locker," Holly explained as we all climbed out.

"Give me a second," I said and fished a pair of gardening gloves out of my glove box. I joined the girls as they approached the garbage can that was, indeed, painted in blue and yellow vertical stripes.

"I can work a reluctance so people won't notice what we are doing," Holly said.

"Good idea." I gave her a minute to work her magick.

Holly softly chanted, and, as I watched, Cypress joined in. In unison they both gestured out with their hands in a circular motion. I saw a shimmer billow out that made me think of a heat wave, and the girls lowered their hands.

"We're good to go," Holly said. "It will last for about five minutes."

"Stand back," I told the girls as I pulled on the gloves. There was no point in all of us digging in the garbage.

Cypress held out the garbage bag. "Go ahead," she said.

I carefully pried open the lid on the can and cringed at the sour smell of food that was several days old. I sincerely hoped I would not ruin my new Ouija board t-shirt. With a grimace, I started to pick through the very full can. *God, what a nasty job.*

Piece by piece I lifted out trash, and set it to the side of the can. When it got to the point that I would have to lean into the garbage can, I laid it on its side in the grass and kept digging. My eyes were watering and I was fighting back the urge to gag as I worked my way to the bottom.

I felt it before I saw it. My glove covered fingers bumped against something, and my stomach dropped. A shiver rolled down my back. "I think I found it," I told the girls. But, instead of feeling excitement... I felt revulsion.

I pulled the poppet free and held it up to the afternoon sunlight. Sure enough, it was another fashion-type of doll wearing a crude imitation of the girl's cheer uniforms. This one had dark hair that was cut to resemble the shoulder length style and bangs of Kate's hair.

"That's nasty." I grimaced and dropped the doll in the new garbage bag.

"By the element of earth, this salt shall contain all evil intent," Holly said as she poured salt down into the bag and on top of the doll.

While Cypress knotted the bag, I put the school's trash back in the can as quickly as possible. Once I righted the garbage can and set the lid back in place, the three of us went directly to my truck.

"Autumn, we need to secure this." Cypress set the bag holding the poppet in the open back of my pickup.

"I'm on it." I climbed up in the bed and scooted my spare tire on top of most of the bag to keep it from flying out as we drove home. I stripped the gloves off and set them inside the truck bed.

"I don't suppose either of you have any hand sanitizer on you?" I asked the girls as I climbed back down over the tailgate.

Holly handed the salt carton to Cypress and reached into the cab of the truck. "I do," she said pulling a mini bottle out of her purse. "It's made with lavender oil. Lavender is cleansing," Holly explained.

"Nice." I held my hands out as she squirted the lavender scented sanitizer. I briskly rubbed my hands together. The girls followed my example, and I glanced down relieved that I had managed not to get any of the nasty on my clothes. That was damn near a miracle.

I was about to climb back into the truck when Cypress put her hand on my arm. “Hang on a second.” Then, to my surprise, she poured a mound of salt into the palm of her hand and tossed all that salt across the bench seat of the truck.

“What’s that for?” I asked wondering how in the hell I’d ever get all that out of my truck.

“To help protect us on the ride home,” Cypress said to me as if I was slow.

I frowned at her. “That’s going to stick to us when we sit down.”

“I could always pour some salt down the inside of your shirt,” she said and started to pour more salt into her hand.

I held up my hands in surrender. “Okay, okay. Point taken.”

“You should see your face,” Holly said and climbed in the cab with a little giggle.

Cypress tossed that second handful of salt into the bed of my truck. It showered down over my gloves, and the tire that held the bag secure. “This is called: covering your ass,” she explained.

“Well, *your ass* can help me clean it up later,” I told her. We climbed in the cab on either side of Holly. Before I could even start the truck, a police car pulled into the school parking lot and slowly headed straight for us.

“Shit,” we all said together.

The officer cruised up and behind my truck. He rolled down his window. "You girls having car trouble?"

I stuck my head out the window, and smiled at him. And for the first time in my life, I lied to a police officer. "Picking up the girls from a late practice. We were just leaving."

Cypress popped her head out the passenger door and gave a friendly wave. Clearly, the cop didn't believe us. So, without another word, I started up the pickup and waited for him to move his squad car. I carefully drove out of the school parking lot and back to the manor. He followed us home and waited as we turned into the driveway.

As if by magick, the big ornate metal gates at the end of the drive swung silently closed behind us right after we pulled into the drive.

"One of these days, remind me to ask how that gate works," I muttered to Holly.

***

We brought our discovery into the garage and handed the bag over to Marie and Gwen. While the three of us scrubbed up at the work sink in the potting room, Gwen and Marie studied the new poppet.

Marie held her hands over the poppets. "We should remove the bindings," she said after a moment.

"Agreed." Gwen nodded.

"Can we watch?" Ivy asked from the doorway.

"You can," Marie said. "But please stay out of the way."

With the okay from Marie, Holly, Cypress, and I gathered around Ivy to watch the proceedings— from the relative safety of the potting room door.

"This is *nasty*." Gwen hissed through her teeth, carefully un-wrapping the dolls from the strips of fabric and twine. "These dolls are filled with very sour energy."

As I looked on, I noticed they were both wearing latex gloves. "What's with the surgical gloves?" I said wondering why two experienced Witches would need them.

"They are protecting their hands." Holly explained patiently.

"From what, chemicals?" I asked.

Cypress nudged me with her elbow. "They are protecting their hands from herbs or oils that may be on the dolls. Plus the gloves protect them from having direct skin contact with any negative energy."

"Oh," I said, feeling dumb. I'd worn gloves— but that was mostly because I was digging through the trash. "I didn't think those two would need to wear them." I shrugged.

"They are Witches, not super-heroes," Ivy said.

Once the dolls were unbound, the women took the fabric and twine to the backyard fire pit. I noticed that they put the disposable gloves in a brown paper bag and dumped more salt on top of those before disposing of the gloves in the outside garbage can. I stood and waited on the back patio next to the cauldron shaped fire pit with the twins, Marie and Cypress.

Gwen came out and joined us carrying a bottle of pure grain alcohol. As I watched, she poured the alcohol over the bindings that had been placed inside the cast iron fire pit.

"Stand back a bit," Gwen said, and, as one, we did.

"By the element of fire," Marie said. "I destroy these bindings and remove all dark magick contained therein." Marie struck a match and tossed it into the fire pit. The bindings went up with an impressive *whoosh.*

"The flames are blue," I said, surprised to see the bright blue flames the alcohol had produced.

"That's the point of using it," Ivy explained. "The high alcohol content makes things burn hot and fast."

Fascinated, I watched as Gwen and Marie tended the blaze, making sure that the fabric and twine burned away completely until it was nothing but ashes.

A short time later, we all stood contemplating the poppets on the garage workbench. Still within the original circle of salt I had poured, the two poppets lay side by side. Kate's poppet was lying neatly next to the poppet that had been in Viviane's back pack. The bay leaves were rearranged around them and even more angelica had been sprinkled on them.

I peeked over at my aunt, curious as to what she'd do now. Her mood was so grim, and I had a million questions, but I didn't think this was the time to ask them. Whoever had created the poppets had put a fair amount of work into them. Well, before they had mangled them. I don't know what was creepier, the effort to make the dolls look like Kate and Viviane in their uniforms or the way the dolls were beaten up.

"There's still a lot of dark energy attached to these poppets," Gwen finally broke the silence.

"So we are dealing with a real practitioner," Marie put her hands on her hips. "Someone with *power* and not a dabbler."

"A dabbler?" I questioned, unfamiliar with the term.

"Someone who plays at magick. They 'dabble'." Marie used her fingers to make air quotes.

"And dabblers are bad?" I asked for clarification.

Gwen crossed her arms over her chest. "A dabbler will try anything with magick, just to see if it works. They play at the Craft, typically disregarding any idea of ethics."

Oh. I supposed that would be bad. I rubbed my forehead as I thought about the situation.

"I'm going to contain anymore dark magick coming from the dolls with silver," Gwen said and went back in the house. She returned a moment later with a white piece of cloth, folded and tucked under her arm, and a handful of silverware. The real stuff. The heavy silver table knives were polished to a soft gleam. I had to admire the way Gwen neatly arranged the nine knives, tip to end, in a circle around the poppets.

"By the power of three times three, I contain any lingering negativity," Gwen chanted as she placed the knives. "Within the silver circle round, all evil is forever bound."

I felt a little tingle from her magick, then she stepped back and directed us to all join hands. I linked hands with my aunt and Holly and watched the rest of the group join hands as well. Gwen asked us to repeat the charm with her twice more, and I felt a little thrill of energy roll through me as we finished up the containment spell.

Merlin came out and went straight for the garage workbench. I started to reach for him as he sniffed at the poppets. However, before I could grab him, Merlin's back arched up. His eyes narrowed, and he let out a loud feline hiss. He backed up, hissed again at the poppets, and hightailed it off the workbench scampering back into the house.

"Well," I said and tried to keep a straight face. "I was wondering why you weren't worried about the cat getting into all of that."

"Merlin's got better instincts than most people." Holly smiled at that.

"The dark magick has been contained for now," Gwen said as she unfolded the white cloth and covered up the poppets. "Viviane and Kate should both be safer and heal quickly."

"What about us, Mom?" Holly asked. "Are we safe with those things in the garage?"

“I want to keep them here for now. It’s fine. Don’t worry about it.” Gwen headed for the door to the potting room.

As if in agreement, everyone went back in the house. I couldn’t help but look over my shoulder at the poppets that lay on the workbench under that cloth. It gave me the creeps knowing they were out there, but if Gwen said they magick was contained, I should trust her.

Shouldn’t I?

CHAPTER FIVE

The day of Homecoming dawned bright, clear and cool. I had no classes that day, and I was secretly looking forward to seeing the parade— especially after being dragooned into helping out with decorating the cheerleader's float. Honestly, I was looking forward to doing something normal. Like attending a local parade and the Homecoming football game... Not to mention my plans with Duncan *after* the game. I tossed on a faded denim jacket over my black lacy shirt. My running shoes seemed to glow with their neon green against my darker skinny jeans. I left my hair down. I tucked my sunglasses in my backpack style purse and stood in the foyer waiting for Ivy.

She had my jaw dropping in shock when she strolled down the main staircase wearing a Senior Homecoming shirt, her brown hair all twisted into a pretty up do. To keep her hair from looking too mundane, Ivy had added blue and yellow hair extensions that were artfully arranged in her hair.

"Festive," I said. I had never seen Ivy display so much school spirit. She merely raised her eyebrows at me and looped her digital camera strap around her neck.

"It is Homecoming," Ivy announced and pulled her cat eye sunglasses out and stuck them on her nose.

As luck would have it, the house Duncan was currently rehabbing was almost at the end of the short parade route. We drove over, and I pulled my truck in the driveway. We unfolded a couple of lawn chairs and sat at the end of the driveway, preparing to watch the local color. Duncan and his crew joined us— and they were sitting on the driveway or on overturned buckets. One of the men from the crew had his wife and toddler join us. The couple introduced themselves as Marshall and Felicia. They sat in the shade talking to each other while the other guys made faces at the little girl in her stroller to make her smile.

I watched people mill around, and noticed that most of the younger children carried plastic grocery bags. I was about to ask what that was all about, but then I heard the marching band. A police car came over the little hill to start the parade and to clear the street. The parade come rolling through. I heard the band before I saw them and noticed a shift in the excitement of the crowd gathered on the street.

"My kid brother is in the drum line," Marshall said to me.

"That's cool," I said, grinning at him. Marshall seemed so proud.

I saw the flag corps leading the way and estimated there were over a hundred kids playing in the marching band. The band marched in perfect time, and in a coordination which made me envious. I smiled at the smart metallic gold and royal blue uniforms and watched dozens of proud parents and grandparents snapping pictures with cell phones and cameras. The crowd did indeed go wild.

Ivy stood up to take pictures. I watched her working, and Duncan put his arm around my shoulders.

"The marching band went all the way to the State Championships last year." Duncan explained to me. The guys on the crew stood and cheered with enthusiasm as the drum line thundered past. Marshall called to his brother, Felicia waved animatedly, and I saw a drummer in the line nod his head in response. Obviously, the younger bother of Marshall.

I had to smile. In the little town I had grown up in, there weren't any Homecoming parades. It had been a fairly rural area, and the students were spread out. This was a whole new experience for me. Looking around at the local people of William's Ford, I sensed a huge amount of home town pride. It was sweet, actually.

The band moved onto a rousing fight song, and they sounded great. Ivy came back and was checking the photos as the Varsity football team rolled by. The team captains were being driven around in a slick convertible sport car. They wore their football jerseys and waved as they rolled past. The rest of the football team was behind them sitting on hay bales inside of a flat bed trailer pulled by a tough looking SUV.

To my surprise, the team threw little mini footballs and candy to the kids in the crowd. I watched the little kids scramble and realized that's why they were carrying bags. I saw candy come winging my way and caught a piece of bubble gum on the fly.

"Hey, Ivy! Catch!" a hunky young man with curly brown hair called out from the football trailer.

Ivy lowered her camera and neatly snagged a little football that he had thrown. The football player grinned in response, and that had me looking at my cousin carefully.

"Is that a friend of yours?" Duncan teased her.

Ivy waved at the football player while his teammates tossed more candy. "His name is Eric; he's the center on the team."

"And?" I poked at her.

"I'm going to the Homecoming dance with him," Ivy said casually. She handed the football to Marshall's little daughter in the stroller. The toddler squealed in excitement.

"What? You never even said anything!"

"We've been friends for a long time," Ivy said as she raised her camera and took more pictures of the team. "He surprised me a couple weeks ago and asked me to the dance," she waited a moment then added. "So I said yes."

"But the dance is tomorrow night. Do you even have

a dress?" I asked her completely shocked that she was playing this so cool. Duncan shook his head at me and rolled his eyes. "Shut up, you," I said to him.

Ivy lowered her camera. "Oh my god— are you playing mom, now?"

"Hey, a Homecoming dance during your Senior year is a big deal. Please tell me you have a dress," I begged.

"Relax, I have a homecoming dress." Ivy shrugged and turned her attention back to photographing the parade.

"Well, thank god," Marshall said with a serious expression. "I don't think I would have slept at all if she didn't." His eyes twinkled as he smirked at us.

Felicia swatted her husband's arm playfully at his at teasing. "Ignore him," she said. "Men don't understand the seriousness of the situation."

I laughed in agreement. "I want to see the dress when we get home," I warned Ivy.

"Well, I could use an opinion on what shoes to wear with it," she admitted as she focused and took more pictures.

"Done," I said.

A group of cheerleaders marched along behind the players, and the banner they held announced them to be the JV squad. Their uniforms were different from the ones I had seen Holly's varsity squad wear. A dozen girls wore white tops with royal blue and gold trim. Their skirts were short with more metallic trim. They were close enough to us that I could see the girls were all sporting matching manis. Good grief. I will never understand the need for people to color coordinate every little thing.

One girl with short dark hair in a pixie cut broke formation from the rest of the JV squad and took off running to an open section of the street. "Hey, isn't that Leilah?" I asked Ivy.

"Yeah," Ivy said and lowered her camera.

As we watched, Leilah did a roundabout, then started on a series of backflips while the squad and the crowd spelled out E-A-G-L-E-S. She landed her sixth flip with a controlled little bounce.

"Wow. She's good," Duncan said. "Somebody's got major gymnastic skills."

I watched her as she waved to the families along the sides of the street that cheered for her performance. "I'm surprised she's not on the varsity squad with those kind of skills."

"It wasn't her talent that kept her off the varsity squad," Ivy confided.

"Really?" I peered at Ivy over the top of my sunglasses. "I smell gossip. Gimme details."

Ivy grinned at me. "Leilah's got an attitude. Let's just say that she's not an easy person to be around."

"Oh, really?" I thought back to when I'd met her while she'd been admiring the Halloween decorations. She'd been friendly enough. But there was no denying that she certainly seemed to be in her element now. Leilah walked several feet in front of the rest of her squad waving to the crowd in a way that made me think of a pageant girl.

As I watched Leilah wave to the parade goers, something caught my eye from directly across the street. Folks were jostling back and forth to get a better view when suddenly the crowd parted, and I saw Thomas Drake. My heart slammed against my ribs as I recognized him. He stood perfectly still directly across the street from us. He was wearing sunglasses, his salt and pepper hair was brushed back from his unsmiling face. It was the formal dark suit that had caught my eyes, I realized. That's what had seemed out of place. As I stared at him, he inclined his head in acknowledgement. Our gazes held— for one heartbeat. Then two.

I jolted hard when Duncan and his crew started to cheer and whistle. I blinked. The crowd shifted, and he was gone. I shivered in reaction. *Why would he be here? Was he watching us? Was something else about to happen?*

The trailer that made up the Varsity cheerleader's float was being slowly pulled along by a red, heavy duty truck. I adjusted my sunglasses and told myself to relax as I waved to the injured Viviane and Kate as they sat on the sides of the colorful float. Several squad members rode on the float, but a few girls marched along side waving metallic pom-poms at the crowd.

As the float cruised slowly by, I noticed a large black dog walking through the crowd on our side of the street.

His leash trailed behind him, and I looked to see if anyone was trying to catch him. As I watched the dog weave in and out of the spectators on the sidewalk, I had the weirdest feeling of déjà vu. My stomach turned over and everything else around me, the people, the floats, Duncan and Ivy, all blurred away.

It was like tunnel vision where all I saw was that dog. His head swept left, then right, and he gathered himself as if he was about to bolt. *The cheerleader's float: Something's going to happen to the girls.* I reached blindly for Duncan's arm and heard myself say, "Something's wrong."

Time seemed to slow down as the dog streaked out into the middle of the parade, directly in front of the red truck. There was a sudden screeching of brakes, and then several screams. Duncan and the guys on the crew shot past Ivy before I could even take a step.

I shook myself out of wherever I had just been. With a snap, time seemed to re-set itself. The crowd pushed forward as one, and even though the float was only about ten feet away from us, for a few moments, I couldn't see anything. Ivy grabbed my arm, and we started to work our way through the crowd.

"Is Holly okay?" Ivy shouted.

"I can't see!" I called back. *Damn it! Gwen had said the dark magick had been contained! Now something else had happened to the squad.* My heart raced as I broke through the people milling around.

I saw Holly and Cypress squatting down beside the

float. They look unharmed, and Holly had her arm around a girl who was sitting on the street and crying.

"Holly!" I called to her.

She motioned us over. "I'm alright. Megan's hurt, though."

As I approached, I noticed a large bump in the middle of the girl's forearm. My stomach turned over. Definitely broken.

The driver of the truck rushed over, and she knelt down next to Megan. "I'm sorry honey, I stomped on the brakes to avoid hitting that dog."

"The trailer jerked hard. I lost my balance and fell off," Megan cried.

"That's the coach," Ivy informed me.

I stepped back and saw that Duncan and his crew were helping the other girls down from the float. Duncan scooped Viviane up, and I went to the float and grabbed her crutches for her. He handed Viviane off to Marshall, and Viviane smiled at him, a little flustered.

Marshall carted her gallantly over to the sidewalk and out of the way. Kate climbed down with assistance from Cypress and a few other adults who had gathered to help. I handed Viviane her crutches and saw Felicia pass over a baby blanket to Ivy. The blanket was passed to the coach who tied it into a makeshift sling to stabilize Megan's arm.

I helped round up the other girls while Holly checked with their coach, and, after getting her consent, we escorted the rest of the girls over to the sidewalk and off the street, keeping them all together. Someone from the crowd pulled the float over to the curb so the rest of the parade could continue. They handed the truck keys back to the coach as a police cruiser rolled up, and a male and female officer got out.

I recognized the female officer as Lexie Proctor from Aunt Gwen's coven. She carefully helped Megan up, and Megan, along with the coach, got into the police cruiser. A few moments later, they smoothly rolled away to the emergency room, no doubt, while the other officer remained to get the street clear. The crowd quickly got out of the way, and the parade continued on.

"We need to get back to school," Kate said as she stood there cradling her wrist in its blue brace against her chest.

"Are you hurt?" Duncan asked her sharply.

"Oh." Kate scowled down at her wrist. "I don't think so. Well, not anymore than I was already."

"Once the last of the parade moves through, we could get the girls back to school easily. We have enough drivers." I motioned to Duncan's crew.

A bit later, Felicia and Marshall took Viviane, Belinda, Danielle, and Jayne in their minivan. The four girls were cooing over the toddler, and they all seemed to be in good spirits. I sent Kate and Lissa off with Duncan. Ivy volunteered to wait for us and promised to send texts to Gwen and Marie so they could contact the other girls' parents. I took Cypress and Holly in my pickup, and we made a caravan to the school to drop the squad off.

I waited until I was alone with the two girls, driving towards the school. "Are you thinking what I'm thinking?" I asked them grimly.

"That hex is still at work," Holly said quietly.

"No shit," Cypress whistled through her teeth.

A thought occurred to me. "I'm starting to wonder if this is like magickal revenge. Who did you girls piss off, anyway?"

Cypress pursed her lips as she thought about it. "I haven't heard any of the other girls talking about a big fight with anyone."

I stopped at an intersection and eyeballed them. "Did any of the girls on the squad steal somebody's boyfriend?"

Holly crossed her arms over her chest. "Not that I know of."

"You know, hell hath no fury like a woman scorned and all that," I said.

Cypress smacked her hand on the dashboard in frustration. "Well, whoever this nasty, spell-casting, bitch is... they've gone and pissed me off now!"

"I wasn't trying to make light of the situation— I was trying to eliminate possibilities. Sorry." I said to Cypress.

"I know." Cypress made an effort to pull her temper in. "Megan is one of my best friends. She's a sweetie. She wouldn't hurt a fly... let alone steal a boyfriend."

Holly rubbed her forehead as she thought. "I hate to

say this, but we've got to get back and figure out how we are going to perform for the Homecoming game tonight. We made do with nine girls when Kellie broke her leg last month. Now Viviane is on crutches and can't cheer at the game. Kate can cheer, but she can't do any stunts with her wrist in a brace."

Cypress nudged Holly. "As your co-captain, I say we pull from the JV squad again to fill the empty spots.

Holly frowned at her. "We're going to have to."

Personally, I thought the mystery of the hex was more important than the Homecoming game, but Holly and Cypress were seniors in high school. This was their big night. To them, this clearly was more important. We pulled up to the school, and I let the girls out.

As the girls climbed out of the cab to go join the rest of their squad, I called to them. "You two be careful, you hear me?"

Holly stood with her hand on the open car door. "We will be. See you tonight at the game."

I waved at them and drove back to the rehab house to pick up Ivy. Ivy put the lawn chairs back in the bed of my truck and hopped in the cab. Duncan came out to give me a kiss goodbye.

Before he could kiss me, I said. "I saw your uncle right across the street before the accident happened with the cheerleader's float."

Duncan frowned. "Are you saying that you think he's involved?"

"No... I don't know!" I said. "It's just weird is all."

“We can discuss it when I pick you up for the game tonight. He leaned in through my open car window and kissed me, lingering over it.

Ivy made a wolf whistle, and, despite all the magickal incidents, Duncan and I grinned at each other.

Tonight was the night. After the game, I was going back to his place.

Tonight. Duncan pushed his thoughts to me.

I smiled at that, but I had to admit that the build up was starting to get to me. I wasn’t sure if that was the stress from the magickal situation the family was dealing with, the ghost, the family tree discovery, or just the waiting to finally being completely alone with Duncan.

“So, what did you think of the parade?” Ivy asked me too cheerfully.

“Well, never let it be said that William’s Ford is a boring place to live.” I left the truck idle in the driveway. “I told Cypress and Holly that I think the hex is still in play.”

Ivy sighed. “I am going to have to agree. This is *crazy.*”

“Did you get ahold of your mom and let her know Holly was okay?” I asked.

“Yup.” Ivy pulled at her bottom lip.

“So what do we do now?”

“I say we break into Megan’s locker and see if a doll has been planted,” Ivy suggested as she stowed her camera away.

I laughed as I put the truck in gear. "Listen Sherlock, we can't stroll into the school and go rifling through her locker looking for clues..."

"Wanna bet?" Ivy challenged.

"Oh shit, are you *serious*?"

"Sure, the squad will be busy, and there won't be many people around." Ivy seemed to consider the possibilities.

I backed the truck out of the driveway and decided on the spot to go back to the girl's high school. At least this was proactive. We were doing *something,* and not just sitting around and waiting for the next cheerleader to get hurt.

When Ivy realized where we were headed, she patted my thigh. "Stick with me and follow my lead, Watson."

I snorted out a laugh. Five minutes later, I found myself skulking along in a hall of Central High. "I swear to God, if we get caught, I'm gonna strangle you."

"Relax," Ivy said, ambling along without a care in the world.

"Would this be considered a misdemeanor or a felony?" I whispered to her.

We had strolled into the school so easily, that it made my hackles rise. I saw one janitor pushing a cart down the hall, and Ivy gave him a cheerful wave.

"Will you calm down?" Ivy hissed at me. She stopped, leaned around the next corner, and gave me a 'come ahead' gesture.

I made an effort to act more casual, and I relaxed my shoulders. "Do I even wanna know how you know which locker is Megan's?" Ivy tossed a look over her shoulder and, like the classic television witch, twitched her nose at me. I clamped a hand over my mouth before nervous laughter could escape.

"Here we go." Ivy said as she approached a row of lockers. While I anxiously kept watch, Ivy laid her hand over one lock and muttered something under her breath. I heard the unmistakable sound of the lock clicking open. "Ta da!" Ivy made a flourishing gesture, and the locker door opened on its own.

"Cool," I said in admiration.

"I love the smell of telekinesis in the afternoon." Ivy grinned at me.

"It does come in handy." I scanned the hallway again. "In case you do find something, don't touch it with your bare hands. Use this." I handed her an old grocery bag that I had picked up from the parade route.

For a few nerve wracking moments, Ivy searched through Megan's locker. She handed me Megan's purse, and I opened it and peeked inside. I found nothing but the typical items: a cell phone, wallet, a few cosmetics. "We should drop Megan's purse off at her house," Ivy told me.

I nodded my head in agreement. "Good idea." A quick search had revealed nothing suspicious with Megan's books, so Ivy patted down the purple backpack that was hanging from a hook inside the locker. When she yanked her hands back from the open backpack, I felt my stomach turn over.

"I think something *is* in there," she breathed, pointing at the backpack.

"Do you want me to do it?" I asked her.

Ivy checked up and down the hallway again. "Nope, I got this." She stuck her hand inside the plastic bag and reached inside the backpack with the bag covering her hand. I watched her dig to the bottom of the backpack. She made a face and pulled out a mutilated doll, wrapped in fabric strips and twine.

"Son of a bitch." I said. I wasn't surprised, but damn it, Megan was a really nice girl, and this seemed cruel. "Isn't it unusual for someone to cast spells like this?" I shook my head as we stood looking down at the poppet.

"The kind of spells that purposefully cause bodily harm?" Ivy regarded me steadily. "Yeah, it is rare." Moving quickly, Ivy grabbed the handles of the bag and pulled the whole bag inside out around the poppet. She wrapped the bag around the doll and handed it to me. She closed the locker herself and, without another word, we started walking out of the building immediately with Megan's purse and the wrapped poppet.

As soon as we stepped outside, Megan's cell phone started to ring.

"Let's go drop off Megan's purse at her house," I suggested.

"I want to text Cypress and Holly and let them know

about the new poppet," Ivy said.

"Oh god, your mom," I realized. "We need to let her know we found another one, as well."

Ivy whipped out her cell phone and started texting. I stuck the bag holding the poppet in the back of my truck under the spare tire as I had with the last doll. Since I didn't have any salt to combat negativity, I improvised a quick protective prayer when I got back in the truck. "By the powers of the earth, air, fire and water; Goddess please protect your daughters."

Ivy reached over and drew a circle clockwise around my steering wheel and drew an upright pentagram over it. "As we will it..."

"So shall it be," I finished. I started up my truck and, following Ivy's directions, drove to Megan's. I drove as carefully as if I had dynamite in the back of my pickup truck.

With that poppet back there— it felt like there was.

CHAPTER SIX

Three poppets lay side-by-side on the workbench. Gwen had closed down the shop early for the Homecoming parade, and I stood with her and Bran in the garage. Once again, the bindings from the newest poppet had been burnt in the fire pit. More bay leaves and angelica were sprinkled, and now the astringent aroma of fresh rue was added around the dolls as well.

I tried to listen attentively as Gwen chanted over the poppets to bind their malicious energy, *again.* Gwen expanded the containment circle of silver to thirteen pieces by adding another knife and three silver spoons. When she finished, she stepped back with the two of us.

Bran stood and frowned at the trio of dolls. He was, as usual, immaculately groomed. Today in the breast pocket of his dark suit he had one of those little pocket square thingies. It matched his burgundy tie, and it irritated the hell out of me. He hadn't even had the chance to unpack from the conference he'd been at for the past few days. His suitcase was still sitting in the kitchen.

I nudged him with an elbow. "See what fun you missed by being at your conference this week?" I whispered.

He patted my arm. "Well, I'm here now," he said in what I'm sure he *thought* was a comforting tone.

He may have been a hero when Ivy was abducted, but he *still* got on my last nerve. I sighed at him. Loudly. "Oh good. That makes me feel *so* much better." My derision rolled right off him.

Gwen rolled her shoulders and rubbed at the back of her neck. "I have never seen anything like this. Four girls have been hurt in the past six weeks. The first with a broken leg, this week Kate sprained her wrist, Viviane injured her ankle during practice, and now Megan's broken her arm from the accident during the parade."

Bran held out his hands over the poppets. He blew out a breath between his teeth. "Do we know if there was a poppet found when the first girl was hurt?"

Gwen continued to rub at her neck, "No one has mentioned Kellie finding one."

I rolled my own shoulders, they were starting to cramp in sympathy as I watched Gwen.

Bran tucked his hands back in his pants pockets, as he seemed to consider. "There was a significant amount of dark magick bound up into these poppets. Whoever created these is remarkably skilled in the arts. I also sense that the caster of the hex is female."

Exasperated by the bizarre events of the day, I

turned my irritation towards Bran. “Golly, do you think?” I snarked. “Well thanks for that brilliant insight, Captain Obvious. This whole thing reeks of jealousy or revenge, and it doesn’t take a genius to figure out that somebody, probably a student, has it in for the girls on the squad.”

“Autumn,” Gwen chided me.

I rubbed at the back of my own neck, unable to ignore the tension that was gathering there. “God this is frustrating!” I snapped. “We are *Witches,* for gods sake. Why can’t we put a stop to this hex? This is getting way out of hand. Holly could be next! I mean, what’s the point of having powers or abilities if we don’t use them to solve problems, or protect ourselves?” Gwen stood there and silently studied me. Fed up, I stormed back into the house.

I tossed my denim jacket down next to a big book on herbalism that lay on the table and blew out a long aggravated breath. I knew that losing my temper wouldn’t solve anything, but I had so much happening in my life at the moment. Grad school, trying to find time to study the Craft, Ro the ghost, my relationship with Duncan, finding my place in the family, the tragedy of my brother, the search for the missing grimoire... and now *this* mess. Even mentally listing everything on my plate made my shoulders tighten up.

There had to be a way to get some control over this situation. I deliberately looked at the pretty bundles of herbs that hung from the beams of the potting room and tried to calm myself down. There was always something about the atmosphere in this room that made me feel better. Gwen had told me that my father had fixed up this room for his mother, Rose. Maybe that was why I tended to be drawn to it when I was at my most frazzled.

I reached out and ran my fingers over the fuzzy leaves of a potted African violet. Looking at all of the blooming plants, drying herbs and the big apothecary chest filled with all sorts of magickal ingredients, I felt my shoulders start to loosen slightly. I flipped open the book on magickal herbs, and out of curiosity, thumbed to the listing for African violets.

I read the magickal properties of the African violet, and had to smile. According to the book, the African violet encouraged protection when grown indoors, and its purple flowers promoted love and spirituality. Why was I not surprised? Aunt Gwen never missed a trick.

I heard them come into the house behind me, and I closed the book. Gwen moved into my line of sight. She stood there, seeming remarkably calm, in a pretty blue tunic sweater and grey leggings. "Autumn, I know that you are frustrated. However, you need to understand that a competent Witch does not go around casting spells indiscriminately. Not without knowing exactly where to focus their talents and energy."

I thought about that for a moment. "But all we are doing is defense. Containing the dark magick from the poppets... It's all *after* the fact, and the damage to those four girls has already been done. Isn't it time to be a little proactive?" I argued.

Gwen gave me a little smile. "As in the best defense is a great offense?"

"Exactly!" I agreed.

"Alright, where do you suggest we focus our magick?' she inquired smoothly. "For example, if you cast a counter spell on the individual that you *think* might be responsible, what do you imagine would happen if you were wrong? Where would that magickal energy go, and what would the price be for casting on an innocent?"

Damn it. I hated it when she was all logical. I also recognized that my aunt was absolutely correct. "Yeah, yeah... I get what you are saying. We need to be totally sure who the caster is. Otherwise, if we throw around more magick—"

"It only creates more chaos," Bran finished for me.

Whatever else was going to be said was cut off by a knock on the door. Bran opened the door to the garage and Lexie Proctor, police officer and member of Gwen's coven came in.

"Lexie." Bran nodded formally to her.

"Hi everyone." Lexie smiled.

I noticed that Bran stood up a little taller as Lexie came in. I *thought* he was dating some snooty chick named Angela. But it was obvious to me that Lexie flustered him. Even in her police officer's uniform, Lexie Proctor was pretty. Her honey blonde hair was braided in a neat bun at the nape of her neck, and she stood there radiating confidence.

I'd been a fan of Lexie's ever since I saw how gentle she'd been with Ivy, when she had questioned my cousin at the hospital the night of Ivy's rescue. Because of her kindness, I tried to work up some warmth into my greeting. "Hi Lexie."

"I'm off shift, so I thought I'd drop by and see what else you've discovered," Lexie explained as we all went through to the kitchen. Lexie pulled up a stool at the breakfast bar and sat, comfortable in her uniform and gun. "I took a look at those dolls out there. That's truly messed up." She shuddered.

Okay, that reaction bothered me— a lot. If a cop— who is also a Witch, shudders over something, that can't be good. Focusing on Lexie, I felt a strong tightening in my solar plexus. "What else has happened?" I asked her following my gut hunch.

She smiled at me. "You are really impressive. One of these days I'd like you to take a look at some of our open homicide cases."

"Ah, no thanks." I tried not to heave. The last thing I wanted to do was to psychically 'see' a murder or to have a vision of someone being killed.

"This is off the record, and is not to be repeated." Lexie waited until we all agreed. "The coach of the squad contacted me because she received a sort of vague threat against the girls, a call to her private cell phone."

Gwen laid her hand on Lexie's arm. "Is the school taking it seriously?"

Lexie frowned. "Well, I went in and had a meeting with the principal. He seems to think it's just a prank. But to be on the safe side, he has taken the precaution of having a few more plain clothes officers as security at the game tonight."

Ivy wandered into the kitchen. "Hi Officer Lexie." Ivy grinned at her. "I have some news," Ivy announced plopping onto an empty barstool. "Holly texted me a little bit ago. Megan's arm is in a cast. She won't be performing at the game tonight, but she's at home and resting now."

"I'm glad she's resting comfortably," Lexie said. "But I'd really like to know how a spell involving so many individuals is being pulled off."

"I have a theory," Gwen began, "the longer the dolls are in close physical proximity to their victims, the more damage or harm they've been able to cause."

"Which might explain why Kate's wrist had only been sprained," I said. "It must not have been in her locker for very long, and she tossed the doll in a garbage can right away."

Ivy drummed her fingers on the counter. "If Viviane, and now Megan, unknowingly carried the dolls in their backpacks for a few days... that would explain why their injuries were worse."

"Here, look at this timeline, Gwen." Lexie pulled out a notebook and showed us a timeline she had created.

"Whoever is planting the poppets on the girls is *close* to them. Close enough that they have easy access to their backpacks and lockers."

"Agreed," Bran said.

"How *did* you find that third doll today?" Lexie asked us.

Ivy squirmed a bit in her seat. I studied the kitchen counter, trying to act innocent.

"Girls?" Gwen inquired.

I glanced over at Ivy before I said anything. "We found it in her backpack," I said finally. *Well, that was the truth.* No sooner had I silently thought that, when Gwen raised an eyebrow at me and seemed pissed. I shook my head. I had to start remembering that her telepathy worked best when she was physically close to you.

"Why am I getting a psychic impression of Sherlock Holmes?" Gwen asked.

I suddenly recalled joking with Ivy about acting all 'Sherlock' on our way into the school. Ivy's eyes flared wide, and she shook her head at me.

With a sigh, I dropped my chin into my hand in defeat. *Freakin' telepaths...* "Oh, go ahead tell them Ivy." I gave up.

"Thanks Watson. You suck," Ivy said to me. She crossed her arms on the counter and explained how we had acquired the third doll. Afterwards, Gwen shut her eyes and shook her head. Bran tossed his hands in the air, and Lexie started to smile but made an effort to look disapproving.

Gwen walked over and dropped a hand on Ivy's shoulder. "What would you have done if you'd have been caught?"

Ivy shrugged. "Well we weren't. So no harm, no foul."

Lexie tapped her pen against her notepad. "It stands to reason if there were four accidents, and three poppets found, then there are probably more poppets."

Gwen nodded in agreement. "We need to see if the rest of the girls have been given poppets— *discreetly*." Gwen emphasized the last word, and gave Ivy and me a withering look.

Bran seemed to mull that over. "How do you suggest we go about doing that?"

I couldn't help it, I grinned at Ivy and said. "I suppose we could have our resident B and E girl go through the rest of the girl's lockers at the school."

Lexie held up a hand. "I did *not* hear that," she grimaced.

"Sorry." I tried to look contrite.

Lexie drummed her fingers on the counter as she thought. "For tonight, we keep an eye on the rest of the girls on the squad. We need to watch and see who is close and who has access to their personal belongings during the game. Tonight is the biggest football game of the year, and if someone is going to try something else, it will probably be tonight."

"I'm going to the game with Duncan. We can help

watch." I volunteered us.

Ivy announced that she was supposed to help take pictures for the yearbook, so she would be on the sidelines of the game with her camera. "I'm supposed to get plenty of pictures of all the cheer squads, and the band tonight. So I can watch and photograph the squad from a different perspective."

Lexie beamed at her. "That's perfect." She focused on Bran. "I'm off duty this evening, but I'd feel better if I was close. Do you have a date to the game tonight?" she asked him.

I had the supreme pleasure of watching Bran be at a loss for words. "Ah, no I don't," he finally managed.

"Well, you do now," Lexie said.

Bran stood there shell shocked, as Lexie continued on as if she didn't notice. "I'll pick you up at six thirty," she told him. Lexie hopped up, told the rest of us goodbye and let herself out.

I bit the inside of my mouth to keep from laughing. Bran appeared a little flummoxed. His mouth worked, but nothing came out. "I've never had a woman ask me out before," he finally said.

Ivy gave him a light punch in the shoulder as she walked past him to the staircase. "Technically bro, she didn't ask you. She *ordered* you." Ivy made a whip cracking sound.

Gwen tried to hide a smile as Bran shuffled his feet and for once did not look all elegant, poised and in control.

Bran ran a hand through his hair. "You know, I am really uncomfortable around guns," he said to no one in particular. He picked up his suitcase and carried it upstairs.

I followed him up to the second level. I had a big night to get ready for, myself. "I wouldn't worry about it Bran— looks to me like Lexie is *very* comfortable with guns." I couldn't resist ragging on him, as it helped keep me from being nervous.

About tonight. After the game. With Duncan.

"What are you so nervous about?" Ivy frowned at me from over her shoulder.

"Nothing. Stay out of my head." I glared at her.

"I'm not in your head. Your emotions are broadcasting way out to here." Ivy stopped, stretching her arms out as if to demonstrate.

Damn! I walked around her, making an effort to yank my emotions back in line.

"You *are* nervous about tonight..." Ivy wiggled her eyebrows at me. "And you're not wound up because of the football game."

"I think you're sensing Bran," I said. "He's the one who's all flustered."

"Shut up, Autumn," he grumbled passing us on the second floor landing.

"You never know..." I teased him. "Maybe if you're a really *bad* boy Lexie will get out her handcuffs."

Bran turned to glare at me, and I wiggled my eyebrows suggestively. Ivy giggled at him and went to her room, and I turned to go to mine. Suddenly I felt a quick burn across my butt. I gasped and grabbed at my backside and looked over my shoulder to see what happened.

There was a little black smudge across the back pocket of my jeans. *Bran.* I glared at him, truly shocked that he had done that.

Bran brushed his hands off, and I saw a little spark of energy fall from his hands.

"Damn it Sparky, these jeans are new! I am *so* telling your mom you did that," I threatened.

Bran tossed back his head and laughed. An honest to god belly laugh. I had never heard him laugh like that before. It reminded me of my father, and I smiled in reaction.

Ivy moved to her doorway and announced in a superior tone of voice, "You kids stop playing with magick before you put somebody's eye out!"

"What's going on up there?" Gwen called from downstairs.

"Nothing." Bran and I hollered back in unison.

Bran grinned at me as he slammed his door. I slammed mine too, and I hurried to get ready for my evening with Duncan. Tonight promised to be memorable... in more ways than one.

***

The first thing I noticed as Duncan and I entered the

stadium was that the stands were packed. The Homecoming game had brought the locals out in droves. We worked our way through the crowd, and the atmosphere was celebratory and electric. The marching band was seated all together in one section and was playing a rousing fight song, while the cheerleaders were standing on the track between the stands and the field, doing a dance routine to the music.

Duncan and I found a seat with the rest of my family, and I noticed that the cheer squad currently numbered eight. The eighth girl had a slightly different uniform, and once the gold metallic pompons stopped shaking, I realized that it was the back-flipping girl from the JV squad. Leilah. I remembered. Her name was Leilah Martin.

Holly and Cypress were in the center of the front linc as co-captains, and they appeared happy. Kate was there doing her best, despite her wrist in a brace. I searched for, and found Viviane sitting in the front row of the stands, right in front of her squad, with another girl who had a hot pink cast on her leg.

Both of the injured girls were wearing their cheer uniforms. They sat with the coach and cheered along with their squad from the bleachers. I smiled when I saw that somebody had decorated both of the girls' crutches festively with blue and yellow curling ribbons.

Duncan and I sat down next to Aunt Gwen and Marie Rousseau. Bran and Lexie followed us up the steps and ended up sitting one row below, and directly in front of us. I saw as Lexie sat down, that she was indeed wearing her gun. The outline through her coat was unmistakable. But I was pretty sure all cops carried a gun, even if they were off duty.

I nudged Aunt Gwen. "Is that Kellie?" I asked, pointing to the cheerleader with the hot pink cast.

"It is," Gwen answered, and handed me a program. Gwen was wearing a large button featuring a photo of Holly in her cheer uniform. The button had blue and gold ribbon behind it, and I saw lots of parents sporting buttons with sports photos of their son or daughter. Even Marie was wearing one.

"Aw, I feel bad for her and Viviane missing out on cheering at their Homecoming game," I said, and glanced over the names of all the players, cheerleaders, and the nominees for Homecoming court. As I read the program, I noted that both Kellie and Viviane were nominated for Homecoming Queen.

I held the program down between Lexie and Bran. "Lexie, did you notice that two of the injured girls are nominated for Homecoming Queen? Could that be connected to everything that's going on?"

"I did." Lexie shifted her gaze from the program to where the girls sat. Then she pulled out her cell phone and sent a few quick texts.

Duncan put his arm around my shoulder and said in my ear. "She's probably contacting the plain clothes officers working security at the game and telling them to move closer to the squad."

While I had told Duncan about the poppets, I had not shared the information about the plainclothes officers. I gaped at him, wondering how he had known, and he leaned over and told me. "I spotted them when we first came in." Duncan smiled. "There's Ivy." He pointed to her as she stood between the squad and the football player's bench taking photos for the yearbook.

As I watched, Ivy swung her long lensed camera directly at our group sitting in the stands. I smiled and we all waved to her. She gave us a thumbs up and went back to photographing the squad and the band.

A short time later, Lexie stood up and told us that she and Bran had decided to sit with her friend. She leveled a look at Bran. His smile was a bit strained, but he stood up, and they moved several rows down to sit right next to the cheer coach and the two injured cheerleaders. I saw Lexie smile at the coach, and the coach look a little relieved to have the off duty cop sitting close by.

I exchanged a significant look with Aunt Gwen. So much for going to the game and having fun.

Gwen patted me on the arm. "Try and enjoy yourself," she suggested.

Duncan squeezed my hand, and I did my best to try and relax. The football game was enjoyable, and as the second quarter wound down, I had almost forgotten about the intrigue. Right before half time, I was standing in line waiting to use the restroom. I could still see the game, and listened with a half an ear while two overdressed women stood in line in front of me, gossiping. I wiggled my toes in my comfortable neon green running shoes and rolled my eyes at the idea of wearing stiletto heels to a high school football game.

"... if it wasn't for that Bishop girl, she would have made the Varsity squad," said woman number one.

I zeroed in on the two women giving them my full attention.

"The girl is a high level competitive gymnast. By all rights she *should* have made varsity," a dark haired woman declared. She had her back to me, and as she straightened her gold sweater, I tried to act casual, as I shamelessly eavesdropped.

Gossipy woman number one leaned into the second woman. "Well, who knows what sort of black magick that family does to get their way?" She wasn't very quiet and I was shocked at her comment.

The woman in gold laughed spitefully. "Well keep watching dear, and you'll see some real *magick* before the game is over." She winked at her friend. I sincerely hoped they were only joking.

I worked hard not to have any facial reaction to what I had overheard. How many times had I been told that my face gave away my feelings? *Be calm... and listen.* I told myself. There were many families in William's Ford with a legacy of magick. It seemed every time I turned around, I was tripping over more of them. I wondered who these women were.

A bit later, as I washed my hands, I saw in the mirror

over the sink, the two women still talking like conspirators. I shook the water from my fingertips and noted that both of them were sporting decorated buttons with a picture of a cheerleader on it. Exactly like Aunt Gwen was wearing. Okay, so these were cheer moms.

"Excuse me," I said politely as I reached past them for a paper towel. I glanced quickly at the photos of the cheerleaders that were on their buttons. *JV uniforms.* I confirmed for myself. I'd seen enough of the varsity squad for the past few weeks to be able to tell the difference. I got a good look at the photo button on the brunette's gold sweater. It featured a girl with pixie length dark hair, and a sleek foxy face. It was Leilah Martin. The girl who was currently filling in on the Varsity squad.

The women seemed to take offense at my reaching for the paper towels and moved farther off to the side. "Well at least tonight Leilah will get to show everyone what she can do!" Woman number one insisted to her friend.

I tossed the paper towel towards the can, and started to walk past the two bitchy women. Seemed like these cheer moms had a bad case of sour grapes. Given their comments about magick, I wondered, were those grapes sour enough to make one of them start hexing the varsity squad? Gwen, Marie and Bran all agreed that the caster was powerful. It was a safe bet that it was also a female. What if it was an adult doing the hexing, and *not* a student at the school as everyone supposed?

My mind on getting back to the family with this newest piece of information, I almost didn't see the group of teenage girls that came racing into the restroom. I tried to move quickly out of their way, and that had me colliding solidly with Leilah's mother. I bumped into the brunette hard, and she teetered on her heels.

"Sorry!" I apologized and reached out to steady her. When I touched her arm I was hit with a hard, nasty snap of energy. I gasped in surprise and let go of her in a hurry.

"Idiot." She glared at me, tossed her head, and sailed past.

I stood there for a moment holding my hurt hand. Leilah's mother had *power.* The last time I had experienced something so nasty was when I'd had an unfortunate encounter with Thomas Drake at the University library.

I checked my hand, half expecting to see blistered fingers, but they seemed the same. I flexed my hand, blew out a long shaky breath, and started working my way through the crowd and back to Duncan and my family as quickly as possible.

I passed Gwen on the crowded bleacher steps. My aunt gave me an odd look, but was jostled past me by the crowd that was heading down. I eventually made my way back up, and sat down between Marie and Duncan. My butt had barely hit the bleachers, and Duncan was reaching for my sore hand.

"What happened?" he asked.

I cradled my aching hand to my chest. "I had a little run-in with some angry cheer moms."

Marie whipped her head around her eyes narrowing. "You smell a little like sulfur,"

"What?" I asked horrified.

She leaned in and sniffed at my jacket. "Some negative magicks leave a trace. Particularly nasty juju smells bad— like sulfur."

"So that brunette *had* been a Wi—" I was cut off as Marie gripped my wrist firmly, and yanked my hand over so she could inspect it.

"Be careful what you say in public," Marie gave me a stern look.

"Sorry," I mumbled.

"Which brunette?" Duncan wanted to know.

I looked around for her. "I'm pretty sure it was Leilah Martin's mother. She had on a gold sweater."

"I'll be right back," Duncan stood up, quickly went down the bleacher steps, and was soon lost in the crowd.

"What's he going to do?" I asked Marie.

"He's going to go scout around, I imagine," Marie said discreetly, laying her hand over my sore fingers. I could hear her chanting under her breath while the majority of the people in the stands rose to their feet to cheer for the Homecoming Court.

A few moments later, Marie gave my hand a gentle pat. "That should do the trick."

"Thanks Marie," I said, looking down at my hand. I was impressed. It did feel better.

"You're welcome," she said, tossing me a wink.

"What about the sulfur smell, will that go away?" I asked. *God, I did not want to smell like sulfur, tonight of all nights!*

"Trust me," Marie stood up to applaud the Homecoming Court. "It will fade away before the end of the third period of the football game.

CHAPTER SEVEN

Duncan held open the little guesthouse door for me. The heavy wooden door made a loud creaking sound. "Very Halloween-ish," I said.

"Enter freely of your own will," he said with a slight leer.

"Funny." I laughed in reaction to his quoting of *Dracula*. Despite the creaking door, the guesthouse looked inviting. The exterior had recently been painted white with blue trim, and it sat centered in the quiet backyard of the older home Duncan was currently rehabbing.

"It's an old door, but it has character." Duncan ran his hand along the stained glass in the heavy wooden door.

"I like the colonial blue color that you painted it." I brushed my fingers along the door as I stepped inside.

"Blue front doors repel negative magick," Duncan said and came in behind me.

"Oh yeah? That's cool."

Duncan smiled. "Let me take your jacket." I shrugged out of it and he hung our jackets on a series of old antique hooks in the entry. When he flipped the lock on the door, my heart jumped against my ribs.

"I'm glad nothing else happened with the girls at the game tonight," I said, as he reached past me to turn on the lights.

"Come on in." He took my hand as we walked over into the combined living room/ kitchen area.

I ordered myself to settle down. Now that we were finally alone, I *was* a little nervous. It's not like I was a virgin or anything... I'd had a few serious boyfriends while I had been an undergrad. But I'd been single for the last year or so, so I was a little anxious. My former partners had been college guys, while Duncan... was a man. He had accomplished a lot by becoming a contractor and running a successful business, and he wasn't quite thirty years old.

God I hoped this went well. Please don't let me do anything klutzy tonight... I realized my thoughts were rambling, and remembered that Duncan could occasionally pick up thoughts if they were loud enough — and he was in close proximity. So, I made an effort to clear my mind.

Duncan moved to the kitchen alcove and got out a bottle of white wine. He poured the wine into two glasses as we chatted about the home team's victory, and I took a deep breath and released it as slowly, and as quietly, as possible. The past weeks had been a slow build up to tonight, and I was torn between a little case of nerves and some serious sexual tension.

I admired the little guesthouse he would be calling home for the next few months. It was charming, really. The walls were painted a warm gray, and the charcoal colored sectional sofa appeared brand new. A huge flat screen TV was across from the sofa, and a little breakfast bar separated the living room area from the small kitchen. An artificial jack-o'-lantern was lit on the counter and cast a warm orange glow on the breakfast bar.

I saw a few weathered looking signs hanging on the kitchen walls, and went over for a closer look.

"These are great." I told him as I studied a large, obviously vintage apothecary sign, and another old metal sign that featured an owl on a crescent moon.

He handed me a glass of wine. "How's your hand?" He asked, as we sat down on the couch.

I glanced down at the hand that had gotten a good zap from Leilah Martin's mother. "Better since Marie worked on it."

Duncan took a sip from his glass, and set his wine aside on a table. He took my hand in his and studied it carefully. When he did, I felt that familiar rush of energy. My face felt warm and as I watched, he raised my hand to his mouth and pressed a slow lingering kiss to the center of my palm.

I hastily took a sip of wine and gulped... Hard. I tried to keep my focus, but he wasn't making this easy. What

I really wanted to do was to toss the wine aside and jump him. However, I really didn't want to come off as some horny co-ed.

So I thought I'd try and go for sophisticated, and have some conversation.

Before.

I hastily chose a safe topic. "I thought it was cute when Kellie's and Viviane's boyfriends scooped them up and carried them out to the center of the field, when they announced the candidates for Homecoming Queen." I smiled, remembering the gallant football player and marching band member from half-time.

"It sure made it a lot easier for both of the girls than trying to get across the field with their crutches," Duncan said as he reached out and began to toy with my hair.

"Bran sure seems nervous around Lexie," I said in my bid for intelligent, adult conversation.

"He's attracted to her." Duncan continued to stroke my hair.

"He is *not*!"

Duncan smiled. "Yes, he is."

"But he's dating that Angela chick." I made a face.

"Have they gone out recently?"

I thought about that. Since Ivy's abduction, I hadn't seen Bran go out... and come to think of it, he never mentioned Angela anymore. I glanced at Duncan, and he was studying me in a way that made my mouth go dry.

My heart thudded against my ribs as I took another careful sip of the wine. “So what do you think about all of the recent weirdness?” I asked him.

“Could you be more specific?” he said.

Good point. This was William’s Ford, where weirdness seemed to happen on any day of the week that ended with a ‘Y’. “I meant,” I explained, “the poppets, the injured cheerleaders, and what I overheard at the game.”

Duncan smiled at me a little, before he answered. “I think it bears looking into... But not tonight.”

He took the wine glass out of my hand, set it aside and stood. He held his hand out to me, I took it, and rose to my feet. We stood facing each other for a moment. He slid his arms around me and kissed me.

I wrapped my arms around him and our chests bumped. Just like the first time we kissed, I felt a blast of energy from the full body contact. After a moment I saw a *flickering* behind my closed eyes. Distracted, I pulled back. I frowned up at the overhead light fixture, as it blinked from dim to bright, and back to dim.

“I think you need to have...” I gasped a little as Duncan’s mouth cruised from my mouth, to my cheek, and down my neck. “...the electrician back in here.”

Duncan paused and raised his eyes to the blinking fixture. “It’s not the wiring. It’s us.” He ran his hands from my waist, under my shirt, and up. He bit gently down on the spot between my shoulder and my neck, causing me to jump. The lights flickered again.

"Oh." I figured it out. I had seen what happened at the manor when my cousin's and I got into a fight. When our magickal energy raised from strong emotions, the lights flickered and sometimes blew out.

Pay attention. Duncan's voice sounded in my head.

You want attention? I projected my thoughts back to him, as I reached up and gave the side of his neck a playful little bite.

Duncan yanked back from me a little bit to meet my eyes. "I heard you. You sent your thoughts clearly that time." His eyes seemed a darker blue, as he swooped down and kissed me harder than before.

I wrapped myself around him, relieved that I had managed to avoid bumping noses, or do anything else uncoordinated. After a few moments I projected my thoughts again. *Duncan?*

Yeah? He was kissing down my neck and unbuttoning my lacey blouse at the same time.

Show me your bedroom. I thought at him, and the overhead lights went out with three soft pops of sound.

I would have laughed at the lights blowing out, if I hadn't been gasping at the sensation of his hands peeling my shirt aside. He unhooked my turquoise lace bra, pushed it and my blouse off my shoulders, tugging it down my arms. The garments fluttered down to the floor as he trailed more urgent kisses from my throat to my breasts.

I tangled my hands in the hair at the nape of his neck and hung on. Duncan reached down, and firmly grabbed ahold of my backside. He boosted me up and I wrapped my legs around his waist. His mouth met mine again as he carried me across the living room, and into the small dark bedroom.

***

I laid in the dark with my head on his shoulder, running my fingers across his chest. A cool breeze fluttered the curtains at the bedroom window, making me shiver a bit. Duncan shifted, pulled the sheet up for me and I cuddled in closer to his warmth.

"What time is it?" I asked around a yawn.

Duncan reached out, fumbling for the clock on his night stand. He turned it around. "4:15."

"Hmmm. I guess we fell asleep after the second round."

"We earned it," he said.

I slid down, and ran a line of kisses from his chest down to his belly. I smiled in satisfaction when his stomach quivered. "I guess I should probably go." I trailed my kisses lower and felt his hands tighten in my hair.

Duncan's hands clenched and he groaned when I ran my tongue across the length of him.

"Unless you'd rather I stayed?" I paused. The light of the waning moon shone through the window and I could see him clearly. His hands tightened in my hair again, and he seemed to be holding his breath.

"Can't make up your mind?" I teased.

"You're not going anywhere," he growled, and yanked me back up to the top of the bed. He flipped me over onto my back and pushed my knees apart. I bit back a moan when he lowered his head between my thighs. I reached my hands back for the spokes of his wrought iron headboard and held on.

Beside us, the bedside clock blinked, crackled, and went out.

***

"Well, holy crap." I panted, sometime later.

Duncan and I lay side by side trying to catch our breath. I felt him reach out for his alarm clock. He banged it against the night stand a few times but it stayed dark. "We fried it," he said, and began to laugh.

I snorted out a laugh as well. I covered my mouth, horrified at the un-ladylike noise, but that only made Duncan laugh harder. I gave it up and let the laughter come. "I'll get you a windup clock," I said. It struck me as ridiculous that our combined energy had literally shorted out the living room lights *and* the bedside alarm clock.

Duncan reached down and took my hand in his. He raised it, and pressed the back of my hand to his lips. "How about a shower and then I'll fix you breakfast?"

I smiled at him. "Sounds good."

The sun was beginning to rise as I stood wearing

only my unbuttoned blouse, bra and panties in Duncan's bathroom. I brushed out my hair, and Duncan sat on the side of his bed, shirtless, in unsnapped jeans, watching me.

"You have a little tattoo on your left hip," Duncan said.

"Too busy last night to notice it?" I grinned at him as I walked in the room. I reached for my jeans and stepped into them. Before I could pull them all the way up, Duncan came over to inspect the small tattoo.

"A blue crescent moon and yellow stars." He ran a fingertip over them.

"You like?" I asked as I hitched the jeans up the rest of the way.

"Yes, I like that little smiling moon. Now I'll see that every time I look at you." He grinned at me.

After a casual breakfast of scrambled eggs and toast, Duncan dropped me off at the manor. The gates were open as we pulled in. We shared a lingering kiss before I hopped out of his blue truck and waved goodbye.

I watched as he backed his truck out of the driveway, and as soon as he cleared the gates, they closed— all on their own.

I dug my keys out of my purse and stood for a moment, enjoying watching the eastern sky brighten. The crisp smell of leaves and mums were ripe in the morning air. How I loved the colors, and scents, of the season my father had named me after. With a happy sigh, I headed for the front porch. My foot had only hit the first step when I heard someone singing.

I cocked my head to the side and listened. Whoever they were, they had a strong voice. Intrigued, I followed the sound. I walked around the corner of the house, and realized I was hearing a woman singing the old Robert Palmer song, "Addicted to Love".

There in the rose garden, kneeling in the plants, was Ro. Her back was to me, and, once again, she appeared with the fuchsia sweater, denim overalls, and that silly straw hat with the pink flowers on the brim.

Seriously? A singing ghost? I stopped for a second, and rolled my eyes to the sky. I took a deep breath to psych myself up, and continued forward. As I walked closer to the rose garden, Ro turned around.

"Good morning," she said turning back to her gardening, and to belting out that song from the 1980's.

"Good morning, Ro." I stopped at the edge of the rose garden. I crossed my arms against the early morning chill.

"Have a nice time with Duncan last night?" she asked.

"What?" I gaped at her.

She continued to sing the song while she fussed with the lavender planted under the roses.

I blushed at the appropriateness of the lyrics. I didn't even want to know how a ghost had kept tabs on my sex life.

While I stood there at a loss for words, Ro turned her head up to me and grinned. "I assume you had a *very* nice time as you are strolling home after sunrise."

"I am so *not* having this conversation," I said and turned away. I managed about two steps before Ro suddenly materialized directly in front of me. I couldn't help it. I squeaked as I came to a halt.

"Did you use protection, young lady?" Ro planted her hands on her hips and raised her eyebrows.

"Dear god," I muttered, shutting my eyes in embarrassment. "Keep your voice down."

"No one can hear me but you." Ro tapped her foot. "Well?"

"Yes! Yes, we used protection." I tossed my hands up in frustration. "And clearly I've had a psychotic break since I'm standing here discussing safe sex with a ghost!"

"Well, a baby would complicate your plans for that Master's degree," Ro pointed out.

A baby would complicate your plans... "Ro, what can you tell me about my father's son? The baby that was born in 1985?"

Ro's image suddenly started to fade. I could see her lips moving, but there was no sound. I reached out, as if that would stop her departure. My hands passed right through her image and felt chilled.

"Ro!" I called out for her, but she was gone— again.

I walked around to the back of the manor on the off chance that the ghost had materialized somewhere else, but found nothing. *Figures, the minute I start to ask the important questions...* My good mood was sliding towards annoyance, and I pulled my jacket closer to ward off the morning chill. I heard the loud call of a crow, and tipped my head up to discover one perched on the peak of the roof of the manor.

"Don't you start with me," I said, and to my amazement the crow launched itself from the roof and landed a few feet in front of me.

The crow folded its wings under. It walked along with its head bobbing. "*Koww, koww,*" the bird called.

"Okay." I stood still, waiting to see what the bird would do. I held my breath, partly curious, and partly thrilled at my close encounter with the large bird.

The crow cocked his head at me and seemed to be waiting. I took an experimental step forward, and the bird flapped his wings as if he wanted to keep me from going anywhere. I stepped to the left, and the bird hopped over playfully as if to block me. I tried going right, with the same result. "Well, aren't you smart?" I said to the bird. "I read somewhere that the crow was thought to be one of the smartest animals in the world."

I started to chuckle as the bird's head bobbed up and down, and he called again. Wondering what would happen, I sank slowly to my knees in the wet grass. I held my breath when the crow ambled over close enough to touch. It seemed to regard me carefully.

"You're very handsome," I couldn't help but grin as the crow held his head a bit higher at the compliment. *I mean, it wasn't any stranger than anything else that had happened recently.* My fingers itched to touch, and

I considered getting my phone out of my purse to get a picture of the crow.

The bird began to pick through his feathers. He pulled a small feather from his wing, and as I held my breath, the crow dropped the feather on my knee. "Thank you," I said.

The crow hopped back, and with a few flaps of his wings that had my hair fluttering, he launched himself back into the sky.

I picked up the feather and rose to my feet. I brushed at my wet knees, and watched the crow circle around the manor and then settle back on a point of the roof. I twirled the feather as I let myself back in the house, thinking about today's ghostly and avian visits.

I quietly went up the stairs, figuring everyone was still sleeping, and eased into my own bedroom. I shut the door behind me and flipped the lock. I walked over to the mantle above the white brick fireplace and picked up the large feather from the crow that had smacked into my truck's windshield last month.

That crow had caused me to stomp on my brakes and avoid a SUV that had ran a stop sign. The bird had probably saved the twins and me from being in a serious car accident. *There's no way this playful bird today was the same bird from before... was there?* I considered the possibility, and tucked the new smaller crow feather next to a few of my favorite framed photos displayed on the mantle.

I wandered over to my bedroom window, glancing

down towards the rose gardens. They looked normal at the moment— whatever normal was around here anyway. Before I could forget, I grabbed my notebook. This was my second ghostly encounter in the manor's gardens with Ro, and I wanted to document it. At her first visitation she had told me to study my family tree. This had led me to uncovering the secret of my father's first child. But when I asked her about that baby today, she had faded away.

Who was Ro, really? And why was she haunting me?

I needed to speak to Gwen. It was time for some answers. Today would be crazy with the girls getting ready for their Homecoming dance. But early this evening, as soon as they left, Gwen and I would be alone in the manor.

I tossed my jacket over the footboard of my bed and stripped out of my damp jeans while I went through various scenarios as to how I could confront my aunt about the ghost in the rose garden *and* the family tree.

A loud knock sounded on my door. Before I could open it, the lock popped, and the glass door knob turned. I knew what was coming and stepped quickly back, right before it slammed open.

Ivy stood out in the hall with both hands full of nail polish. "Good! Your back! What color should I paint my nails tonight?"

"Using your magick to open locked bedroom doors isn't polite, Ivy," I said, standing there is my underwear.

"Whatever." Ivy shoved the bottles at me.

I glanced down at the nail polish. “Every one of these polishes are black.”

“Hey! Is that a tattoo on your hip?” Ivy grabbed at my hips and turned me around.

“Aack!” I jumped back to evade. “Hands off my butt!”

“What’s going on in here?” Gwen stood smiling from the doorway. Wrapped in a plush hunter green robe, she wore flannel pajama pants and was sipping calmly from a mug.

“Mom, check this out!” Ivy turned me so Gwen could see my back. “Autumn has a design close to the family’s magickal crest tattooed on her hip.”

“Family magickal crest?” I asked them, my hands still full of bottles of nail polish.

Gwen stepped into my room setting the mug on my dresser. She unbelted her robe, turned her back to me, shrugging her right shoulder free. As the robe dropped down, I saw above the tank top that she’d slept in, a large black crescent moon tattoo. The crescent was made up of Celtic knot work, and three small stars were sprinkled around the moon.

“Your father also had this tattoo.” Gwen pulled the robe back into place. “His was centered—”

“On his back,” I said, handing the polish back to Ivy. A little shaken, I went to my dresser for a pair of yoga pants. “That was the reason I got this little blue moon,” I admitted. “It was a way to honor his memory after he died. I didn’t realize that the crescent was a family crest."

"It's a cute tattoo, but you need a bigger one," Ivy suggested.

"It's an interesting coincidence," I said.

Gwen picked up her mug and moved to the doorway. "I don't believe in coincidences." She smiled, but it didn't reach her eyes.

Before I could call after my aunt, Ivy was waving nail polish at me and demanding to know which was better, shiny black, black glitter, or a flat black for her manicure.

I pulled my yoga pants on and helped Ivy pick out a sparkly black polish. It was at that moment that I realized I had found my opening for the discussion I needed to have with my aunt. A discussion about our resident ghost, my father's past *and* his son.

While I listened to Ivy's happy chatter, I considered what I had learned. I didn't think it was a fluke that the family's magickal crest was a crescent moon, and we were now searching for a grimoire tied into the magick of lunar eclipses.

I was starting to think that Gwen was right. There was no such thing as *coincidence.*

CHAPTER EIGHT

I had never seen such a commotion in all my life as the twins getting ready for Homecoming. I was roped into their preparations for the rest of the day, whether I liked it or not. Once they were ready, the sheer amount of pictures Gwen took was staggering.

The girls posed on the decorated staircase, and Ivy's halter top style black polka dot dress was perfect for her. She paired the knee length dress with red chucks, and somehow it worked. Holly's dress was also above her knees, and was a strapless number in a pretty aqua-blue. Their dates, Travis and Eric, arrived, and the photos started all over again.

Still, I was determined to have a private talk with Aunt Gwen. So I stayed at the manor, and tried to be a good sport. While I watched the girl's photo session with their dates, I decided— for the time being—not mention the information about my father's son that I'd found. Instead, I wanted to bring up the subject of the ghost and see what, if anything, Gwen could tell me about her. Then depending on that, I'd broach the other sensitive topic. We'd had enough drama at the manor lately.

I bided my time, and waved goodbye to the girls and their dates. It was late afternoon, and apparently they were supposed to meet up with a large group before the dance for dinner. As soon as I heard their car leave, I followed Gwen into the kitchen and, verbally, pounced. "Did you know that we have a ghost?"

Whipping her head up, Gwen stopped looking at the images on the digital camera. "Come again?"

"I said, did you know that we have a ghost?"

Gwen set the camera on the counter. "What makes you think we do?" She smiled as if I was making a joke.

"I don't think we have a ghost," I bristled with indignation. "I *know.*"

"I've seen plenty go on around the manor, but I've never seen a ghost." Gwen started to walk by, patting me on the arm as if to reassure me.

While she may have meant to be kind—the arm patting pissed me off. "That's interesting Gwen, because she told me that you *knew* she was here!"

"You interacted with another spirit?" I had Gwen's full attention now. I could almost see the wheels turning in her head. "*Where* exactly did you have your encounter?" she asked after a moment.

"I first saw her the other day when I looked out my window and spotted someone working in the rose garden. I thought she was a real person so I went to find out who she was, and what she was doing in the yard."

Gwen's eyes grew large. "Describe her to me. What did she look like?"

"She's an older middle aged lady, blue eyes, gray hair, and she was wearing denim overalls with a bright pink sweater. Goofy clothes for a ghost, if you ask me. Oh, and she had this crazy straw gardening hat on, with bright pink flowers on it."

Gwen made a sound somewhere between a sob and a laugh. "Did she tell you her name?" She pressed a hand to her heart, and her eyes shimmered with tears.

"She told me I could call her Ro."

Gwen suddenly burst out laughing. "She did, did she?" Gwen wiped at a few tears that had spilled over, and cleared her throat. "When did you see her again?"

"This morning after I came home from Duncan's."

"I see." Gwen slanted me a look. "Did she communicate with you today?"

It wasn't a secret that I'd spent the night with Duncan, but still... I struggled not to feel embarrassed. "For a short time, she did talk to me." I hedged, not wanting to discuss my sex life.

"Come with me. I want to show you something." Gwen motioned for me to follow her.

I trailed along as we went upstairs and into Gwen's bedroom suite. We walked through the turret space and Gwen went immediately to a gorgeous antique wardrobe in her bedroom. She opened it and pulled out a storage box.

She sat on her bed and patted the yellow and white quilt next to her in invitation. Gwen pulled up the lid on the box. As I sat beside her I saw dozens of old photos inside, all stacked neatly. She rummaged through, pulling out a snapshot. Gwen studied it carefully for a moment, then, finally, handed it to me face down.

"What's this?" I asked. As I reached for the photo, I saw the year 1992 printed on the back.

"You tell me," Gwen said.

Flipping over the photo, I got a good hard jolt of recognition. A middle age woman seemed to smile at me from the snapshot. She was wearing jeans, a hot pink sweater and a silly straw gardening hat decorated with pink flowers. This was absolutely the woman who'd appeared to me. *Ro* was kneeling in the rose garden of the manor with her arms around a laughing, pigtailed toddler.

It wasn't so much seeing a photo of the ghost—when she'd been alive, that had me jolting. It was the sudden realization that the little girl who stood grinning in Ro's arms, was in fact, me.

"Ro told me she had changed my diapers," I whispered to Gwen.

"*Now,* do you recognize your grandmother, Rose?"

"She told me to call her Ro—" I shook my head over that.

"My father—your grandfather, used to call her Ro," Gwen explained.

"I don't remember her." I felt sad about that. *No wonder she told me to look at my roots. My grandmother had probably been miffed that I hadn't recognized her!* I replayed in my mind everything Ro had ever said to me.

Remembering our conversation this morning, I shut my eyes in mortification. *That had been my grandmother asking me about my sex life!* While I sat there and wondered if it was possible to die of embarrassment, Gwen pulled out a stack of photos.

"I have some other pictures in here of your grandparents, and your father. Would you like to have them?" Gwen asked kindly.

"I would." I accepted a neat bundle that had been tied together with a blue ribbon. I flipped through them, thinking about the date 1992, written on the back of the photo of Ro and me. That was the year the Blood Moon Grimoire had been stolen. Afterwards, Thomas Drake had hexed the thieves, because of this, my grandparents and Duncan's father had all died.

I held up the picture of Ro—Rose and me. "How long was this photo taken *before* she and my grandfather died in that accident?"

"A few months before." Gwen closed the photo box and left it on the bed beside her.

"Thanks for these, Gwen." I said of the photos, meaning it.

"If you have any other questions about the photos or your grandparents feel free to ask me."

As I thumbed through them, one in particular caught my attention. The photograph was of an older man sitting on the back patio of the manor in an Adirondack chair. What was unusual was the crow perched on the arm of his chair. "Who's this?" I held up the snapshot.

Gwen glanced over. "That's your grandfather, Morgan."

My heart started to beat a little faster as I thought about the weird encounters with crows I'd been having. "This is an interesting picture," I said and tried to sound casual. "Tell me about it."

Gwen smiled. "That's a picture of him and Midnight."

"He had a pet crow?"

"Not so much a pet..." Gwen chuckled a bit. "Let's just say your grandfather had a way with animals..."

"Are you telling me the crow was his familiar?"

"Of course."

"Really?"

"My father was able to communicate with animals. All sorts of animals," Gwen said proudly.

"Can you, Bran, or the twins do that?" I wanted to know.

"Holly can with song birds. I can a little—though I have a better connection with cats," Gwen said. As if she'd conjured him up, Merlin jumped up on the bed and climbed into Gwen's lap.

That explained the comment she'd made about having an agreement with Merlin about leaving the

Halloween decorations alone. Oh, and how Holly had gotten those birds to eat out of her hands at the pool. *Well, well, the things you learn...* I stacked the pictures together and retied the ribbon around them, while Merlin purred contently from Gwen's lap. "Did anyone else in the family have the ability to communicate with ghosts?" I thought to ask.

"Your Great-Aunt Faye is a Seer. And a Medium, like you are."

"Are you still in contact with her?"

"Yes. She's a widow, in her seventies now. She lives in Hannibal." Gwen started to root through the box again, and after a bit handed me another older photo. This one included Morgan, my grandfather, and two other women. One was smiling, while the other appeared intense and serious.

"Who are these ladies with my grandfather?"

"His two sisters, Irene and Faye." Gwen pointed to one of the ladies who had piercing pale eyes. "That is Faye Bishop."

"So, Hannibal's only what, a couple of hours north from here?" Gwen nodded her head in confirmation. "Can you arrange for me to speak to her?" I asked.

"Of course." Gwen ran a hand down my back. "I'll contact her tonight. You'll like Aunt Faye. She's quite a character."

I added the picture of my grandfather and his sisters to the stack. "It'd be great to speak to another Seer and Medium. The sooner the better," I said, thinking of Ro.

I thanked my aunt for the photos and took them back to my room. I spread them out across my bedspread to study them more carefully, in private. There were about a dozen photos. A snapshot of my father and his father, Morgan, was there. They seemed to be grilling on the back patio. I saw several photos of my grandmother working in her gardens- always with the silly hat.

The photo of Morgan, Irene and Faye was stamped 1990, and I wondered at Faye's serious expression. Finally, I studied a cute picture of my grandparents sharing a kiss. When I flipped over the back of the photo it said "30th Anniversary Mo and Ro".

Oh god. They called themselves Mo and Ro. It was silly enough to make me smile. I pulled the photo of the anniversary smooch, the shot of Grandpa Morgan and Midnight, and the photo of myself in the rose garden with Ro, and put them in an envelope. I had seen an arts and crafts store in town, and I thought I'd take some time this afternoon and get some pretty frames for the pictures. I wanted to display them on the fireplace mantle in my room. They would be perfect next to the framed picture of my father. While I didn't remember my grandparents, they seemed very determined to interact with me—even from the other side. I wanted to honor them in some way, and this seemed appropriate.

No sooner had I made the decision, when the scent of roses bloomed in the air. "Okay, Ro. I mean *Grandma* Rose. I understand what you were trying to tell me. No worries, I'm honoring my roots." I sat on the padded bench at the foot of the bed, waiting to see if she would reappear, but the scent of the roses faded away.

I thought about the family tree in the journal, and those mysterious lines. If I left now, I'd have time to hit the local library before they closed and do a search on *W Sutherland.* I could also research the local newspaper's archives and see if I could find any birth or death records for my father's son.

My mind made up, I pulled the family tree book out, added the envelope and the rest of the photos from Gwen, gathered my things and headed out. As I walked to my truck, I heard crows calling in the distance. I smiled to myself, and wondered if that was my grandfather, making his presence known as well. Somehow, I didn't doubt it. Seems my ancestors were determined to show me more of the legacy of magick, no matter what.

***

I stood at the information desk of the William's Ford public library and waited. I had turned in the form to get a library card, and had spent the last hour going through the archives, killing time, while I waited for them to process my application. My newspaper search had yielded no results, but I wasn't ready to give up. Finally, I had been paged to the desk, and a middle aged woman with a short brunette bob approached me.

"Bishop?" Her eyes narrowed suspiciously as she scanned the application. She wore a gorgeous stone pendant over her dark sweater, and was frowning.

"Yes, Ma'am," I said.

She shifted her eyes back and forth, from the application to my face. "So you are a resident now?"

I pulled my university ID badge out, wondering why she was being so hostile. "Yes, I am in the Museum Studies Master's program at the university."

As she took the ID and scrutinized it, I resisted the urge to salute. Talk about a tough librarian... If I hadn't sworn I would never scan another person's mind without permission again, I'd have been damned tempted to take a walk through her head, if only to see what all the hostility was about.

A shame about the unfriendly attitude, because the pendant she wore was beautiful. It seemed to glow against her dark sweater. I wondered what sort of stone that was? It was a cloudy, soft purple color, but it didn't look like an amethyst. I thought I'd try a compliment, and see if that helped move the library card process along.

"Your pendant, it's gorgeous. What kind of stone is that?" I asked.

She seemed to be sizing me up. "It's a purple sapphire."

"I didn't know sapphires came in purple. Where did you get it?"

"My husband made the pendant for me." The

librarian went to her computer and started to enter in my information.

"Does he sell his jewelry?" I asked her.

The librarian seemed to be softening up. She actually gave me a polite smile. "Come back to the desk in a little bit and I'll have your temporary card ready for you."

I took my ID back from her and headed into the stacks, looking for books on local history. While looking through the books, I had the oddest feeling I was being watched. I deliberately strolled along acting as if nothing was amiss, but I stretched out with my magick and waited. I turned a corner and saw Thomas Drake standing at the front desk. He was staring right at me. I jolted, dropping the books I was carrying.

I cringed at the racket and automatically picked up the fallen books. A few seconds later, when I stood back up, he was gone. I shifted, looking towards the exit and saw that the door was closing.

I tried to sense the area— to double check, and everything felt normal. The atmosphere of the library seemed different now. I figured my magickal senses were telling me he had left. Relieved, I leaned against the bookcase for a moment. The last time I'd been in a library with that man had been less than pleasant, and I was shaken at the sighting.

My close encounter over, I went back to the information desk with my books, and my temporary card was ready. The librarian handed it over, along with a business card.

"That's my husband's card. He has a little shop on Main," she said. "Tell him that Sarah sent you." She didn't smile, but she didn't frown at me either.

"Thanks, Sarah." I smiled at her anyway.

I was walking out to my truck, my new library books tucked under my arm, when I glanced down at the jeweler's card. I stopped dead still in the middle of the parking lot as I stared in disbelief down at the card.

Sutherland's Gemstones and Jewelry

"Sutherland," I breathed. Not sure if this was magick or merely a happy coincidence of living in a small college town, I read the address on the card, noted they had evening hours, and decided to go straight to the store.

It was a long shot, but maybe someone in the shop would know who the W. Sutherland was from my family tree. I drove downtown, and tried to work out in my head how to politely ask if a woman in their family had given birth to a son back in 1985. There really *wasn't* a polite way to ask, so I guessed I'd have to ask for straight up information, and see how it went.

I found the shop easily enough, and I swung my truck into a nearby parking space. Before I could chicken out, I hitched my backpack style purse over my shoulder and marched directly into the store. The shop's door jingled as I let it close behind me. I quickly took in the cases of jewelry, and I moved closer to admire the display cases that were filled with stones in a rainbow of sizes, shapes and colors.

Rough crystals and beautifully cut and polished gems were arranged on pale gray velvet. I went straight to the nearest case and peered down at all the specimens of crystals, gems and stones. “Wow,” I said.

“Can I help you?”

A young woman and a middle aged man had come out. The man came forward with a pleasant smile, and took up position behind the jewelry case.

“Hi. Sarah sent me,” I said. “I was complimenting her on her purple sapphire pendant and she told me to come and speak to her husband.”

“Sarah is my wife. I made the pendant,” the man said politely.

The store phone rang and the young woman went to answer it. “Sutherland Gemstones and Jewelry, may I help you?”

I psyched myself up. “Sir, I was wondering...” I began.

“You’re not here to shop for jewelry... are you?” The man smiled down at me his eyes intense.

“No sir,” I said. “Actually I was hoping you might be able to help me with some research. I’m a grad student here at the University, and I’ve been looking into my ancestry.” I peeped up to check his expression. He still seemed friendly, so I continued. “I came across an entry in my family tree of a *W Sutherland*. It was noted that she gave birth to a son in 1985. But other than that I don’t have any information on her.”

The man studied my face intently, but his hazel eyes didn't seem angry. More like curious. "What is your family name?" he asked.

"Bishop," I said meeting his eyes trying to look non-threatening. "My name is Autumn Bishop."

He blinked at me. "Your father is Arthur?"

"He was. He passed away about two years ago."

"I'm sorry to hear that." Mr. Sutherland rubbed his hand across his chin. "I'm not sure what I can say to you."

"I should have phoned first. Not just dropped in. But I didn't know what else to try."

"Come in the back and let's talk privately." Mr. Sutherland went to an open doorway and I followed him into a little office. He gestured to a chair and I took a seat. He had a quiet word with the sales person, then came in and sat across from me.

Since the door was open, I lowered my voice. "I'm sorry. When I saw the name on the business card, I followed my gut." Saying that, I pulled the book out of my backpack and opened it to the marked page. "I only recently found my family tree, and was *very* surprised to see that there had been a connection to a W. Sutherland— and my father." I turned the book around and pointed out the entry.

He slipped a pair of reading glasses on his nose and leaned forward to study the page. "Yes, I see," he said softly.

"Do you know anyone by that name, Sir?" I held my

breath.

"W. Sutherland would be my sister, Winifred."

Whoa. Jackpot. "Would it be possible for me to speak with her?" I asked.

Mr. Sutherland sat back in his chair with a sigh. "She relocated to the west coast almost thirty years ago. We've lost touch."

"So," I asked as carefully as I could, "did your sister have my father's child in 1985?"

"Yes. It was a difficult time for my sister. She was barely nineteen when..." he trailed off, and seemed to be composing himself. "When she left town."

I tried to think of the most delicate way to ask my next question. Mr. Sutherland seemed like a nice man and I didn't want to upset him. I put the book back in my backpack. Taking a deep breath I asked, "What happened to the baby? Was he stillborn?"

Mr. Sutherland flinched. "Why would you think that? My sister gave up her rights to the child, and went to California to go to college, and for a fresh start.

It felt like I'd had the wind knocked out of me. "So you are telling me that the baby born in 1985, my father's son, is still *alive*?"

"Yes, of course."

"What happened to him? Was he given up for adoption?"

"You don't know…" Mr. Sutherland trailed off as he studied me.

"Excuse me," the salesperson interrupted. "Dad, we

need to close up."

"I'm sorry, Miss. I've said enough." Mr. Sutherland stood up and formally held out his hand.

"What?" I balked, knowing I was being dismissed.

"You need to speak to your family about this. They will have the answers you are looking for. I can't tell you anymore." His expression was kind, but he appeared determined.

Numbly, I shook his hand. Obviously I wasn't going to get anything else out of him. I slung the backpack purse over my shoulder, and followed him to the main door while my mind raced. *Alive! My brother was out there somewhere!*

"Thank you," I said as he opened the door for me. "Thank you for telling me the truth."

"Good luck." Mr. Sutherland smiled, and gently closed the door in my face.

I heard the door give a solid 'click' as it was locked, and I walked away blindly in the general direction of my truck.

I found myself sitting in my old pickup a while later. But did not remember getting there. I groped for my keys and started up the engine, while I tried to put together the pieces of what I knew.

It wasn't uncommon for teenage girls to put their babies up for adoption in the 1980's. In fact, keeping the baby was pretty unusual back then. There was a chance that my father and Winifred had known who the adoptive parents were *if* it had been an open adoption.

I wondered, had my mother known about that child? Unfortunately, now that my mother had basically disowned me for embracing the family's legacy of magick, there would be no help from that quarter.

The legacy of magick... Did that mean that my brother was out there dealing with the same things I had? Knowing he was different, having abilities but never understanding why or where they had come from? With the birth mother's location unknown and my father being deceased, how the hell would I go about finding my half-brother?

Did Ro know? Maybe that's why she sent me looking for the family tree. Not only to remember her and my grandfather, but so I would find out about my half-brother. Obviously dad's parents and sister had known about the baby...

His sister. Gwen was four years older than my father. She probably knew most if not all of the details. And that thought propelled me into action.

"I've been tiptoeing around this issue for way too long." I grabbed my phone, and called the manor. It went straight to the answering machine. Next I dialed Gwen's cell, that too went to voice mail. She had to be around somewhere. I disconnected, clicked my seatbelt into place, and took off for the manor.

CHAPTER NINE

"Aunt Gwen!" I called as I opened the front door. "Anybody home?" I laid my bag on a table in the foyer and headed to the kitchen. Merlin came scampering down the stairs and ran to me like he hadn't seen me in weeks instead of a few hours.

"Hey, where's Gwen?" I asked the cat.

Merlin studied me for a moment, stuck his tail up in the air and strolled off. I went through the family room, peeked in the dining room, and checked the downstairs bedroom that Gwen used for an office. *Nothing.* I went through the kitchen and discovered Merlin sitting in the doorway of the potting room. There, I found the remnants of a spell that had been cast on the work table. Incense smoke still hung in the air, and a candle was burning inside of a large iron cauldron. Herbs and flowers surrounded the outside of the cauldron, and were arranged in a circle on the butcher block counter.

So somebody had been home and was casting. I held my hands out over the cauldron trying to get a picture of what sort of spell had been cast. I got a quick flash of Gwen, chanting and scattering the flowers, but other than that... nothing.

I stuck my head in the garage and saw that while Gwen's car was gone, Bran's car was here. I bolted up the stairs searching for him. But other than Merlin, who seemed to think me running around the manor was a great game, I saw no one else. Usually I couldn't even move around the manor without tripping over someone. But now that I really needed to speak to Gwen, she was nowhere to be found.

Damn it! I sat on the top step of the second floor landing, studied the Halloween tree, and blew out a frustrated breath. *Maybe I should try and scry for Gwen? If I only knew where she'd stored that scrying mirror...* My thoughts were interrupted by Merlin. He sat in the back area of the second floor hallway, and gave a quiet kitty type of chirp.

"What?" I glanced over my shoulder in time to watch Merlin raise a white paw up in the air, as if he was batting at something. Curious, I got up and walked to the back part of the hall outside of Bran's room, and promptly tripped— over thin air.

Now while 'grace' has never been my middle name, there was nothing on the floor for me to have tripped over. I backed up and considered the hardwood floor. I started forward very slowly with my hands out, in case I needed to catch myself—and again, felt one of my feet catch on something.

I literally couldn't go any farther down the hallway. It felt like it was blocked. Merlin gave a soft meow and I realized what I was running into was *magick.* I dropped down to my hands and knees, without a clue of what I was searching for. But when I hunkered down and squinted at the floor, I could see a tiny ripple in the air, like a shimmer, or a heat wave coming off the asphalt on a hot day.

I pursed my lips as I stood and considered what I had walked in to. I couldn't even get a sense of what was behind that magickal barrier, which made me feel very uneasy. I was starting to consider calling Duncan and asking for advice, when I heard the first moan.

My heart slammed into my throat as I listened intently. Yup, there it was again, and it sounded like a woman. Standing there in the hall— with my way blocked by magick— I imagined the worst. *What if Gwen was hurt, or trapped? What if Thomas Drake had gotten into the house and she was being tortured?*

Because whoever was making those noises beyond that barrier, was in a world of hurt. I remembered Ivy's black eye and bruises when we had rescued her from Julian Drake, and I panicked.

"Stand back, cat," I said, and Merlin scampered back a bit. I concentrated on the magickal goal of raising energy, threw my hands down and out to my sides. For the first time, I felt power burning across my hands. I felt a rush of power roll through me, and my hands grew hot. I glanced down and saw energy building in my open hands.

Before I could really appreciate what I had accomplished, I heard a muffled scream. “That’s it,” I growled. I pushed the energy out in front of me, and ran forward as fast as I could— straight towards Bran’s room. I passed through that barrier with only a slight hitch in my stride, hit the bedroom door at a full run, and it crashed open.

The door bounced off the wall, as I came careening into Bran’s bedroom. It was dim, but I could see easily enough. What I discovered in a split second, was *not* someone being tortured.

Lexie and Bran were tangled together on Bran’s bed. Lexie’s back was to me, and she was naked as the day she was born. She was sitting in Bran’s lap, her legs wrapped around his waist, and her head was thrown back. Bran’s hands were gripping Lexie’s long blonde hair as it trailed down her back.

Bran’s head whipped up, and he looked at me mouthing the words, “*Get out!*” with a snarl.

Mother of god! I slapped my hands over both of my eyes. I spun around and felt a solid push of energy hit me in back. It propelled me out of the room, and I quickly shut the door behind me.

Mortified, I bolted down the stairs with Merlin hot on my heels. I could hear Lexie’s screams reach a crescendo, and I grabbed my heavy bag and keys, and was running out of the house as fast as my legs would carry me. I dove into the truck, and the cat jumped in after me. He tucked himself on the floorboard of the passenger's side. I slammed the door, started my truck, and spun out of the driveway, through the open gates and towards Duncan's place.

I didn't start to giggle until I was a few blocks down from the manor. *It was not funny.* I gave myself a lecture.

Aw hell, yes it was.

I couldn't hold it back anymore, so I pulled my truck over to the side of road, dropped my head on the steering wheel, and howled with laughter. Oh. My. God. *And here I'd thought someone was being tortured...*

The scene played back in my mind. Me banging down the door, thinking I was rescuing my aunt, when I had actually burst in on my cousin and *Officer Lexie*. I don't think Lexie had even noticed that I was in the room, as she had been kind of— distracted. I cringed and tried to wipe the image of them together on the bed, from my mind.

Nope. It was burned there. Probably for the rest of my life.

Well at least there weren't any handcuffs... and that thought had me losing it all over again. I wiped at the tears running down my face from laughing so hard, and pulled myself together. Merlin yowled from the floorboard, it sounded pathetic.

"You wanted out of there too, eh?" I turned on the truck radio to the local university station, and found they were playing Halloween music. I drove the rest of the way to Duncan's little guest house, singing along with Michael Jackson's "Thriller" on the radio, while Merlin seemed to caterwaul in time with the song.

A short time later, I stood on Duncan's little front stoop and tried to knock while I juggled my heavy purse and a squirmy fifteen pound cat.

"Autumn!" Duncan seemed genuinely surprised when he opened the door.

"Got room for a couple of refugees?"

"What happened?" he asked and stepped aside to allow me to come in.

I set Merlin down immediately, and he began to nose around Duncan's little house. "It's kind of a long story."

"Are you okay?" Duncan reached out and tugged me close. "Have you've been crying?"

I pulled back to smile at him. "Give me a glass of wine and I'll tell you everything."

"Deal." he said, and kissed me.

As I related the events of my day to Duncan, Merlin deigned to join us on the sectional. He was sprawled across Duncan's lap, and purring loudly in contentment. Duncan was fascinated at my encounters with Ro, and the possible crow/ familiar connection to my grandfather, Morgan. He agreed with me that Gwen would likely have more information about what had happened all those years ago to my half-brother. We also discussed the possibilities of trying an online search, or hiring a private investigator to find him.

I probably should've waited for Duncan to swallow

his beer *before* I explained what I'd burst in on, during my tragic "rescue attempt" at the manor. I came to this brilliant conclusion about a second too late, as his reaction to that was to choke, cough, and laugh— all at the same time.

"Oh my god!" Duncan thumped his own chest with a fist, and tried to set his beer on the table. Disturbed by Duncan's reaction, Merlin jumped off his lap and the beer was knocked over spilling on the floor.

"Sorry!" I said, and scrambled to grab a dish rag from the kitchen.

Duncan didn't seem to mind. He was still laughing while we cleaned up the spill from the hardwood floor. "It never occurred to you, the barrier outside the room was for privacy?" Duncan wheezed.

I scrubbed harder at the sticky floor with a soapy washrag. "No," I admitted. "I heard the moans and screams, and thought somebody was being tortured."

That only made Duncan laugh harder.

"I guess she's a screamer." I shrugged trying not to let it embarrass me.

"Well. Go Bran!" Duncan hooted at that. "Got a show, did you?"

"All I could really see was Lexie's bare back. And I'll thank whatever god is listening— that I did *not* see any more," I said, and meant it.

Duncan was still laughing as Merlin came to sit next to me, in a sort of survivor solidarity, I suppose. Merlin narrowed his feline eyes at Duncan's mirth, and gave a kitty mutter.

Duncan smiled down at the both of us. "Look at you, sitting there on my floor. You're so damn cute with your trusty familiar at your side."

"I'm pretty sure he's Aunt Gwen's familiar."

"Have you asked him?" Duncan reached down and tugged me to my feet.

"Are you serious?" I raised an eyebrow.

Duncan took the soapy rag and tossed it towards his kitchen sink. "Sure, the familiar chooses their Witch. Not the other way around."

"I didn't know that." I thought about it while Merlin regarded me with unblinking golden eyes.

Duncan put his arm around my waist. "Hey, Autumn?"

"Yeah?"

"Let's see if I can make you holler louder than Lexie." Duncan swung me up, and tossed me over his shoulder

I burst out laughing. "I wasn't issuing a challenge," I said, upside down.

"That's okay. I'm just a competitive type of guy." He gave my butt a playful swat as he carted me towards his bedroom.

***

The theme song from the 1960's classic television show *Bewitched* sounded in my ear, jolting me awake. I frowned for a moment before finally realizing that it was a ringtone playing. As it started to play again, I realized someone had changed the ringtone on my cell phone.

Damn Ivy and her warped sense of humor. I fumbled in the dark, before finding the phone. "'Lo?" I mumbled.

"Autumn?" I heard Gwen's voice. "Where are you right now?"

The urgency in her voice got through to me and I sat up. "What's happened?"

"What is it?" Duncan said, and I felt more than I saw him start to reach for his clothes.

"Where are you?" Gwen repeated, her voice shrill.

"I'm at Duncan's place."

"You're there with him, right now?"

"Yes. Why?"

"The manor's been ransacked."

"Ransacked?" I said feeling my heart slam up to my throat. "Is everyone okay?"

"The family is all accounted for."

The Blood Moon Grimoire. Someone, I realized, had been looking for it and decided to toss the manor. Odds were the cops were already there, and listening. So I chose my next words carefully. "Is the item I found a few weeks ago still intact?"

"Yes," Gwen answered, then was speaking to someone there with her, so I jumped up and starting patting around for my clothes.

"How's Bran's tie collection looking?" I asked, meaning the hidden panel in his closet that housed the Bishop family's collection of antique journals and spell books.

"He said his ties were all accounted for."

"Good." I said and was thankful that the backup flash drive with digital pictures of the grimoire pages had been locked in a safe deposit box at the bank.

"I want you home. Now," Gwen snapped.

"Shit." I stubbed my toe on the corner of a dresser. "I'm on my way." I hung up.

Duncan slapped the lights on, and I winced at the brightness, but got dressed as fast as I could. "Were they robbed?" he asked.

"She didn't say so, I think someone tossed the place." I found my other shoe sticking out from the end of the bed, grabbed it and wiggled my foot down into it.

"Looking for the Blood Moon Grimoire, no doubt," Duncan said, and tucked a worn t-shirt into his jeans and pulled a brown 'Quinn Construction' sweatshirt over that.

I was suddenly glad I had taken the family tree book along with me this evening. I ran my hands through my hair trying to pull myself together. What the hell time was it anyway? I grabbed my phone to check and frowned at the time. It was a little after one o'clock in the morning.

I went out into the living area and found Merlin snoozing on the sectional. I borrowed a hoodie from

Duncan, and fished my keys out of my big purse. Duncan scooped up Merlin, and I waited on the stoop while he locked his door and set the alarm.

In silence, we both jogged towards my truck. Merlin seemed to enjoy the truck ride home. He sat easily in Duncan's arms and gazed out the window as I drove quickly back to the manor.

"With everything that's been happening— grad school, me and you, the girls on the squad being under attack, and the family tree discoveries..." I said. "I haven't been focused on finding the rest of that damn grimoire."

"I'm sorry," Duncan said quietly. "I'm the one who told you to let it go for a while."

As I pulled into the driveway, we saw several police cars. "Looks like we all have been given a reminder to keep searching."

The police asked where Duncan and I had been all evening as soon as we walked in the front door of the manor. Holly and Ivy let out a happy squeal when they saw Merlin.

"We thought something had happened to him!" Holly cried and took the cat from Duncan's arms.

While Duncan and I spoke to the police officers, I saw Bran out of the corner of my eye, and I felt myself flush. No way was I making eye contact with him. I saw a few things knocked over, but weirdly, the Halloween tree and the decorations were untouched. That made me frown. An officer asked me to go check my room to see if I noticed anything missing. So I gave Duncan's hand a squeeze, and I went up with Gwen and the officer. I stopped in the doorway and surveyed the wreck that was my room.

Every dresser drawer had been dumped on the floor. The closet doors were open and most of my clothes had been knocked off their hangers. My books and papers from class were left alone, maybe because they were obviously text books? My laptop was open and with the officer present, I checked my school files and saw that everything was still there.

"Is everyone else's room as bad as this?" I asked Gwen.

"I don't think they made it into Bran's room or mine. The girls' room is much worse than yours," she said, looking tired.

"I want to see," I turned down the hall. There were three other officers in the twins' room, and the cop who had accompanied us shot out his arm and blocked me from going in the room.

"We are still processing the scene," he explained.

"Okay, I won't go in," I said, staying outside.

What I saw when I did look in scared me. The girl's bedroom was destroyed. The big mirror above their dresser was shattered. The curtains had been ripped down, and the beds were slashed. I could see the stuffing from their mattresses. From out in the hall, it looked like someone had thrown paint across the ivory walls. Then the smell hit me. It was nail polish, and the bottles had been smashed against the floor and walls. There was another scent though... It was coppery and sweet. I realized I was smelling blood.

"Shit," I said. I turned my head and saw a capital letter 'H' smeared across the white paneled closet door. My head spun and I grabbed at the door frame.

The vision I'd had. *A red letter 'H' smeared across a white paneled door...* I tried not to breathe through my nose anymore, since the smell of blood was really nasty. My heart beat hard in my chest as I saw the physical reality of the vision I'd had the day I tripped over Cypress.

I shifted so I could see the whole set of closet doors. The word 'WITCH" was scrawled in huge capital letters, in what had to be blood, over the white closet doors. I saw the officers taking photographs of the room, and I gulped hard. No wonder the girls were afraid for Merlin.

"Let's go downstairs, now," Gwen said and put her arm around me.

With a nod in agreement, we went down to join Duncan, and the rest of the family, in the kitchen. The potting room had taken some abuse as well. I could see from the kitchen that dozens of drawers from the apothecary cabinet were dumped, and dried herbs were everywhere. Potted plants were overturned, and I winced as I saw the pretty African violets uprooted and their broken pots discarded on the floor.

I sat my purse down on the counter and joined my

cousins. "Does anything seem to be missing?" I asked.

"A little cash, some of Mom's jewelry," Bran said. "But other than that, no."

"No electronics were taken?" Duncan asked as he came to stand behind my chair.

"They weren't after electronics," Bran said. "We all know what they were looking for."

"Well, they did a hell of a number on the girls' room," I muttered. "That was blood on their closet doors."

"Bran told me about their room," Duncan said. "The girls shouldn't stay here tonight."

While Gwen and Bran agreed with that, the girls immediately argued against it.

"Marie is already coming to get the girls," Gwen said speaking of her coven sister and friend. "There's no safer place."

Holly had yet to let Merlin down. She sat on the kitchen barstool, still wearing her pretty party dress, with the cat in her lap. "I want Merlin to come with us," She said.

"Fine," Bran said. "I'll go get his cat carrier out of the laundry room."

I heard boot heels clicking across the hardwood floor, and I knew who had arrived. Marie stalked into the kitchen, and did she look *pissed.* She reached in her jacket pocket and slapped a couple of small glass bottles on the counter.

"This here is Indigo Water. You use it everywhere

you can tonight. I'll bring more back when we can get started working on the girl's room."

"Thank you." Gwen smiled.

"Don't you fret," Marie told Gwen and grabbed her up in a hug. "I'll look after them and be back in the morning with reinforcements."

Gwen and Marie exchanged parting hugs. I had no doubt the coven would be here as soon as they were able. If I'd learned anything about them, it was that they rallied together in a crisis.

Bran came in with the carrier, and Merlin went in with a minimum of fuss. Gwen hugged her daughters goodbye. I gave Ivy's arm a squeeze as she passed me.

"Girls, let's go." Marie nodded at us as the twins followed her out.

One of the police officers asked to speak to Gwen, and she excused herself from the kitchen going to him. We all waited, and I wondered what we were going to do next.

"As soon as the police give the all clear, I can have a crew in here to repaint the room and refinish the floors in their room, if necessary." Duncan said as soon as Gwen came back in the room.

"Thank you. I'll take you up on that." Gwen sat on the barstool next to me. Bran got a few bottles of water out of the fridge and passed them to each of us.

I scooted my backpack style purse over to give Gwen some counter space. I could feel the family tree book in there as my hand lay across it. Not the best time, perhaps, for me to ask, but at the rate we were going, I'd never get any answers.

"Gwen, I know things are a little crazy right now," I said. "But you told me you'd answer any questions I had about the family."

"We might as well. They aren't going to let us back up there to clean for a while."

I pulled the book out of my bag. "I found this recently." I flipped open the book to the illustrated pages of our family tree, and I felt Duncan's hand on my back in support.

"I haven't seen that in years," Gwen said setting her water bottle aside.

"I was looking through this, and noticed that there was an extra line filled out in my father's section of the family tree." I pointed to the section.

"Oh?" Gwen leaned forward, and Bran stiffened.

"I was pretty shocked to see that there was a line filled out for a son, born to my father in 1985."

Gwen swung her gaze to my face and she seemed pale... but said nothing.

I continued. "Since the name of the birth mother is listed as W. Sutherland, I did a little digging today, and found relatives of hers that still live in William's Ford."

"I see," Gwen said.

"At first I thought—because of the way the family tree had been filled out, that the baby had died, or been stillborn. But after interviewing Mr. Sutherland, he explained that his sister, Winifred, had given birth to my father's child. He also told me that she gave up her rights to the baby, and then moved away."

The silence in the kitchen was deafening. The police team continued their work in the rest of the house, but it was like the four of us were completely alone. Gwen sat and mutely stared at that name on the family tree, so I continued on. I *had* to know.

"I'm asking you Gwen, to tell me the truth. No more secrets. What happened to my half-brother? Do you know who adopted him? And if so, where can I find him?"

Gwen cleared her throat. "Autumn, you have to understand—"

"No," I cut her off. "No. I don't *have* to do anything.

"When the baby was born, your father was completely unprepared and incapable of caring for him." Gwen shut the book and met my eyes. "He tried at first, but Arthur was very spoiled and selfish as a young man. Your grandparents always gave into him, and eventually your father turned over the raising of his son to the person who had cared for and loved that baby from the moment he came home from the hospital."

"Give me a name," I said, and didn't care that my voice was flat, and angry. "I want to know who adopted him, and where my brother is."

"He's right here," Bran said.

I whipped my head up. "Don't cover for your mom, Bran. I am sick to death of the lies and secrets that come with being a part of this family."

"I suppose you are." Bran crossed his arms over his chest.

Alarm bells started to sound in my mind. Between his stance, and the look on his face, my stomach dropped. *What are you holding back, Bran?* I stared him down. "What the hell do you mean?"

"It's me," Bran said. "Arthur Bishop and Winifred Sutherland were my biological parents."

I tried to say something. I opened my mouth, but no sound came out. My chest heaved up and down from the force of holding in a huge feeling of betrayal. *How could they do this? Why would they all lie to me?* I felt Duncan's fingers squeeze down on my shoulder and I blindly reached up and covered his hand with mine.

Bran mirrored that move, placing his hand protectively on Gwen's shoulder. "*This* is the only mother I have ever known," he said.

I sat there, silently staring at Bran, as the pieces started to click together. *The way I could link psychically with Bran. I'd read his memories and he'd scanned mine, again so easily. I could send him visual images over distances... and I'd thought it was from the blood bond of being cousins, when actually it was because we were siblings!*

"God," I finally said. "That day Thomas Drake used magick on me in the university library, those snide comments Drake had made about mine and Brans' *close* personal connections... He knew." I felt like I was going to be sick. My stomach clutched as I worked through the facts.

Duncan squeezed his fingers on my shoulder, silently letting me know he was there to support me.

"How could I have missed it?" I whispered to myself. "Why didn't I see the truth?" I thought back to the first time I'd heard Bran laugh, and how it had reminded me of my father. And finally, the comment he'd made when my own mother had turned her back on me... What had he said? *I know only too well how much it hurts to be rejected by a parent.*

Gwen cleared her throat to get my attention. "I went from being Bran's legal guardian to officially adopting him, after your father gave up all of his parental rights." She tried to explain.

"When did you officially adopt Bran?" Duncan asked her, before I could.

"Twenty two years ago, shortly after my parents died, and Arthur left town with Autumn and her mother," Gwen said.

"So my mother knew about you?" I asked Bran, still trying to process this revelation.

"Yes, but she wanted nothing to do with me. Even when I was a child, she hated me. It was the magick." Bran stepped away to pace the kitchen floor. "Your mother was always terrified of the legacy of magick."

After all of the lies and secrets, I knew the truth when I heard it. My mother despising her husband's illegitimate child didn't surprise me at all. It actually fit her right down to the ground. Another thought occurred to me. "Do Ivy and Holly know?" I asked Gwen.

"That Bran is adopted? No, they don't." She shook her head.

"You're going to have to tell them now. Because I gotta tell ya, accidentally discovering your parents knowingly lied to you about your sibling hurts incredibly bad. And that is not something I would wish on those girls. So, if you don't tell them immediately, I will," I stated.

Gwen nodded at me, and crossed her arms over her chest.

I forced myself to look Bran directly in the eye. "No wonder you hated me when I first came here to live," I managed after a moment. *God, he was my brother!*

"I was jealous," Bran admitted. "Jealous that our father chose you over me."

I understood where he was coming from, but, "I want to know something before we discuss anything else," I said to Bran.

"Yes?"

I stood up and walked over to face him. "If I hadn't found out on my own, would you have continued to lie to me?"

"Yes, I would have," Bran sighed.

"Then I feel totally justified in doing this."

"Doing what?" Bran frowned at me.

"This," I said, and punched him right in the nose.

CHAPTER TEN

I only got a single punch in, but it wasn't for lack of trying. It took Duncan and one of the police officers in the house to keep me from hitting Bran more than once.

When all was said and done, Bran's nose had bled all over his nice button down shirt and a little blood had managed to splatter on the kitchen floor. Gwen was horrified at my outburst, and Duncan carted me out of the manor promising not to bring me back until I had cooled off.

A policeman asked Bran if he wanted to press charges, and I heard a couple other officers chuckle as Duncan hauled me out while I shouted curses at my *brother.* Duncan stuffed me back in my truck, shoved my bag at me, and backed out of the driveway. I made it half way down the block before tears of frustration began to fall.

"First to find out there had been a baby— that I thought had died. And I *mourned* for him. That was horrible enough..." I said.

"Breathe," Duncan suggested as he drove capably down the dark neighborhood streets.

"Then I had that little bit of hope from Mr. Sutherland. The hope that my brother was alive and out there somewhere... only to find out that it's *Bran*."

"I think he was shocked that you figured it out. Autumn, he lost his temper too. You two are more alike than you realize," Duncan said.

"Insulting me is *not* helping right now!" I fumed at him, and the dashboard lights flickered.

"Pull that anger back, before you fry the electronic systems in the truck," Duncan suggested.

"Well damn it I *am* angry!" I glared out the windshield, and saw two street lamps flicker and blow out. I squeaked, as a shower of sparks spilled onto the hood of the truck.

"I know you're pissed, but reign that shit in!" Duncan snapped.

Duncan was right. I *had* to calm myself down. I stared up at the waning moon overhead, searched for my center of energy and worked hard at evening out my breathing and slowing my heart rate.

"Better?" Duncan asked after a few moments.

"Yeah." I blew out a long breath and told myself to try and let the rest of my anger go. We drove along and no other street lamps flickered. Everything seemed almost normal. "The picture that is being painted of my father..." I said to Duncan working to keep my voice even. "I tried to convince myself that he was noble;

binding my powers, keeping the legacy of magick a secret. But knowing that he basically *abandoned* his own child makes me angry and a little sick."

"I think there is someone who might be able to give you an honest perspective on your father," Duncan said as he parked.

"Who?" I asked.

"My mother."

***

Rebecca Drake-Quinn arrived at Duncan's little guesthouse right before sunrise. He opened the door for his mother and kissed her cheek. She smiled up at him, and when she walked in the room I was surprised to see her dressed in black yoga pants and a light blue and black matching jacket. I'd never seen her dressed so casually before.

Rebecca came straight over and sat beside me on the big sectional sofa. "How can I help you?" she said.

"You can tell me about my father. What you remember, about when my brother was born, and what sort of man my father *really* was."

Rebecca reached out for my hand and held it. "I first met Arthur when I was dating my husband, David, back in college." She smiled at the memory. "Arthur and David had been friends all through school. They were even roommates together in college at the fraternity house. It was Arthur that introduced David to magick.

While David didn't have any aptitude for the Craft, he appreciated it, and loved the history behind it."

"Maybe that helped him accept the Drake's magickal legacy." Duncan seemed to consider that. He sat beside me on the sofa, and I leaned into him while listening to Rebecca.

"Which is why— when Arthur came to him about finding the Blood Moon Grimoire, David wanted to help." Rebecca explained.

"I don't suppose it ever occurred to my father that there might be a price," I muttered. "What was my father like when he was in college? Aunt Gwen said he was spoiled."

"He was, to an extent. Your grandparents doted on him. Arthur had led a life of privilege as the only eligible son of the Bishop family line. From what I know, after Bran was born, and Winifred gave up her parental rights, your grandparents planned to raise the baby themselves. Your father was still in college, you see. But it was Gwen who bonded with the baby and your father left the child care mainly to his mother and sister, while he lived on campus."

Rebecca didn't say so, but I got an intuitive hunch that my father hadn't been as concerned about his studies as he was his frat-boy party lifestyle. "He was too busy partying to take care of his own child?"

"Your father was very popular, and he... had plenty of female companionship." Rebecca explained.

I thought back to Mr. Sutherland's comment about

his sister wanting to start her life over. "I'm really afraid to ask, but did he abandon Bran's birth mother when he found out she was pregnant?" I held my breath.

"Winnie was fresh out of high school when she and your father became involved. The young women of the other magickal families pursued your father, because of who he was. And well… I'm not sure how to say this." Rebecca grimaced.

"Say it straight out."

"Alright, it was quite the gossip in the magickal community all those years ago. Arthur spread the rumor that she'd tried to trap him by becoming pregnant on purpose. And poor Winnie was devastated when she realized that he wouldn't be marrying her."

"You knew her personally."

"Yes, I did."

Internally, I cringed at this confirmation of my father's character as a young man, but damned if it didn't ring true to me. I tried to reconcile the quiet man that I'd known, the hardworking man who had let my mother run the show— to the spoiled, privileged, partying womanizer from his past.

"Rebecca, did you ever see my parents interact with Bran?" I figured out the timeline in my head. "Bran would have been around three years old when they married."

"No, I did not. Bran and Gwen had a bond, they were inseparable. Folks in town came to think of him as

Gwen's child before long." Rebecca sighed, and it seemed she was trying to choose her words with care. "As to Arthur leaving Bran behind... I think Arthur thought he was doing the best thing, leaving your brother with Gwen, where he would be loved."

"You mean it would have been better for *him*," I said, meaning my father.

"After David and your Grandparents died, the families were broken. I was mourning, and trying to protect Duncan. Your Aunt Gwen was devastated, as you can imagine. She hadn't known about the Blood Moon Grimoire back then." Rebecca's tone of voice had stayed matter-of-fact while she spoke.

"I'm surprised you can even talk about this so calmly. Don't you hold a grudge?" I asked her.

"Your father, Arthur, admitted to me that he was ashamed of what he'd done. That he hadn't protected his parents or his friend, and had lost all of them to the curse." Rebecca paused, and seemed to be composing herself. "A few weeks later, I'd heard he had left town."

"He felt guilty, so he ran away," I said realizing another truth. "He *was* a coward, after all."

"I'm sorry, sweetheart." Rebecca gave my hand a little squeeze.

"No, no, don't apologize for my father." I waved her apology off. I stood up and paced to the other side of the living room. "That day in the library, when your brother used magick on me. He told me, but I didn't believe him." I thought back to that day, and recalled

Thomas Drake's words...

My dear, your father ran from this town with your mother over twenty years ago. He turned his back on his legacy, his blood, and then he obviously bound your powers. Those are the actions of a coward.

"Autumn, are you okay?" Duncan asked me.

I shook my head as I thought everything over, and sat in the nearest chair. "It's a hell of a thing to find out that my family has lied to me, in one way or another, my whole life... while the bad guy has actually been telling me the truth."

There was a knock on the front door. Duncan went to answer it, and I saw Holly and Ivy, still in their homecoming dresses standing on the stoop. Duncan stepped back and they came in together.

"Shit!" I said. "Please tell me you didn't walk over here by yourselves! With everything that's happened, the manor break in and the poppets—"

"We didn't." Ivy stopped me.

"Cypress drove us over," Holly said. "She's watching Merlin for us."

As the girls walked farther into the living room area I could see by their posture and faces that they knew. "You've had a talk with your mom," I said.

Rebecca offered up her spot on the sofa. "I'm going to make everyone some tea," she said going into the kitchen. Duncan followed her to allow us a little privacy.

The twins sat side by side staring at me. I waited to

see what they'd say. It was so quiet that I could hear the old clock on the mantle ticking. "I can't believe no one ever told us." Holly broke the silence first. "In all these years..."

"Bran's technically our brother, since mom adopted him. But he's your *biological* brother," Ivy said.

"Half-brother. Technically," I corrected.

"The fact that they kept this a secret from us, is such bullshit," Ivy said, succinct as always.

"I'm gonna have to agree with you on that one, Shorty." I leaned back in my chair. *God I was tired.*

Holly scrubbed her hand across her face, smearing what was left of her makeup. "Mom said that you figured it out because of an old family tree you'd found?"

"I've actually got it with me," I said to the twins. "Are you up for seeing the book?"

"Bet your ass," Holly said.

I had to smile at the combination of the grim voice, and the smeared all to hell makeup, on my normally flawless cousin. I went over and pulled the book out of my backpack for the girls to see.

While the sun brightened the eastern sky, my cousins and I sat with the big old book on Duncan's coffee table and studied the family tree. Rebecca fussed over us, which I found endearing. She passed out mugs of tea and offered support in her calm and gentle way. Duncan scrambled up a big batch of eggs for everyone, Rebecca handed Holly a washcloth and suggested she wipe off the rest of her makeup before she eat.

After breakfast, we were all pretty wiped out. Rebecca offered the girls a blanket, and Holly and Ivy crashed on the big sofa. The girls lay together, and within minutes they were asleep. As I watched, Rebecca murmured a few words, pushed her hands out in front of her, and a ripple of energy rolled out in an expanding circle. I felt a warm comforting energy hit me, and it spread throughout my whole body.

"For a little extra protection, I'll check on everyone later," she said, leaving quietly. Duncan locked the door behind her and we went to go lay down in his room.

"Your mom is one talented Witch. I could see and feel that spell ripple out. I wonder if she'd work with me. I really need to learn more, and I have to learn fast."

"She'd probably love that." Duncan toed his shoes off.

I yawned as I laid down on top the covers, still in my clothes from the day before. "Thanks for cooking breakfast for everyone." My mind was spinning with everything I'd learned. "I owe you a dozen eggs," I said randomly.

"No worries." Duncan spooned up behind me and wrapped his arm around my waist. "Turn off your brain, and try and get some rest," he suggested.

"I'll try." I yawned again, cuddled back against him and somehow managed to fall sound asleep.

***

There was only so long we could avoid returning to the manor. Holly, Ivy and I decided we'd imposed on Duncan long enough, and by Sunday afternoon, we were ready to go back and face the inevitable. Duncan had called Officer Lexie, so we knew the police had concluded their investigation, and had finally left the house. I couldn't quite manage a conversation with her after what I'd walked in on. *God, had it been only yesterday?*

The ornate wrought iron gates at the end of the driveway swung open as we approached. I pulled my truck in behind several cars that were parked along the double driveway.

"I see Cora's car, Marie's car, and Violet's van for the flower shop," Holly said.

I pulled up behind a sleek hybrid car. "Whose car is that?" I nodded at the expensive midnight blue vehicle. There were vanity plates on the hybrid that read 'I SEE U'.

"I don't know." Ivy frowned at the car.

The three of us trooped up to the front porch with me leading the way. I tripped over the last step when I spotted a quaffed elderly woman sitting on the porch swing. She had long white hair pulled back into a sleek braid that trailed over her shoulder. Boxy peach colored sunglasses covered her eyes, and she wore a patterned shirt in shades of red and yellow. Trim faded jeans ran down her legs and ended at brown leather boots.

"Hello?" I said, struggling to think of the last time I had seen an elderly woman look so fashionably put together.

"Well," she tucked the sunglasses up on top of her head, and stared at us out of pale and piercing eyes. "The three of you decided to come back, after all." She began to drum her fingers on the arm rest of the swing, and I saw large stone rings flashing on every manicured finger.

"Great Aunt Faye!" Holly and Ivy leapt forward, and the woman stood up to embrace the girls.

I stood back, studying my grandfather's sister. This was the relative who was also a Medium and a Seer, like me. The old photo I had gotten from Gwen hadn't done her any justice. She had the face and build of a fashion model. As she embraced the twins, I wondered what she was doing here. Then with a sudden flash of insight; *I knew.*

Faye looked over the top of the girls' heads and studied me in return. "Hello Autumn," she said to me formally.

I hooked a thumb over my shoulder towards the hybrid. "Nice vanity plates on your car," I heard myself say.

"Yes, they are very appropriate," she said as she continued to watch me.

"Gwen called you."

"She did." She made no move to embrace me as she

had the girls.

"Are you here to help me *or* to help smooth over the recent family dramas?" I asked her flat out.

Ivy shook her head and laughed a bit. "Hard ass."

"She needs to be." Aunt Faye gave the girls a hug then focused on me. "You shoot straight from the hip. I like that. Honesty is a vital quality in a Seer."

"But not a vital quality found in a large percentage of this family— apparently," I said.

"I understand that you are upset…" Great Aunt Faye began.

"Lady, you don't know the half of it," I snarked back.

"We still have time to sort all of this out." My great aunt walked to the front door and shooed the twins inside.

Holly and Ivy glanced back at me. "I'll be right in," I promised them. I hoped the girls were up for facing their mother, and when I heard voices raised in greeting, I knew that Violet, Cora and Marie were there, and were running interference.

"You're protective of the girls." Aunt Faye crossed her arms, regarding me steadily.

"Yes, I am."

She nodded at that. "Good. They'll need you."

"What's that supposed to mean?" I asked her.

Aunt Faye waved my question away. "Some of Gwen's coven is here, helping to put the house back in order." She held the door open for me, giving me a look that was clearly a dare to go inside.

I raised my eyebrows at her and strolled in.

"For now," she said, "I want you to sit with me and tell me about this grimoire, the encounters you've had so far with ghosts, and what's been happening here."

"That might take a while," I warned her.

"Then let's get started."

***

I liked her. I hadn't expected to. I'd figured Gwen had called the old Witch in to run interference, but damned if Great Aunt Faye hadn't started to grow on me. I tried to figure out if her eyes were a pale green or icy blue. Maybe they were gray, but no matter their color, her gaze was startling and direct. I had no doubts the woman was a Seer. When it came to the subject of me interacting with ghosts, she'd smiled and simply assured me that she could help me gain a little control in that area. I sincerely hoped she would.

Aunt Faye and I had been sitting at the worktable in the now cleared potting room, when Bran walked by us with a bag of trash, and then past us again as he came back inside. He tried to ignore me, but Great Aunt Faye, it seemed, had other ideas.

"You, young man. Stop your sulking and show me these pages my great-niece has found."

Bran's head had whipped around. "I would be happy to show you the pages, Great Aunt Faye. If you'd follow me," he said. While he was polite and formal to our great aunt— he still glared at me. "And for the record. I am *not* sulking."

"Whatever." I rolled my eyes. Now that I had gotten a good look at him, I could see that his nose was swollen. I tried not to feel proud that I'd done that, and failed.

That's nothing to be proud of, young lady. Aunt Faye's voice was crystal clear in my mind, as we followed Bran up to his room to view the pages of the Blood Moon Grimoire.

I stared at the back of her silver head and concentrated on sending my thoughts back. *The condescending asshole had it coming.*

Her shoulders shook from holding back laughter. Ah, so my message had been received. She could both send *and* receive thoughts. That made her a true telepath. I wondered what other tricks she had up her high fashion sleeves. And more importantly, would she teach me?

Oh, I'll teach you, my dear. I give you my word. I 'heard' her say in my mind.

I tried to repress my excitement at the hope that someone could teach me some control with the psychic abilities. So far, Gwen had taught me psychic self-defense, a little protection magick, Craft basics, the Witches holidays, and rules... Lots of rules. It was frustrating, but I'd tried to be patient.

I'd actually learned more of what I was capable of from spending time with the twins and Duncan than formal lessons from Gwen. Ivy managed to sneak in a few more lessons over the past weeks, and Duncan had asked his mother to work with me. Learning from many different sources might be a good thing. At least I had a hunch it would be good for me.

We filed into Bran's room and waited while he retrieved the pages from the hidey hole in his closet. To my surprise, the pages were now inside of a locked heavy box.

"You have the pages contained inside of lead," Aunt Faye said.

"Yes," Bran said as he flipped open the outer box to reveal the archival box. Inside the archival box, wrapped in acid free tissue paper, the pages of the grimoire waited.

"That's new. Why a lead box?" I asked.

"Lead helps dull any magickal vibrations coming from the pages," Bran said.

I frowned at him. "That's a little bit of an overkill, isn't it? It's not like the pages are radioactive."

Aunt Faye held her hands out over the pages, but did not touch them. "The pages do emit a very strong energy, and it *is* negative."

"I have a hard time touching the pages, even with gloves on. They make me feel sick," Bran admitted.

I glanced at the pages, and felt nothing coming from them. If anything, they made me want to pick them up to study them. I watched Aunt Faye. She carefully took cotton gloves from Bran, put them on, and then, using a pair of tweezers, turned a few pages. When she flipped over a third page, it slid off the tissue paper and landed on the floor.

She and Bran both jumped back.

I rolled my eyes and gently picked up the page by the outside edges. "Don't you guys think you are overreacting?" I was more worried about the page being on the floor than touching an outside edge. But I still set the page directly back in the open archival box. "The pages are so pretty, why are you two acting so weird?"

I took a pair of gloves from the stack Bran had out, put them on, and rearranged the pages into two neat stacks. After I finished, I glanced up to find them both studying me.

"What?"

"Do me a favor." Bran pulled a glove off my hand. "Touch the grimoire pages directly with your hands again."

The look on both of their faces kept me from making a snide comment. So I peeled off the gloves, and gently set my fingertips at the edges of the pages, making sure to keep my fingers away from the illustrations and the printed words.

I felt a little tingle in my fingertips. My hands grew warm and a little hum of energy rolled up my arms. I smiled down at the pages. This particular one had an illustration of a rose bud in front of two overlapping triangles. Words in what looked like Latin were written around the central symbol. The various phases of the moon were beautifully drawn, curving above the rose and overlapping triangles. The design was stunning.

Bran said the pages made him feel sick. But to me, the sensation was warm, and it made me feel stronger. Almost as if the pages were infusing me with energy. I gazed down at the pages and blinked in surprise. *Wait a second, was something changing on the page?*

I gasped, realizing that the illustration had started to move. "Wow, can you guys see this?" I asked them.

The images shifted as I held my fingertips on the page. The drawings and the print actually reformed, becoming something else. As I watched, the illustration of the rose bud transformed into a fully open rose. The pages seemed brighter, almost as if they were alive. Unsure of what to do, I peeked up at Aunt Faye.

"Hold on," Aunt Faye said.

Bran had whipped out his smart phone. He was taking a video of the shifting images on the pages. "Autumn," he said after a few moments, "let go of the pages and step back."

I lifted my hands, and the images stopped moving. That strange illumination faded, and I made myself take a few steps back. It was hard though, I wanted my hands on the grimoire again.

Bran and Aunt Faye exchanged glances, then they both stared at me.

I crossed my arms over my chest. "I take it from your reaction, that hasn't happened to anyone else?"

"No. It hasn't." Bran shook his head.

"Well shit," I said.

CHAPTER ELEVEN

Fun Fact: If you want to freak out a family of Witches—all you have to do— is be the only person able to handle antique grimoire pages, full of dark magick, without suffering any nasty physical side effects. Oh, and if you *really* want to make them jumpy... make the pages come alive and light up with your touch.

On the up side? My *brother* gave me a very wide berth for the next few days. If I would have known that's all it would have taken, I'd have slapped those pages in the middle of the kitchen counter and showed off my mad 'make-the-grimoire-come-to-life' skills weeks ago.

Things at the manor were more insane than usual. Great Aunt Faye had announced she was moving in. She'd had the girls and I haul in a huge set of leopard print luggage to the downstairs guest room, formally known as Gwen's home office.

Gwen's computer and desk were relocated into a

corner of the dining room. Holly efficiently set up her mother's work station, while Ivy and I freshened up the downstairs room and adjoining bath. Aunt Faye watched over the proceedings and sat back in a curvy chair, announcing that she'd prefer the bedroom furniture to be rearranged. So, Ivy and I put our backs into it and rearranged. Then vacuumed again.

I think we'd still be at it if not for Ivy, who'd — out of sheer frustration—levitated the chair the older woman had been sitting in. When Great Aunt Faye realized the chair was several inches off the ground, she'd suddenly announced the room was sufficient for her needs. As soon as the chair hit the floor again, we were excused.

Marie, Violet, Cora and Gwen had saved whatever clothes and personal items that they could from the girls destroyed bedroom, and discarded the rest. The back bedroom was stripped now, except for the splattered floors, walls, and stained closet doors. My bedroom only needed to be put back to rights, as nothing had been broken or destroyed in there, merely tossed around.

Marie had washed the hardwood floors, stains and all, with a mixture of cleaning supplies and what she called 'Indigo Water'. When I'd asked what that was, Marie had informed me that it was a magickal mixture used for spiritual protection and to ward off evil. When she poured some of the contents from the bottle into the mop water, I could have sworn I'd heard drums beating from somewhere. Like the old tribal kind. I'd offered to help her, but she'd asked to be left alone to do her work. A little spooked by the phantom drumming. I'd backed out of the room and left her to it.

Things were still uncomfortable between Gwen and me. We were polite to each other, but, for lack of a better word, Gwen was distant. I imagined she was not happy that I'd forced her hand into telling the girls about Bran's parentage. Holly and Ivy were quieter than usual, and Ivy was bunking in my room. Holly was sleeping in her mom's room while they waited for their new mattresses to be delivered. There was plenty of room in their mother's suite for the pair of them, but Ivy had admitted to me that she wasn't quite ready to forgive her mother for keeping secrets. Personally, I was relieved to go back to my classes at the Museum, if only to get away from the pandemonium.

On Wednesday afternoon, I shut the front door of the manor behind me. Fall break had officially begun, and after everything that had been happening, I was really looking forward to some down time. Halloween was two days away, and I was excited to see the kids in the neighborhood come to the house for trick-or-treating. I was about to head up to my room when Marie strolled into the foyer.

"Good. You're home." Marie— seamstress extraordinaire, smiled and waved me into the living room.

"Where's Gwen and Aunt Faye?" I asked.

"Your great aunt wanted new window treatments for her room, so Gwen took her shopping," Marie said.

"Typical." I rolled my eyes.

I set my things down, and walked into the living room to see Holly standing on a chair wearing a billowy, long, pale pink tulle skirt. Cypress waved at me from the couch, and when my cousin turned to face me, my mouth fell open.

It wasn't Holly at all.

It was in fact, Ivy. She had on what appeared to be a Glinda— Good Witch of the North costume.

Saying nothing, I stopped, backed up, and walked out of the room. I waited a second, and entered again. Nope. Ivy was still in a Glinda costume. "I've passed into an alternative universe," I said.

Cypress and Ivy giggled at my reaction. Marie let out a booming laugh and went to fuss with the length of Ivy's tulle skirt.

"Holy shit, are you wearing *pink*?" I staggered towards the couch. "My heart… it can't take the strain."

"I know, right?" Cypress said.

"Very funny," Ivy frowned. "It's actually pale peach."

"Yeah, and you have sequins and sparkly butterflies sewn onto your shirt…" I said.

I sat down next to Cypress and stared at Ivy, my mind reeling. Before I could comment further, Holly came strolling in from the foyer. She carried a classic pointed Witches hat, and wore a gothic style, corseted gown. The dress was gorgeous and long in charcoal with black trim. The material swished as she walked in.

Suddenly, I got it and started to laugh. "Oh my god. *Good Witch* and *Wicked Witch,* right?"

"We thought it would be more fun if we switched it up," Holly explained.

I went to admire the gown Holly wore. "I'm digging those Victorian style sleeves, Blondie." The sleeves were large and poufy from shoulder to elbow and became snug below the elbow, ending at a point over her hands.

"Didn't Marie do a great job?" Holly said proudly.

"It was an old 80's style wedding dress. I dyed it first, then embellished it." Marie said from down on the floor where she shortened the hem of Ivy's tulle skirt.

"Good god woman, is there *anything* you can't do?" I said to Marie.

"Well, I didn't have time to make the corset," Marie said.

"I lent Holly one of *my* corsets," Ivy said.

"Why am I not surprised that you own corsets?" I said to Ivy.

"You should see the props she made for the Halloween Ball," Cypress said. "They're really awesome."

I eyeballed Marie. "You're an artist, a seamstress, you design props, and you run your tattoo shop?"

Marie stopped from trimming off the excess tulle from Ivy's skirt. "It's all art in one form or another."

I made a circling motion with my finger for Holly, and she turned around for me. "This is amazing," I said as I checked out her costume. The black under-the-bust-style corset cinched around her middle, and gray ribbons laced up her back.

"Marie, I brought the hat." Holly held up the pointed hat.

"Great." Marie tipped her head over towards the coffee table. "Hand it to Cypress and we'll decorate it for you so it matches the gown." Marie stood up and held out a hand to Ivy. "Come on down, and let's see if it's the right length now."

Ivy hopped down, and I saw sliver ballet slippers flash from under that massive tulle skirt. Ivy took a few steps forward, then more confidently started strolling around the room. "This length will work. I'm not tripping anymore," Ivy said to Marie.

Cypress handed her a large rhinestone crown, and Ivy went to check her hair in the ornamental mirror that hung in the living room. She brushed her long choppy bangs aside and stuck the tiara on her head. With a dramatic indrawn breath, Ivy spun and started to parade around the living room. Waving to imaginary Munchkins, I supposed.

Holly shook her head at her sister's theatrics, and took her turn up on the chair so Marie could check the length of her *Wicked Witch* costume.

"Those the shoes you'll wear the night of the Masquerade Ball?" Marie asked Holly.

"Yup." Holly lifted the skirt and stuck out a toe.

I saw black lace up boots with a low heel and, of course, a pointed toe. "Nice witchy boots," I said to Holly.

"Click your heels together three times, and think to yourself... " Ivy simpered and waltzed by us.

"Autumn." Marie ignored Glinda and caught my attention. "See that garment bag draped over the chair? That's yours. Go try it on for me."

"It's done?" After seeing what she'd pulled off for the girls, I couldn't wait to see the final outcome of my costume. I picked up the garment bag and went into the powder room to change.

I closed the powder room door behind me, toed off my sneakers, and stripped out of my jeans and shirt. Last I had seen the old black bridesmaid gown— it had been a long, sleeveless crepe gown. At the first fitting, Marie and I had discussed how to turn the thrift store find into a dress that would look more like Morticia Addams.

"Wow," I breathed. The dress had been transformed. Amazing what a little black lace and tulle could do.

"Autumn!" Cypress banged on the door. "Hurry up. I wanna see!"

"Okay, okay," I muttered. I pulled the zipper down the back of the dress, and slipped the gown over my head. There was no way I could pull the zipper up myself, so I left it and came out of the bathroom.

Cypress pounced. "Nice!"

"Ooh," Ivy said, and wafted down the hall past us.

"Zip me up, will you?" I turned around, and Cypress tugged the zipper up.

I took an experimental step forward in the slim fitting skirt. I found that I still had room to walk. Relieved that my range of movement was not too restricted, I went into the living room with Cypress carrying the garment bag and Ivy/ Glinda flouncing around behind us.

Holly was stepping down from the chair. She squealed when she saw me. "Hey, that's very Morticia!"

I walked to the long mirror to look. Now, the deep neckline was trimmed in gothic black velvet ribbons. Marie had added long, black lace sleeves that ended in artfully shredded black tulle. It gave the sleeves a dramatic look. The dress was creepily elegant, streamlined, and not too fussy... Which is exactly what I wanted. "It's wonderful. What do I owe you?" I said to Marie.

"Nothing. Gwen took care of the bill," she shrugged my question away.

"But, I—"

Marie cut off my argument. "Be sure to leave your hair down and loose that night... Like you have it today." She held up a finger. "Wait a second. I have a few things to jazz up the costume." Marie dug around in her sewing box and came over to the mirror. She handed me some silvery dangle spider earrings and a matching spider shaped pendant on a black cord.

I slipped the jewelry on and grinned at myself in the mirror. "Once I use that temporary black hairspray, it will look perfect."

"You sure you don't want to wear heels?" Marie asked me and knelt down to check the hem.

"I have some flats," I told her. "I'd trip in the heels. It's risky enough with me wearing a long dress."

"I dropped off Duncan's, 'Gomez Addams' costume this morning," Marie said as she continued to tug at the hem.

"How'd that burgundy smoking jacket turn out?"

"Very well. I watched my DVD of *The Addams Family* so many times to get the right look for that smoking jacket." Marie finished her adjustments and stepped back.

"So what are your costumes for the big Halloween Masquerade Ball?" I asked Marie and Cypress. "You've never told us."

Cypress took her phone out of her back pocket. "I'm going as a Wood Nymph." She pulled up a picture of herself in her costume. "See? I have wings, a green dress, with flowers and leaves for my hair," she explained while the girls and I all gathered around.

"That suits you," Holly said.

"So, Marie?" I raised my eyebrows at her. "What's your costume?"

Marie flashed me a grin. "I want to surprise you."

***

After the costume fitting was over, the twins and I put the gowns away in my bedroom closet. Cypress and the twins left me and went off in search of a glue gun to trim out Holly's Witch hat. Once the girls were gone, I stacked my books on my desk and tried to settle down. But I found I couldn't sit still. Something was pushing me.

I wandered over to the mantle and my growing collection of framed family photos. The picture of my Grandmother Rose, and a two year old me, was front and center. The photo Gwen had given me of my grandfather Morgan with his crow, Midnight, sat next to that. The romantic anniversary photo of my grandparents was now showing, to its best advantage, in a fancy antique looking silver colored frame. It still made me wish I could remember them. One of the selfies Duncan had taken of the two of us at the house I'd landscaped for him turned out so well, that I'd framed it too. It made me smile every time I looked at the picture.

Next to the photo of me and Duncan was my birthday present from the twins— a framed black and white photo of the two of them sitting with Merlin. I adjusted the framed photo of the girls and the cat a bit, but otherwise left the display of photos alone. That first framed picture of my father and I was still there, but I'd moved it to the back of the collection.

With the mixed feelings I had about my father, I

wasn't comfortable looking at it any longer. While I didn't want to pack it away, I also didn't want to see it every day, either. I realized as I studied my little collection that I had no photos of Gwen or Bran. While I mulled that over, the scent of Roses came out of nowhere.

I turned my head slowly, half expecting to see Ro in my room. But there was nothing to see, only smell. Come to think of it, I'd only ever seen my grandmother's ghost in the gardens— so far, anyway. I rushed to the window and there she was— puttering away in the rose garden. In the fading light just before sunset, she appeared real.

I grabbed my jacket, clattered down the main steps of the manor, straight past Gwen and Aunt Faye who'd come home from shopping.

"Autumn!" Gwen called after me.

"Not now, Ro's back!" I said and hit the front door at a dead run. I raced around the side of the house, my heart pounding.

"Ro!" I called skidding to a halt at the edge of the formal rose garden.

"Hello, sweetie." Ro stood up from where she was kneeling wearing the same outfit I'd seen her in before. She pushed her garden hat back, and held out a purple rose from our gardens.

I held my breath, wondering what would happen if I tried to take the flower, and reached for the stem. When my fingers closed around it, I gently took the rose from her.

"You can stop holding your breath now. I'm going to be here a little while," Ro told me.

I blew out a shaky breath. "Well, give a Witch a break will ya? I'm trying to wrap my mind around all of this." I lifted the rose, which was very real, and sniffed. "Thanks, Grandma."

"So, you've learned one of the secrets." Ro crossed her arms.

"Yes, I know that you are my grandmother, and I know about Bran."

"You've had a hard time... adjusting to all of this," Ro said. "I'm sorry."

I wanted to ask my questions quickly, before she faded away like before. "Ro— I mean Grandma Rose. What can you tell me about the Blood Moon Grimoire?"

"That it is best left buried."

"It's too late for that—I already found a part of it. I know it was torn into three pieces."

"Four pieces." Ro frowned at me. "There are four."

"My vision showed me three."

"Three sections of pages, and the cover—four," Ro insisted.

Aw hell, we had more to find? "Okay, four then. Where are they?" I asked.

"You may search far and wide across the land, but a house divided cannot stand," Ro said.

"Seriously? You're going to rhyme at me?"

The ghost of my grandmother gave me a chastising look.

I held up my hands in surrender. “Okay fine. But is that a spell, or a *warning*?” I noticed her image began to waver. “Hey, you said you would be here for a while. Don’t go!”

“Trying,” Ro frowned, as if in concentration. “Trying to stay.”

Suddenly I figured it out. It took real effort for Ro to appear to me. “It’s hard for you to look corporeal, isn’t it?”

My grandmother’s image nodded in confirmation. She was slightly less ‘there’ when she moved closer to me and reached out. “Tell no one there are four. Promise me.”

“Okay. Nobody will know about the four sections. I promise.”

“There are alliances to be drawn, dark magicks to neutralize, and enemies to defeat—”

“Who?” I asked. “*Who* is our enemy?”

“You must discover these things for yourself.”

“You don’t understand what’s been happening around here,” I said.

I saw her reach up, and I swear I felt my hair being touched. “I am bound. I cannot tell you directly.”

“Bound?”

“The spell that brought my death. I am bound.”

“You have to help me. The family is in danger. Give me a clue. *Something*!” I begged her.

“Only you can know.”

“Only me,” I promised again, as I watched a tear slide down her cheek.

“Sub Rosa,” she whispered and gestured to the rose I held.

“Sub Rosa,” I repeated.

My grandmother nodded once, blew me a kiss, and faded away.

Darkness fell, and the gardens were hushed. I heard the neighbors pull into their driveway of the cottage next door, and they waved cautiously at me from the other side of the wrought iron fence. I grimaced and waved back, trying to look casual. The older couple scurried inside, and I couldn’t have cared less what they thought of me standing out here.

Alone in the dark.

Talking to thin air.

The decorative solar lights in the rose garden came on, and I noticed the orange Halloween lights that decorated the front of the house had also popped on, thanks to their dusk to dawn timer. I was thankful that they had, as it made it slightly less creepy being outside by myself. Overwhelmed, I sat on the concrete bench in the garden.

Good god. There were *four* pieces of the Blood Moon Grimoire. And I was to tell no one about that. Our house was divided— weakened, and we were under attack. Now that I thought about it, that statement made sense— considering what had recently happened.

The manor had been ransacked and the witchy wards hadn't even slowed the vandals down. The revelation of Bran's parentage had caused a big tear down the middle of the Bishops. Ro had warned me of alliances to be drawn, enemies to defeat, bad magick to stop... No, to *neutralize.* She'd said.

At least she'd given me some information and a clue. Sort of.

Information and a clue that I'd promised not to reveal— to anyone. "Thanks for that," I muttered and dragged a hand through my hair. As much as I hated secrets, damned if I'd found myself forced to keep one. I let my hand fall in my lap, and it landed on the rose, the gift from my grandmother.

I gently picked it up, and my gaze swung from the flower to the family rose garden surrounding me. *Sub Rosa?* I knew the phrase from an Ancient Civilizations class I had taken as an undergrad. Sub Rosa was Latin. It literally meant 'under the rose', and was an old term for secrets. As a matter of fact, some occult societies still used the term, and it was usually illustrated as a rose being held upside down.

And she'd handed me a rose. Was it that simple? I jumped to my feet and started to pace. I stopped in front of the pretty garden statue of the Goddess Diana. My grandmother had left a flower there once, was it an offering? Or had it been a clue to where to find another piece of the Blood Moon Grimoire?

She'd said buried. It was best left buried... "What if

a piece of the Blood Moon Grimoire was buried under the roses?" I asked myself.

My heart started to pound in excitement. I needed to get the shovels, flashlights, maybe a metal detector... Nope. Scratch that. Paper pages wouldn't show up with a metal detector. I could try dowsing for the pages. I had read about using a pendulum to show you where things were buried. My mind raced as I considered the possibilities.

"Autumn... " The voice floated out of the dark.

My head snapped up, I spun to face the direction the voice had come from. I braced myself, wondering who or *what* was coming at me now.

CHAPTER TWELVE

A dark shape slowly moved out of the shadows and into the soft lighting of the rose garden. I heard my own heart pound, and then I recognized the figure.

"Aunt Faye!" I pressed my hand to my heart. "You scared me!" My great aunt walked towards me in a flowing black caftan. Her silver hair was long and loose and streamed around her shoulders. Standing there in the night, she *looked* like a Witch. The kind you read about in the very old, very creepy fairy tales.

"Did you see your grandmother's ghost again?" Aunt Faye asked.

"I did."

"Did she communicate with you?"

Aw hell. What to say that wouldn't be a lie, but would still keep my promise? Stalling, and trying to gather my thoughts, I walked out of the garden and towards Aunt Faye. "Well, I told her that I knew she was my grandmother... And that I'd learned about Bran."

Aunt Faye fell in with me, as we walked towards the front of the manor. "What else?"

"She said she was sorry I was having a hard time adjusting to everything," I said truthfully.

"I see." Aunt Faye nodded and hooked her arm through mine. "Sorry if I startled you."

I tried to change the subject. "You know, if you wore this outfit on Halloween and answer the door for the trick-or-treaters, you wouldn't even need a costume."

Aunt Faye smiled as we went up the porch steps. Before I could duck inside, she latched onto my arm with a surprising amount of force. "I hope that when you are ready, you'll come to me. I would never betray your confidence."

I regarded those pale colored eyes. *She knew.* She knew that I wasn't telling her everything. I felt a pulling sensation around my temples, and realized that she was trying to read me. I yanked back so we were no longer touching. "Stay out of my head, and maybe I will tell you... Eventually."

"Felt that, did you?" Aunt Faye grinned. "Excellent. You are much more sensitive than I thought. I look forward to working with you, to help you refine those gifts." She patted my arm like she was proud of me. "For now, I will leave you alone with your thoughts. *And* with that gift from your grandmother." She nodded towards the purple rose in my hand, and she opened the door.

I frowned after her. There wasn't even any point

asking how she had known.

Aunt Faye turned. "Oh, and tell Duncan I said hello. He's such a handsome young man." She winked at me and went inside.

As if she'd conjured him up, my cell phone started to play the *Bewitched* theme song. Proud of myself for not even flinching at Aunt Faye's prediction, I pulled my phone out of my pocket and checked the read out.

That canny old Witch.

"Hi, Duncan. What do you know about dowsing?" I said.

***

Thursday morning, I pretended to sleep in. Behind my locked door, I waited— fully dressed, until I heard the family leave for the day. As luck would have it, everything had worked out perfectly. Bran had meetings, Gwen was off to Enchantments, the twins were at school, and even Aunt Faye had plans- she was getting her hair trimmed... or something.

Last night, Duncan had suggested that I try dowsing using a pendulum. I had practiced using one of Ivy's before I went to bed and was optimistic with the results I'd achieved. She and I had sat up for hours working with the quartz crystal pendulum. All I had to do was casually mention to Ivy that I'd read about pendulums and wanted to try one, and she'd morphed into witchcraft instructor mode. Looking forward to trying it out all by myself, I opened my bedroom door slowly and stuck my head out.

Besides Merlin sitting in the hall and giving me the kitty stink eye, there was no one home. Humming the theme song from *Mission Impossible*, I scurried to the garage, grabbed my shovels, cut through the back yard, and headed for the rose garden.

I set the tools down. The breeze was chilly this morning, so I tugged my hood up, and pulled the crystal pendulum out of my jacket pocket. I figured a little magickal back up wouldn't hurt, so I held out the pendulum and improvised a quick charm. "I seek to find what was buried. By the powers of earth, pendulum show me where to dig."

The pendulum began to move in a lazy circle. I moved carefully forward into the rose garden and following my hunch— headed towards the statue of the moon Goddess Diana. Step by step I went forward, trying to hold my arm steady, watching the circling pendulum. I'd gone about five feet when the pendulum dramatically started to swing side to side. I backed up, it circled. I moved forward— it went side to side.

"Ha!" I was about two feet in front of the statue, so I set the pendulum down to mark the spot and started digging in the middle of the garden path with a hand shovel. Gleefully, I dug up the path. I'd dug down about six inches when my shovel struck something.

I dropped down to my hands and knees and started to paw at the ground. *Oh my god, this was so fast!*

Delighted with my sleuthing abilities, I pulled the earth away in handfuls, and saw a glimpse of white. I pulled more dirt away and my ‘discovery’ came to light.

I’d found something alright. The damn irrigation system.

I shook my head at myself and blew out an aggravated breath. What had I improvised with that charm? *I seek to find what was buried?* Well shit. Annoyed at myself, and my less-than-stellar attempt at sleuthing, I covered back up the PVC pipe and filled in the hole. I had barely finished smoothing the mulch path back into place when I heard a *click.*

I saw several sprinkler heads rise up out of the ground, and before I could stand up—I got sprayed straight in the face with water. With a shriek, I fell back onto my butt. Apparently, the sprinkler system was scheduled to come on and water the roses in the morning.

“Damn it!” I scrambled back, and for a second I swore I heard my grandmother’s ghost laughing at me. “That’s not funny, Ro!” I grabbed my stuff, got out of the line of fire, and hurried out of the garden. Even though she did not appear to me, I had a hunch she was around somewhere. *Probably laughing her ghostly ass off.* I wiped some water off my face with my jacket sleeve and stomped to the back patio. I stood there soaking wet, annoyed, and dripping on the brick pavers.

I caught my own soaked reflection in the glass of the back door, and my anger turned to laughter. Nancy

Drew I was not. Thankfully, no one as at home to witness my little screw up. I sat in a patio chair and tried to figure out where to look next. Clearly, *under the rose* did not mean 'under the rose garden'. While I sat there, the back door of the manor suddenly opened.

Aunt Faye stepped outside wearing a tiny pair of blue, round sunglasses, a paisley shirt, skinny jeans and a denim jacket. Chunky turquoise jewelry dangled from her ears and wrapped around her neck. "Watering the gardens, were we?" She arched a brow.

"I thought you had a haircut appointment."

Aunt Faye flipped her hair over one shoulder, "I came back because I forgot my cell phone." She held it up.

"You look like you are off to a photo shoot or something." I said, hoping to distract her. But invariably, it was true. The old woman had an impressively stylish wardrobe. And an amazing sense of fashion for a senior citizen.

Aunt Faye pulled her glasses down and peered at me from over the rims. "You're trying to distract me from whatever mischief you are up to."

I felt the tug on my thoughts. "Stay out of my head," I grumbled.

"Well, I'm off to my hair appointment and manicure." She regarded my filthy hands and frowned. "Darling, you could use a mani yourself."

I had to laugh. "Yeah, I suppose I could. I've never had a manicure before."

"*What*?" Aunt Faye sounded horrified at the thought.

"I used to work at a nursery, remember? You plant things, you get dirty hands."

My great aunt shuddered. "Why don't you clean up and come with me? My treat on the manicure, and then we could go to lunch."

Call me psychic, but I had a hunch that she was not going to leave me alone today. Especially now that she suspected I was up to something. I sighed, my master plan foiled by a seventy year old. "Okay, give me five minutes."

I put the tools away, scrubbed off the dirt in the potting room sink, and went up to my room to change. I tossed on my favorite persimmon colored sweater, a fresh pair of jeans and my neon green running shoes. I ran a brush through my hair, grabbed my pleather jacket, and jogged down the stairs. As my hand trailed along the banister, I noticed, for the first time, that five petal roses were carved into the wood trim along the main staircase.

I slowed down and looked with a new awareness at the architecture of the manor. I walked through the family room, and realized there were floral carvings on the mantle, too. Come to think of it, there were art nouveau roses in the stain glass windows in the attic... I went out through the potting room, and as my eyes scanned the huge apothecary cabinet that took up one wall, I was unsurprised to note more five petal roses worked into the décor. *There were* roses *all over the house.*

Was the *Sub Rosa* clue my grandmother had given me pointing to the house itself? Holy crap! It would take a couple of weeks to discretely work my way from room from room. But even though it would be a huge undertaking, at least I had a direction in my search for the rest of the grimoire pages.

***

A short time later, I was riding shotgun with Aunt Faye as she drove through town in her fancy hybrid car. "This will be fun!" She beamed over at me.

"Maybe I could get black nail polish for Halloween and my costume for the Masquerade Ball," I said. I stared down at my beat up hands as if I was considering colors, but was actually plotting what room I should start looking through first, for the grimoire pages.

"We call it *Samhain*, dear."

"Oh yeah. I forgot."

"Did you celebrate the holiday when you were a child?"

"Well... it was always a battle," I recalled. "Mom *hated* Halloween, and Dad loved it. So he would take me out trick-or-treating when I was little, while mom usually went to church. Come to think of it— I can't remember a Halloween when they didn't have a big fight..." I trailed off as I thought it over. Knowing what I knew now, I grimaced.

"Susan was always a fussy, frightened little twit," Aunt Faye said of my mother.

I stayed silent, but I had to agree with my great aunt.

"I am sorry that she has rejected you." Aunt Faye reached out and gave my hand a comforting squeeze. "Gwen told me."

I nodded, but didn't comment.

Aunt Faye whipped her car into an empty parking space at the salon. She turned off the engine and glanced over at me. "Listen to me— even though the house is divided at the moment, we will get through this. And we *are* your family."

I felt a little chill at her comment. It sounded very similar to what my grandmother had said, *a house divided...* But I gave her a little smile anyway, and opened my car door.

Aunt Faye got out and waited for me to join her. "You have never been, nor will you be, alone, Autumn."

I stopped and studied her. She stood in a beam of October sunshine, looking like a page from some classy, mature fashion magazine. She was nosey, demanding *and* pushy. But she was really starting to grow on me. "Thank you, Aunt Faye," I said.

She stuck her elbow out and I threaded my arm through hers. We walked to the entrance of the salon together. "I have really been meaning to talk to you about your choice of footwear." She gestured to my neon green running shoes.

"Hey, I like bright colors!" I told her.

"I'm not surprised. Seers tend to be attracted to color."

"Really? That's interesting," I said and meant it.

"But dear, you *always* wear tennis shoes. Do you own any heels, or dressy boots?"

I fought against smiling. "I have work boots."

Aunt Faye shuddered in mock horror. "That's it. After lunch I'm taking you shopping."

"You don't have to..." I tried to argue.

"My girl, the shoes you *do* own are a crime against nature." Aunt Faye pulled a face as she opened the salon door. "Don't argue with your elders. Instead, smile and say, 'Thank you Aunt Faye.'"

"Thank you Aunt Faye." *You pushy old Witch.* I aimed the thought at her.

"I heard that." Aunt Faye grinned and held the door open for me.

By the time we returned to the manor it was late in the afternoon. I now had manicured, black fingernails, and I had to admit they did look pretty cool. I now also possessed two new pairs of dressy boots. I had flatly refused the three inch pumps. My great aunt walked around in them with no trouble at all, but I knew better. *God, I'd kill myself trying to walk in heels.*

However, I had fallen in love with the boots. I let myself in my room and set the boxes down. I shrugged off my jacket and noticed that the central botanical print that hung above my bed was crooked on the wall. I straightened it, and sat down to open up the boxes.

Both pairs of boots came to right below the knee. One was black suede with a thick heel. They were bad-ass and witchy. Laces went up the front, but the boots actually had a side zipper. The second pair was more serviceable. They were a dark brown with a low heel and reminded me of riding boots. I switched out my running shoes for the brown boots, stood back up, stuck my toe out, and admired them.

Gwen stuck her head in the doorway. "Hey! I like those!"

"Thanks." I gave her a little smile.

"Aunt Faye?" Gwen asked as she pointed at the boxes.

"Yup. She took me shopping. I tried to tell her no..."

"I see how well that worked out for you," Gwen said while Merlin nosed past. He headed for the empty boot box, and hopped in.

Gwen and I stood there awkwardly, she in the doorway and me by the bench at the foot of my bed. Neither of us seemed sure of what to say next. I saw her start to say something, and then she shut her mouth.

Merlin popped his head up and meowed at the two of us. I watched his feline eyes narrow. The cat made a growl that sounded like a feline version of muttering, and after making his kitty opinion known, he proceeded to snuggle back into the box.

"I agree, Merlin." Gwen came in and shut the door. She stopped, patted the cat on the head, and came over to sit on the bench.

"Did we just get a lecture from the cat?" I wanted to know.

Merlin yowled.

"I do believe so." Gwen's lips twitched.

I crossed my arms and recalled what Ro had said. *A house divided could not stand.* I decided, then and there, to get this over with. "I think it's time you and I clear the air." I sat next to her.

"Yes, I agree. But first, I want you to tell me about your latest visitation from my mother."

I took a deep breath. Carefully, so as not to divulge any of the secrets my grandmother had told me about the Blood Moon Grimoire, I filled Gwen in— on what I could.

"I wish I could have seen or heard her." Gwen's eyes welled up with tears.

"She's never here very long. She told me she was 'bound'. Something about the spell that had caused her death?" I frowned over that.

"To be clear, she actually told you that we had alliances to make, and dark magicks to neutralize?" Gwen asked.

"Don't forget the 'enemies to defeat' bit." I sighed. "But yeah. That's pretty much it. And honestly, that sounds like a hell of a lot to me."

Gwen sat silently for a moment. "Autumn, I am sorry that you found out the way you did about Bran being your brother." Gwen studied my expression before she continued. "I would have told you eventually, but everything happened so quickly. I wanted to give you time to settle into everything first."

"Bran said he wouldn't have told me at all," I pointed out.

"Bran still believes that you *not* knowing would keep you safer."

"How's that?"

Gwen shifted to meet my eyes. "He was worried that someone would have tried to manipulate you, and turn you against us. He's still worried about how the information about your father could affect you."

"Yeah, well, it wasn't easy finding out about my dad's past."

"Oh? And what *did* you learn, and from whom?" Gwen raised her eyebrows.

"Rebecca filled me on what my father was like when he was a young man— and how badly he treated Winnie, Bran's birth mother." Hoping for more insight, I shared what I had learned.

Gwen cringed. "I'm sorry you had to hear all of that. Arthur was a very spoiled young man."

"The stories about him are true?" I asked.

"Yes, I'm afraid they are."

"So, he abandoned Bran's birth mother—" My temper was making my voice raise, but I didn't care. "He dumped Bran on you and my grandmother to raise, then turns around and marries my Christian mother a couple of years later— like Bran never even happened?"

"Arthur was captivated by Susan," Gwen explained. "She was beautiful and adored him. Plus, she knew nothing of our world, nor was she interested in that side of your father's heritage. After being pursued for who and what he was for so many years, I think that was part of the attraction for your father."

"You said that they lived here at the manor. Did she know about Bran *before* she married my dad?" I asked.

"No, they eloped, and she didn't find out until afterwards."

"I bet that went over well."

"That's an understatement." Gwen rolled her eyes.

"What were my parents like when they were newlyweds— were they happy?"

"At first they were, but your mother did not react well to the family's magickal practices." Gwen's voice toughened. "I'm not ashamed to admit that your mother and I never got along. There are certain things that I cannot forgive."

Sitting there, I had a horrible thought, or maybe more like a hunch. "Was my mother unkind to Bran?" I was almost afraid to ask.

"Only once," Gwen practically growled and rested her hand on mine.

As soon as she touched me, the room we were sitting in fell away. A scene rolled out in front of me.

My mother, so young, stood and shouted at a little red-haired boy. She was pregnant and wore a loose fitting blue dress. The child glared up at her with one red cheek and a defiant expression. It was Bran. He cringed away from my mother, even as she raised her hand to slap him again.

Suddenly, Gwen came running up the stairs, her expression murderous. With a gesture— she had my mother flying backwards and pinned against the wall in the upstairs landing. Gwen scooped up Bran and held him while he cried. My father came running to stand between them. He shouted at the both of them while my mother, still pinned up against the wall by Gwen's magick, screamed her head off. The vision melted away.

I came back to present time with the sound of my own breathing loud in my ears. The room lurched, and I felt sick to my stomach. "Oh my god." I dropped my head between my knees.

"What did you see?" Gwen asked and rubbed my back.

I kept my head down as the room spun in sick circles around me and told her what I had *seen*. "It's like I was there," I said, my voice thick with tears.

"Take a breath," Gwen suggested calmly. "In through your nose... Hold it... Now blow it out," she suggested.

"What made my mother do that?" I asked after I blew out a few slow breaths.

"Bran had been playing in the nursery your mother had set up for you. He broke a trinket, and your mother was angry."

"He was only a little boy..." I closed my eyes, but it didn't help much. To me, it felt as if it had only happened a moment ago. It made me feel badly for Bran and left me so angry at my mother. I glanced at Gwen. "Please tell me you scared her so badly that she never touched him again."

Gwen smiled slowly, and it wasn't a nice smile. "I promise you. I absolutely *terrified* her."

"Good, I'm glad," I said, and meant it. I slowly lifted my head. Fortunately, the nasty after effects of the postcognitive vision seemed to be over.

Gwen started to reach out to me, and thought better of it. "I want to apologize. I need to remember how sensitive you are to memories. Especially strong ones."

"The more I find out about my parents, the more they seem like strangers."

"And that is why I tried to protect you." Gwen stood up and began to pace the floor.

I watched her walk back and forth and struggled to calm myself as well. "*Why?* Why did he turn his back on Bran, but yet, he loved me?"

"Because you were your mother's daughter." Gwen stopped, and her eyes were intense. "He once told me that he thought you would be free from the legacy of magick."

Time to let my super power, sarcasm, off the chain. "Did my father take *any* science classes at college? Or, did no one explain to him how genetics work? Some physical traits *are* hereditary!" I knew I was shouting, but I didn't care. "I am half tempted to ask Aunt Faye how to do a séance just so I could chew my father out!"

Merlin started to growl from the box, and he rose to stalk closer to where I sat.

"I'd like to see that. Samhain *is* almost upon us..." Gwen said as if she was considering it.

Merlin let out an angry sounding wail and took a swipe at my jeans. Clearly, he didn't like my idea about the séance, or Gwen's comment.

"Hey!" I yanked my leg back. The cat sat there glaring at me. "Do you expect me to apologize?" I asked the cat.

Merlin made a noise between a wail and a growl.

"Fine! Fine! I'm sorry," I told him. Merlin hopped up on the bench and head butted my arm. I blew out a breath. "I just got bitched at and had to apologize to... a cat." I rubbed Merlin's ears and shook my head. "I'm going to end up in a home for the 'forever weird' if this shit keeps up."

Gwen laughed and covered her mouth. "I'm sorry. I'm not laughing at you..."

"Yes, you are." I pretended to glare at her. "Go right ahead because I'm going to book *your* room at the home, right next to mine."

"Maybe we can crochet pot holders together," Gwen suggested brightly.

"I'm thinking more along the lines of finger painting."

Gwen burst out laughing. "You remind me so much

of your Grandmother Rose at times."

I grinned. "Really? How?"

"It's the temper and the sarcasm," she explained.

The scent of roses bloomed in the air. Strong and sweet, like there were dozens of the flowers in the room. I breathed deep enjoying it. I felt a laugh bubble up as I watched Gwen's eyes flare very wide. So, she could smell them too. "I suppose Ro, I mean Grandma Rose, liked that comment."

"Will she appear, do you think?" Gwen asked softly.

"I've never seen her inside the house— only outside in the rose garden. The 'strong smell of roses' thing... she does that in here off and on. It's sort of her way to get my attention."

The scent faded away, as if it had never been. I saw Gwen's chest rise up and down, and heard her breath hitch. "Come over here," my aunt said holding out her arms. I went to her and hugged her, hard.

Like the day in the park when Ivy and I had broken through the old spell that had bound my magick, I felt something else shatter and fall away. "I'm glad we've cleared the air," I said as we held onto each other and those old, negative feelings faded away.

"Love you." Gwen pressed a kiss to my hair.

"Back at ya." *We couldn't be divided any longer.* I thought. *Maybe after today, the gap between us will begin to close.*

"We won't *be* divided anymore." Gwen picked up on my thoughts and squeezed me tight.

Damn telepaths. I thought at her and smiled when Gwen laughed in response.

CHAPTER THIRTEEN

Trick-or-treaters paraded up and down the streets of the neighborhood. I sat with Duncan on the manor's decorated wrap around porch watching as the little ones passed through the black metal gates. The tall gates were open tonight, and had been decorated with spider webs and bundles of cornstalks. Groups of flickering jack-o'-lanterns were grouped around the entrance. Once past the gate, the children were confronted by fabric ghosts that fluttered from the branches of trees. As they strolled up the front sidewalk, they wandered by fake tombstones and a creepy scarecrow who held court over the front gardens.

More jack-o'-lanterns lit up the front path and also shined from each porch step. Decorative orange lights and glowing spider webs were draped all over the front porch, while festive orange mums, spiked with twisty black branches, stood in tall urns at either side of the front door. Duncan and I waited for the children at the little bistro table and chairs the family normally kept on the far side of the porch. Tonight, the table was centered on the porch and boasted a long orange tablecloth with the large, candy filled plastic cauldron resting in the middle.

Holly and Ivy flitted to and fro, looking like specters in pale gray hooded capes and white face makeup, while they greeted the kids at the gate, and, sometimes, even escorting the more timid trick-or-treaters up to the house. The girls were having a blast, and were also keeping an eye on all of the flickering pumpkins and props in the yard.

Parents posed their children for pictures in the front yard. The mood was fun and festive with the cornstalks rustling in the breeze, the spicy scent of chrysanthemums in the gardens, and the tumbling autumn leaves crunching underfoot. The fog machine hissed, and 'fog' rolled across the lawn as more groups of children marched up the front steps to claim their candy.

Compared to the lack of Halloween decorations I had grown up with, the Bishop's front yard was an extravaganza. There were over two dozen jack-'o-lanterns displayed, and I had personally carved six of them. The pumpkin carving party had taken place the night before. We'd had made a hell of a mess in the potting room, but we'd had fun. Together... as a family. Which was nice after the tense week we'd endured.

Gwen and Great Aunt Faye would come to the door off and on during the evening to see the trick-or-treaters, but for the most part, they were busy inside prepping for a big Samhain gathering and feast with the coven that would begin at 10:00 pm.

"Trick or treat!" shouted a little angel, a winged fairy princess and a super hero.

Keeping in the spirit of things, I wore my new black boots, a long midnight blue broomstick skirt, and my favorite black lace top. A miniature Witch's hat, attached to a headband, perched at an angle on my head — courtesy of Ivy. I'd left my long hair down, but the decorated headband kept it out of my face.

"Here you go." I handed out candy bars to the trio of kids. Beside me, Duncan, who wore a black button down shirt and jeans, talked to the super hero who was proudly showing off his costume.

Ivy came at us in a full sprint asking for candy. "I've got a couple of little ones who are afraid to come up to the porch."

Before I could scoop a few candy bars out of the big plastic cauldron, I saw Holly leading a pair of preschoolers up along the path.

"Oh. Never mind." Ivy snatched the candy anyway, tucked it in her cape pockets and darted back down the sidewalk. I guessed Ivy knew the father, as she stopped and chatted him up while the little ones dressed as Cinderella and Sleeping Beauty walked up to the porch hand in hand with Holly.

I saw 'Cinderella' was having problems navigating the stairs with her big blue skirt, while her older

'Sleeping Beauty' sister hiked up her pink skirt, flashing jeans and tennis shoes, and climbed up the front porch steps. Holly solved the little one's problem by scooping the giggling Cinderella under the arms and hoisting her up to the top of the steps.

"Twick or tweat," said Cinderella, holding out her plastic pumpkin.

"Hi sweetie." I smiled at the shy little girl, and my heart melted. *Oh god, I want one!*

"Fanks," she said as I dropped a couple of candy bars in her plastic pumpkin.

"Hi!" said Sleeping Beauty. "I can do a trick!"

"Okay..." I dropped the candy into her bag, "...what's your trick?"

Sleeping Beauty looked back at her father who was talking animatedly to Ivy about the yard display. She giggled and held her hand out, palm up. I watched her frown in concentration, and, in the middle of her palm, an orange spark popped.

"That's awesome!" Duncan said.

Holly gave the little girl's shoulder a squeeze, "Well done!" she told her.

"Wow," I managed. That little girl, who I'd estimated at maybe five years old, had done magick—raised energy right in front of us.

"Not supposed to do magick in front of people, Sissy." Cinderella made a face at her big sister. "I'm telling Mommy."

"Don't be a tattle-tale." Sleeping Beauty sneered.

Cinderella was clearly not intimidated. She started to cock back her candy laden pumpkin, and Holly neatly stepped between them before Cinderella could bean her big sister with it.

Their father arrived on the porch a second later. “Girls, behave yourselves,” he said cheerfully and was wearing a sweatshirt that said, *It’s Halloween, Witches!*

I tried not to laugh as the little girls glared at each other.

Daddy scooped up Cinderella in one arm and took Sleeping Beauty firmly by the hand. “Girls, say thank you,” he told them.

“Thank you,” they chimed.

“Happy Halloween,” I said to the girls and their father.

“Happy Samhain.” The father tossed me a wink and strolled off down the sidewalk with his happy little family of Witches.

I sat there stunned for a few seconds. Holly picked up the candy filled cauldron and handed out to the next round of kids.

“You can close your mouth now.” Duncan nudged me.

“What? Oh.” I watched as Sleeping Beauty and her father, who was still carrying little Cinderella, moved off down the sidewalk and on to the next house. “Those little girls are Witches too. Aren’t they?” I shook my head in amazement and a tiny bit of longing.

“Sure.” Duncan shrugged like it was no big deal.

"Wow, they were so *open* about it."

"Well, it is Samhain," Duncan pointed out reasonably.

I had to laugh. "I see your point. That little Cinderella was awesome."

"You want one of those for yourself?" Duncan grinned at me.

Damn it. He'd heard my thoughts. "Well, not today. But some day I would like to have kids."

"Yeah, those two were great." Duncan winked at me. "I bet they keep their parents on their toes."

"Oh man, I never considered that," I started to smile, but a stray thought had me frowning instead. *How different would my life have been if Bran and I had grown up learning magick together?* It made me a little wistful, so I pushed it aside, determined to let nothing ruin the night.

Duncan peeked in the cauldron that Holly returned to the table. "When Julian and I were kids, away at boarding school, we used to try and outdo each other with magick."

I blinked in surprise. "I didn't know you'd gone to school together."

"Yeah we did, up until college." Duncan seemed to shrug the memory away. "We're running low; I'll go get more candy from Gwen," he told us and went inside the manor.

This left me with Holly on the front porch. After the current group of kids skipped away, Holly took

Duncan's vacated chair. "Cinderella and Sleeping Beauty are part of the Jacobs family. They're actually our second cousins."

I knew that name. "Jacobs was Grandma Rose's maiden name," I realized.

"Yup." Holly pulled her gray hood farther over her hair. "I babysit for them sometimes."

"Those two little girls were adorable," I said

Holly laughed. "Oh, well, it's *adorable* that you think so." She stood up and seemed to float gracefully down the steps. Her gray cape billowed romantically behind her as she moved farther down the front sidewalk.

"I have provisions!" The screen door slapped closed behind Duncan. He ripped open a bag of chocolate bars and started to pour them into to plastic cauldron. I smiled at him when he snagged one for himself.

"Those are supposed to be for the trick-or-treaters," I reminded him.

"No worries. I can do a trick to earn my candy."

"It better be good," I said, thinking he would tell a joke or something.

Duncan tucked the candy bar in his shirt pocket. He stepped back from me and off to the left side of the porch. He shut his eyes and lifted his hands out to his sides, palms up. I could see that he was controlling his breathing as he stood there concentrating.

I swung my gaze nervously around, relieved we were having a lull in the trick-or-treaters. I turned my gaze back to Duncan and was startled to realize that he was glowing. A thin outline of light had flared out around his body. A breeze carrying fallen leaves came rushing across the porch, strong enough to send all of the decorations swaying back and forth.

As I watched, the light around his body seemed to pull in and become a bit more defined. The leaves that had blown across the porch suddenly, and impossibly, switched direction. They began to rise up and swirl around Duncan in a continuous tumble of some kind of wonderful enchantment. His eyes slowly opened and met mine.

Elemental magick. I realized as my mouth went dry. *He was calling on the element of air. Working with it, directing it...*

It felt incredibly intimate, watching while the spell swept all around him. He held his hand out to me, and I felt the pull of his magick. I stood and went to him, no questions asked. As soon as I clasped his hand, a blast of air had my hair streaming back. I felt the familiar rush of our combined energy. Those spinning leaves made a cheerful rustling sound as he pulled me to him, and I became a part of his magick. Spellbound, I raised my mouth to his.

As we kissed, my hair billowed everywhere, and the tumble of leaves increased in speed and noise. For a few wonderful moments, I totally forgot that we were in plain sight standing on the front porch.

"Ahem." Someone cleared their throat loudly.

Duncan and I broke apart, and the happy little whirlwind of autumn leaves stopped spinning. The leaves floated naturally and quietly back to the front porch. I pushed at the tangle of my hair to see who had interrupted us.

Aunt Faye stood there, her arms crossed over her chest. "I realize that it is Samhain, however, you two might want to be a bit more discreet with the public displays of magick." She tried to look disapproving, but I could see she was fighting against a smile.

My face went red. I'd been so wrapped up in him that I'd forgotten the trick-or-treaters. "Sorry," I said, trying to smooth my hair back in some semblance of order.

Duncan grinned unrepentant at Great Aunt Faye. "I had to earn my treat." He patted the candy bar in his pocket.

Ivy came bouncing up the steps. "I want to hand out the candy for a while." She snatched up the cauldron and took position on the porch. "Hey, Autumn. Your hair is full of leaves," Ivy pointed out.

"I'll help her with that," Duncan said and plucked a few out of my hair.

Aunt Faye reached into a pocket of her velvet fringed kimono. "Here, I knew there was a reason I put this in my pocket." She held out a small hairbrush to me.

I bit my lip to hold in the laughter and silently took the brush.

"You two... behave yourselves," she suggested gruffly, and went back inside.

Ivy passed out candy to the next round of kids. As soon as they had run down the porch, Duncan took the brush from me and motioned for me to turn around. I tugged the headband out of my mess of hair and handed him the brush. He began working the tangles and bits of leaves out of my hair.

I turned my head to look at him. "I've never seen you do a spell like that."

"Well, I didn't want a five year old out-doing me on Samhain," he said cheerfully as he brushed out my hair. "Besides, I really wanted that candy bar."

"Oh my god. Competitive, much?" I rolled my eyes.

"What did you think of the spell?" Duncan asked a moment later.

I turned around to meet his gaze. "It was impressive *and* beautiful. I've never seen you work with an element before."

He shrugged. "I have an affinity with the element of air— the same way that you do with the element of earth." He finished brushing the leaves out of my hair. "I have a small connection with fire too, but air is my strongest element. I can teach you how to access their powers, if you like."

I thought about that for a moment. "Yes, I would like that." I smiled at him as he handed me the brush. I stuck the headband with its sassy miniature hat back on my head. I returned to my position on the porch in time to see a large group of kids walk through the front gate.

"Hey, Duncan. I might need your help in a minute," Ivy said.

"Back to work." Duncan winked at me, turning his attention to the trick-or-treaters. A large group of young teens was loudly critiquing the front yard display while they shuffled up the path to the manor.

Beside me, I felt Ivy tense up. Before I could even comment on her reaction, one teen shoved another, and that kid shoved right back. Shouting started between the kids in the group. Someone kicked a pumpkin, and next, a 'tombstone' toppled over.

"I don't think so," Duncan said— and he was gone. He had been standing on the porch one second, and then he suddenly appeared in the middle of the group of teens.

I blinked in astonishment. I hadn't even seen him move.

"Did you see that?" Ivy let out a delighted cackle. "I've never seen someone cloak their movements so smoothly before. That was awesome!"

Cloak their movements. His mother could do that too... I tried not to feel uneasy about what I'd witnessed — every time I thought I was figuring out magick, something new popped up.

"Come on." Ivy grabbed my hand, and we hurried down the steps to Duncan.

I couldn't hear what he'd said to the teens, but they'd all stopped in their tracks and listened respectfully to him. By the time we got to the group, the young teens had all apologized and were straightening up the display.

Ivy passed out candy to them, which they all accepted politely. With no other issues, the kids went back down the path, past Holly at the gate, and out to the sidewalk.

"Trouble?" Holly strolled up to us.

"A minor skirmish," Ivy laughed. "Duncan straightened it out."

I righted the pumpkin that had been knocked over and pulled off the lid. Melted wax pooled inside the jack-o'-lantern. The votive candle inside its holder had been snuffed, so I pulled the candle and holder out.

"Here, let me," Duncan offered and took it from me.

"I'll go get the lighter." I started to take a step towards the front porch where we had extra candles and a lighter for the jack-o'-lanterns.

"Nope. I got this." Duncan plucked the candle out of the glass holder and held it up to eye level. He narrowed his eyes a bit, and I managed not to jump back when the candle flared to life.

"Cool," Ivy and Holly said in unison.

"Whoa," I managed.

Duncan placed the burning candle back inside the glass holder. He casually set it back in place. He stood brushing off his hands and burst out laughing. "The look on your face... I told you, I have a small connection to the element of fire, as well."

"So you did," I managed. Holly and Ivy simply grinned at him and took up positions for the next round of kids.

I studied him as he went and straightened out some of the props in the front yard. In the past few moments, I'd witnessed Duncan calling on the element of air. He'd cloaked his movements so well that he seemed to reappear somewhere else in the blink of an eye. And now, he'd lit a candle with the power of his magick. *What was a magician with those kinds of skills doing with a new, bumbling Witch like me?*

"I heard that." Duncan walked over to me and slung his arm around my waist.

I really had to remind myself to watch my thoughts around him. That was twice he'd *overheard* them. But it did make me wonder why someone with those kinds of talents was wasting his time with me.

"Stop it." He gave my waist a gentle squeeze as we returned to the front porch. "You think too little of yourself and worry way too much."

"You've never done magick like that in front of me before," I pointed out.

Duncan ran a hand down the back of my hair. "I was waiting for you to be more comfortable with your own magick."

"You caught me off guard, that's all."

"Well, now you know, so relax and enjoy the evening."

I made a conscious effort to stop worrying and enjoy

the evening. I had to laugh as a little pirate and a killer clown came racing up the path for candy. Here I'd figured that the Samhain ritual with the coven later tonight would be the big magickal 'treat' for the evening. Looks like the best show was, in fact, out here with Duncan.

Halloween was turning out to be a most illuminating night.

***

When Duncan and I entered City Hall the following evening, arm in arm as Morticia and Gomez Addams, the Halloween Masquerade was in full swing. Privately, I had wondered if we were over dressed. The costumes Marie had created for us were amazing, but I'd never seen adults go all out for a masquerade before. My hair felt stiff with all of the black hairspray, but it looked the part and hung straight down my back. Ivy had painted a Gomez style mustache on Duncan who had slicked his blonde hair back with gel.

Once we entered the ballroom, I took a good look at the revelers and realized that William's Ford took their Halloween Ball very, very seriously. I saw everything from tuxes and Venetian style masks on the men to elaborate ball gowns and glittering masks on sticks for the ladies. There were lots of upscale costumes ranging from glamorous to ghoulish. It was incredible. I smiled and gave Duncan's arm a squeeze. "Oh god, this is *amazing*!"

We had only entered the room when a photographer stopped us to pose for a picture. We posed, and I blinked the flashbulbs away. Holly and Ivy, a.k.a. Wicked Witch and Good Witch, joined us a moment later. Each of the girls were sporting a neon yellow wrist band which marked them as minors. Adults were given an orange and black wrist band. I'd been informed by the girls that the age limit for the event was seventeen and up. So this was Holly and Ivy's first year at the Halloween Ball, as well.

The photographer snapped pictures of the girls too. And they really got into it, doing various poses, smiles and sneers for him. Duncan and I waited while Cher's "Dark Lady" blasted through the DJ's speakers. An impressive light show spun in patterns of light across the room. Once the girls were done, we shuffled forward through the crowd and over towards the table reserved for us.

As we worked our way across the room, I thought I saw many people I knew from the museum and from the coven. At least, I was pretty sure I knew them. The costumes and masks the attendees wore were incredible. On each round table, a real pumpkin was centered. Fresh flowers in oranges, purples, and crimson, were beautifully arranged inside. Little candles flickered around the arrangements. Black and orange crepe paper streamers and white spider webs dripped from the ceiling of the ballroom. Various artificial tombstones lined the walls, and there was a crypt set up around the DJ's stand.

Holly and Ivy saw some of their friends and stopped to chat. I caught a glimpse of Ivy's boyfriend, Eric. He was dressed as a Victorian-era vampire. My lips twitched. No wonder Ivy liked him. I waved to a dazzling Cypress, who wore a strapless neon green gown with shimmering fairy wings, a crown of ivy leaves, and body glitter across her shoulders. We found our reserved table, and I couldn't help but laugh when I saw Lexie and Bran who were dressed as Alice and the Mad Hatter— Tim Burton style.

Lexie grinned up at us. "You guys look wonderful!"

"Let me see that dress!" I demanded as Lexie stood up and showed off her tea length blue and black dress. With her hair down and loose, she resembled a Victorian Alice. Bran wore a version of the Mad Hatter's crazy suit, oversized tie and top hat. His face was pale, his red hair stuck out a bit from under the big hat. I had to give it to him, I'd never have expected him to loosen up enough to have gone all out with his costume. "You look good Bran," I said.

"So do you two." Bran nodded.

I suppose that was his way of being nice. *The pompous ass.* As I was the more mature and evolved individual, I smiled in reply and let his 'less than sincere' comment go without any verbal retaliation.

A woman walked towards our table wearing a white, off the shoulder style blouse. A crimson shawl was cinched around the waist of her snowy peasant style skirt, and a red and white striped scarf was tied around her thick braided hair. As she approached, I saw tattoos running from her wrists to her collarbones. "Marie!" I finally recognized her.

Duncan gave a wolf whistle as she approached. "Don't tell me... Marie Laveau the Voodoo Queen?"

Marie laughed, her golden hoop earrings brushed her shoulders. "Of course, *cher.*"

"Has anyone seen Gwen and Aunt Faye?" I asked. Lexie turned and pointed. I saw Gwen in a long red and black gown, with Great Aunt Faye— who was rocking a black and gold column style sequined gown. Her silver hair was twisted up and back in an elegant chignon.

Marie set her bag down at the table and glanced over at Aunt Faye. "You gotta hand it to her. The old girl's got style."

Great Aunt Faye walked up to the table with all of the attitude of a model working a catwalk. Duncan held out a chair for her, and she gracefully took her seat. Gwen followed behind, holding a sequined red mask on a ribbon trimmed stick.

"I'd like a gin and tonic," Aunt Faye announced. She looked pointedly at Duncan and me.

Which is how we found ourselves in a long line waiting at the bar, shortly thereafter. I felt a tap on my shoulder and turned to find Zack and Theo from Gwen's coven.

"Hello gorgeous!" Dressed in a white toga, Zach gave me an exuberant hug.

I hugged him in return. "Don't tell me, let me guess." I studied their costumes. Gilded laurel leaves were in a crown around Zach's blonde hair. A golden cloak hung at the back of his toga. Theo wore a toga as well, but a grapevine crown with tiny grapes rested in his dark hair. I smiled at his purple cloak. "Apollo and Dionysus?"

"Yes! And give us a turn, Morticia!" Zach said.

I did my best at attempting a runway turn and almost pulled it off. Almost. I grabbed at Duncan's jacket sleeve when I wobbled.

"Steady." Theo reached out to me as I righted myself.

"Thanks, Theo." I gave his supporting hand a squeeze. Note to self: *No more quick spins in the costume!*

Zach straightened the lapel of Duncan's smoking jacket, then stepped back. "There, that's better. You are rocking that costume, Gomez."

The music changed to Rob Zombie's "Living Dead Girl", and it took everything I had to stand still in line. I could see Eric and Ivy, Holly and Cypress, and a few other couples out on the dance floor.

Duncan gave me a gentle elbow nudge. "Go on. I know you want to dance."

"I *love* this song." I grinned at him.

Theo grabbed my hand. "Let's hit it, Morticia."

"God. Do you dare?" I asked.

"I'll live on the edge," Theo said.

I laughed in delight. Theo was normally quiet when I was around him. Happily, I let him lead me out of line and towards the dance floor. We worked our way over to Holly and Ivy, who let out a cheer when we'd joined them... and I didn't worry about being clumsy anymore. I just followed the music and danced.

Theo had some impressive moves, but it didn't intimidate me. Dancing always made me feel like I was someone else. A more coordinated and cool someone else. Apparently, the song had inspired other dancers as the floor went from less than a dozen dancers— to crowded with people— in a heart beat.

By the next song, Zach and Marie had joined us on the dance floor. Violet O'Connell, from the flower shop, shimmied up wearing a purple and black, sexy Witch costume. I danced a few more songs, and then made my way back to the table and to Duncan. He was having a conversation with Aunt Faye and Cora O'Connell, Violet's mom. Cora was dressed in a white flowing gown with white sprayed hair and gray face paint.

Cora stood up to give me a hug and an air kiss. "Enjoying the Masquerade, Morticia?"

I carefully hugged her back, staying clear of the makeup. "Ooh, Victorian ghost?" I asked.

"Ooooooooh," she let out a ghostly wail.

Duncan handed me my drink. I sipped at my wine,

noting how it all felt very surreal surrounded by the music, the party-goers and the real life Witches in various costumes.

"Did the floral centerpieces come from your shop?" I asked Cora as I ran my hand over the long trailing red flowers that reminded me of fuzzy caterpillars.

"They did," she said. "That trailing flower is called amaranth or 'love lies bleeding'."

My stomach lurched, and I pulled my hand away from the flower. Standing there in a crowded ballroom I got a precognitive flash; *Long stemmed, white roses arranged in a pentagram on a polished wooden surface.* Carefully I set my wine down. I smiled at Cora and did my best not to let my unease show on my face.

What is it? I heard Duncan's voice clearly in my mind. I glanced over at him and smiled, determined not to let anything spoil the night. A Marilyn Manson song began to play, and I grabbed Duncan's hand. "I'm going to steal him from you, Aunt Faye."

She waved us away. "Go on, have fun."

"I'm not much of a dancer," he said.

"Hello, have we met?" I called over my shoulder as we worked our way to the dance floor. "I'm lucky not to have *injured* anyone out there."

Duncan pulled up beside me. "You had some pretty good moves. I watched you while you danced."

I leaned close to his ear so he could hear me over the music. "I took some belly dance classes a couple years ago with my roommate in college."

Duncan stopped and raised his eyebrows at me. "Well, well. Aren't you a surprise."

I laughed at the look on his face and tugged him forward to an open spot on the dance floor. Over the music I said, "I took the classes to help improve my coordination. Learning some moves for the dance floor was a nice side effect."

Duncan threw back his head and laughed.

As if by magick, the next song was slower—Sinatra's "Witchcraft". Duncan took me in his arms, and we slow danced to the classic song. Many of the younger people left the floor, and the older crowd took over. I watched Bran and Lexie dancing, and it struck me as charming. I saw a flash of red and black sequins, and Gwen and a gentleman danced past us. They were doing the foxtrot, old school style. They were pretty good. The man she danced with wore a tux, a long cape, and a *Phantom of the Opera* style mask that hid his face. I wondered who he was, but Gwen was smiling, so I shrugged it off and turned my attention back to Duncan.

***

A few hours later, I had gone outside to the terrace to get some air. It was easing towards 1:00 in the morning. The little tables that had been set up on the terrace were full with couples who sat and sipped drinks or talked away from the throbbing music. I leaned against the iron balcony and took in some of the cool night air while Duncan went to get us drinks. I gazed over the town square and smiled as I thought about how I'd done "The Time Warp" with Duncan and my *entire* family. Gwen, Bran, the girls, and even Great Aunt Faye. She'd strutted out there and belted out the words to the song, dancing in time with everyone else. I didn't think I'd ever forget that, not as long as I lived.

People were still dancing away, and the music was a fun mixture of Halloween themed songs and, of course, anything that mentioned vampires, monsters, or Witches. I could hear the theme from *The Phantom of the Opera* being played, and it made me wonder at the identity of the man I'd seen dancing with Gwen. As if I'd conjured him up, the man dressed as the Phantom walked outside.

"Hi," I said as he joined me at the balcony. "I love your costume." I smiled up at him figuring he was an acquaintance of Gwen's.

"Thank you," he said.

My head whipped around at the familiar voice. The Phantom was none other than Thomas Drake.

CHAPTER FOURTEEN

A couple of things occurred to me now that I knew the elegant, masked *Phantom of the Opera* was actually Thomas Drake. One: I wasn't alone out on the terrace. I was protected by the crowd of people. And Two: Gwen had danced with him, seemingly enjoying herself. I wasn't sure what that meant quite yet, but as talented of a Witch as my aunt was— she'd had to have *known* who her partner was.

Thomas stood with all the ease and charm of a snake. "How goes the search for the grimoire?" he asked in a pleasant, conversational tone.

I was surprised at the change of his approach. Compared to how strong he'd come on magickally in the library back in September, he was acting very differently tonight. In a bizarre way, he seemed almost courtly. *What was he up to now?* "The search goes slowly," I said.

"Why is that?"

So he wanted to play innocent, did he? I blew out a

breath in annoyance. The various conversations by the other folks out on the terrace were allowing us a little privacy, but I still tried to keep my voice down. “There have been complications— *other* magicks to deal with. Some nasty poppets, girls getting injured... which really sounds like *your* style.”

“Poppets, you say?” He blew out a long breath, shaking his head slightly.

“Someone broke into our house recently.” I raised an eyebrow at him. “Too impatient to wait, were you?”

“Rest assured, *I* did not break into the manor. It would be impossible for me as there are magicks in place.” To my complete shock, he sounded almost offended that I would suggest such a thing.

“Well, *someone* did break in,” I said. “They ransacked the twins’ room, stole what cash they could find, and took some of Gwen’s jewelry.”

Thomas tipped his head to the side. “Has it ever occurred to you that the other magicks, and the break in, are merely distractions?” His voice sounded almost reasonable.

“No, but it had *occurred* to me that *you* are the most logical person behind all of our problems.”

Thomas stared down at the town square for a long moment. “What happened to Julian on the eve of the sabbat...” He stiffened and turned to look at the crowd on the terrace. I saw his eyes behind the mask shift and survey the area. “There is more going on than you know... We can’t speak here. We might be overheard.”

"I'm not going anywhere with you."

He sighed. "To the dance floor only." He stood waiting, leaving it up to me.

I was curious but didn't want to appear too eager, so I scowled at him. "Okay fine. After you." I gestured to the ballroom.

"Follow my lead," he said holding out his arm.

Maybe it was the Morticia costume that made me brave. Or, maybe it was the couple glasses of wine I'd had, but I placed my hand on his arm— the way you see people do in the old movies— and we walked coolly out to the dance floor. He held out his arms in a formal pose, and I stepped into a polite dance with Thomas Drake.

I was silently congratulating myself on my own chutzpah when I realized the song playing was Alanis Morissette's "Uninvited." It took everything I had not to shudder at the creepy and haunting song.

He pulled me a fraction closer as we danced. "There are competing forces at work. More than you know," he said close to my ear.

"Such as?"

"There are *other* parties that want the Blood Moon Grimoire."

"I don't believe you."

"I have never lied to you— not about your father, or the grimoire. I admit I handled things poorly at the library, but consider what you have learned since you moved here. Everything I've ever said to you was the truth."

My father. Bran... and all of the family secrets. I felt a wave of shame about my father and his past. It was a hell of a thing to recognize that Thomas was right. He'd never lied to me.

Thomas gave my hand a sympathetic squeeze. "You have nothing to be ashamed of."

I jolted, realizing that he'd either read my face *or* my thoughts. I started to reply, but, stepping on the hem of my dress, tripped. Without missing a step, Thomas righted me.

"Are you alright?" Thomas asked.

"Don't act all nice to me. It doesn't suit you." I frowned at him as much as I dared. I could *feel* eyes on us. We danced with a good ten inches of space between us. To anyone who watched, it probably seemed perfectly polite. The music swelled and offered me cover from eavesdroppers. "I'm dealing with my family. You should deal with your own," I said.

"Families are complicated affairs," he agreed. "Nevertheless, we are running out of time."

"We have until April before the next lunar eclipse, if you want me to find the rest of the book, back off and give me more time."

"The 'rest of the book'?" His voice was low as he zeroed in on that statement.

Damn it!

"You have a part of the grimoire?" he asked.

I said nothing; instead, I flashed a fake and brittle

smile. *Why had I thought I could handle myself with this man?*

"Listen to me," Thomas' voice was soft but urgent. "You are not safe with *any* part of that book in your possession. For your own sake— bring it to me."

"How very philanthropic of you." I met his eyes, and watched his pupils dilate behind the mask. Something was frightening him, and I wasn't foolish enough to think that it was me. I could *feel* the anxiety coming off him, and that fear was contagious. My own heart sped up in response to the emotions radiating off him.

"You're in danger, more than you can possibly realize." He gave my hand a squeeze. "Damn it," he muttered, catching me off guard by turning us into an elegant little spin.

I struggled not to trip at his surprising dance move. "No more turns, I'll fall on my face," I warned him.

"If I solve one of the magickal problems your family is currently dealing with, would that prove to you that I'm sincere?" he asked.

"And you'd do that because you're such a stand up guy?" I whispered back.

Alanis crooned through the speakers about wanting a moment to deliberate.

God, how freaking appropriate. I caught movement out of the corner of my eye and saw Duncan walking towards us. "Here comes Duncan. How do you want to play this?" I asked Thomas.

"If you return to the manor within the next hour, one

of the problems your family is facing will be solved," Thomas said. He stopped dancing and stared into my eyes. "My word on that."

I recalled my grandmother's warning at her last appearance. *Alliances to be drawn...dark magicks to neutralize, and enemies to defeat.* "Okay, one hour," I said to Thomas.

"I'm cutting in." Duncan reached out, taking my hand away from his Uncle's grasp.

Thomas stepped back without a word and gave a slight bow. Duncan pulled me close as the song finished. Safely in his arms, I shivered in reaction.

"Thanks," I smiled at Duncan. To my relief, the song the DJ played next was an old classic.

He frowned after the Phantom. "Who the hell was that?"

I hated lying, and I didn't want to start now. "I'll tell you later."

"This old song suits you," Duncan said.

I laid my head on his shoulder, and we swayed back and forth in time to the song. "You think I'm a spooky little girl?"

"Absolutely," Duncan pulled me closer.

***

I kept track of the time. As luck, or fate, would have it, most of the family had decided to call it a night within the hour. Ivy had gone off with Eric and his family to get breakfast. The O'Connells, Cypress, and Marie were heading home. Gwen was still speaking to a few folks from the chamber of commerce. Great Aunt Faye had announced she was going to stay a while longer. At the moment, a dashing older gentleman was sitting with her, and they were talking.

Duncan and I drove Holly back to the manor. I resisted the urge to rub my eyes, I was so ready to get my contacts out. We pulled in the driveway and Holly climbed out, tugging her witch hat off. Her hair was still pinned up in an elaborate up-do. I gave Duncan a kiss, held onto my little clutch purse, and scooted over on the bench seat. I attempted to slide easily out and managed to ease down to the driveway in my long dress.

"I'm ready to get this spray out of my hair," I said to Holly, scratching at my scalp.

"Talk to you in the morning." Duncan smiled at me.

"It *is* morning," I said, fishing in my little bag for the house keys.

"You're going to want to wash that hair spray out in the kitchen sink. I could help—" Holly stopped talking, and her head whipped up. I watched her eyes narrow. "Someone's here. The intruder's back." She tossed her costume hat to me, and took off at a dead run around the back of the house.

"Shit! Holly, wait!" I hissed.

"Holly!" Duncan turned off his truck and was next to me a second later. Together, we went after her. I moved as quickly as possible, but form fitting, long dresses were simply not designed to run in. My heart pounded. It felt a little déjà vu as we ran together in the dark. *Like the night we'd rescued Ivy.* That realization pushed me into moving faster— long dress or not.

We skidded to a halt on the back patio. To my shock, my sweet, empathic cousin had a small person pinned to the wall next to our back door. In a spilt second, I saw that the glass in the door was broken, and the intruder was holding a backpack. The person was dressed all in dark colors and wearing a ski mask.

Holly's forearm was up against the intruder's throat. She leaned in, applying pressure, looking ready to do some serious damage. While the other person choked, Holly reached up and pulled the black ski mask off the intruder's head, revealing a familiar brunette with short spiky hair.

"Leilah?" I sputtered, shocked to see the JV cheerleader. I glanced over at Duncan.

"Give me one good reason why I shouldn't kick your ass!" Holly growled.

The tone apparently spurred Duncan to action. He rushed to the girls. "Okay Holly, stand down." He reached up and tried to pry Holly's arm away from Leilah's throat.

I approached them while Leilah coughed and wheezed, even as she glared defiantly at us all. I reached out, placing a placating hand on Holly's arm. "Blondie, I think your Wicked Witch costume has gone to your head. Where'd you learn a choke hold?"

My attempt at humor did not go over well. Holly snarled at me. Literally snarled. She showed her teeth and everything. Startled, I took a step back from her. I'd never seen her act like that before.

Duncan wasn't fazed by the snarl. "Enough," he said pulling Holly back. When he did, it caused Leilah to drop her backpack. When the bag hit the patio, something fell out. Time seemed to slow down as a poppet rolled and came to a halt face side up.

"What's that?" Duncan asked.

Using my cousin's costume hat, I reached down and picked up the poppet. The poppet obviously represented Holly. The red-gold curly hair was a dead giveaway. Wrapped in twine, this doll had the same type of cheerleading outfit as the other poppets had. However, this one's face was melted off. I gulped as my stomach rolled. *Well, mystery solved as to the creator of the poppets.*

Leilah laughed when she saw my reaction to the poppet. Duncan and I exchanged glances. Which was a mistake, as we'd taken our eyes off of Holly.

"You bitch," Holly said to Leilah. There was no inflection in her voice, and I felt the hair rise on the back of my neck.

Leilah sneered at Holly, "You deserved it! I would've made the varsity squad if not for you! The *perfect* Holly Bishop, captain of the varsity team—thinking you're so much better than everyone else!"

"You hurt my friends to try and get on the varsity squad?" Holly asked very quietly.

"Yeah? What are you going to do about it?" Leilah practically spit at my cousin. "A perfect little princess like you?"

Holly surged forward, but Duncan stepped between the girls. "Cool off, Holly." Duncan warned.

"I'll call the police," I said. I reached in my purse for my phone while Duncan pushed a swearing, spitting and shouting Leilah against the side of the house. He held the girl firmly in place with a hand on her arm.

Leilah continued to shout insults even as Holly walked away and over to the edge of the patio. Holly turned her back to all of us, hugging her arms over her middle.

"That's right," Leilah yelled at Holly's back. "Walk away, you prissy little bitch! You don't have the guts to come at me with magick."

"Shut up, Leilah!" I snapped. I started to dial 9-1-1, but I'd only managed the number nine when a violent wind ripped through the side yard. The wind was unnaturally strong. Duncan, Leilah and I all struggled to stay on our feet. "Are you doing that?" I asked Duncan.

"No," he said over the roar of wind, his eyes wide. "I think it's your cousin."

I swung my head to check on Holly. She had turned and was now standing in the darkness with her feet planted apart, facing Leilah. The look on my cousin's face had my stomach dropping. "Uh oh," I said dropping my phone back in my purse. "Shit just got real."

The howling wind tore Holly's carefully styled hair apart. It snapped in long coils behind her. "You wanna see magick?" Holly growled at Leilah, and then she tossed her hands down and out to her sides. I heard a low rumble of thunder as Holly slowly raised up one hand and bunched her fingers closed into a fist.

Instantly, Leilah fell to her knees, her hands tearing at her own throat. Her eyes bulged as her color changed dramatically.

"Holly, stop!" Duncan shouted, spinning to help Leilah.

Stunned at the transformation, I watched my cousin. Tipping her head slightly to one side, she maintained eye contact with Leilah. A vindictive little smile crossed Holly's face as she squeezed her fingers into a tighter fist. Horrified, I realized that my cousin was actually *enjoying* this. With a terrible gagging sound, Leilah dropped farther down to all fours. I turned to the girl, amazed that I could see her belly heaving.

"Help—" Leilah made an awful gurgling sound and began to violently cough up water— seemingly out of her lungs.

"Shit!" I said. I jumped back away from where Leilah expelled the water, dropping my purse, the hat, and the poppet.

"Leilah!" Duncan grabbed for her.

My mind raced as I tried to make sense of what I

was seeing. *Holly must be tapping into the element of water.* But she was using her elemental affinity to fill up someone's lungs with water—someone who was standing on dry land. "Holly, stop!" I shouted.

As the wind tore around us, Holly didn't react to me in any way. She was lost in her own spell— too angry and wrapped up in revenge to stop. The winds shrieked, and rain started to pelt down from the sky. Holly continued to focus, unblinkingly, on Leilah, who collapsed to her belly making a horrible rattling sound.

"What can we do?" I yelled to Duncan.

Duncan turned Leilah onto her back and pressed his ear to her chest. "Break Holly's concentration!" Duncan shouted over the roar of the wind while starting CPR on Leilah.

"Damn it!" I snarled. *How to break her concentration?* I'd never seen anything like what Holly was doing. But I couldn't stand by and watch my cousin *kill* someone with magick. I did the only thing I could think of: I hiked up my dress, kicked off my flats and ran full out, and straight at Holly. I hit her hard— a full body tackle— and we went down together with a hard bounce on the lawn.

Several things seemed to happen at once: The wind stopped as if it had never been, and the rain disappeared. Leilah started to gag, cough, and finally breathe on her own. I kept Holly pinned but raised my head, glancing over at Duncan.

"Is Leilah okay?" I asked him.

"I think so," Duncan said. He rolled Leilah on her side in case she coughed up more water.

"Holly?" I checked my cousin. Her red-gold hair was tangled around her face, and I felt like I was looking at a stranger. Holly's aqua eyes focused on me. "Hey," I gave her a little shake. "Are you back?"

Holly sat up and seemed to come back to herself with a shudder. "Leilah," she said in a grim tone of voice. But she scrambled up, going to the girl.

Duncan started to block her. "Holly?"

"I'm okay, now. I promise," Holly told him. She reached past him and laid her hand on Leilah's chest. Leilah began to breathe more easily. Leilah took several more ragged breaths, then opened her eyes.

Duncan stood over them ready, I think, to forcibly separate them if necessary. With a ragged shudder, Leilah was able to sit up with help from Holly.

Pale and shaken, Leilah sat on the patio. When she realized Holly was sending her healing energy, she recoiled and grabbed ahold of Duncan. "Keep her away from me!" Leilah's voice was raspy.

"What the hell happened here?" Aunt Gwen ran across the lawn, still in her ball gown. "I could feel that elemental magick before I pulled in the driveway. Which one of you did that?" Gwen was furious, but she hadn't returned to the manor alone. To my amazement, Thomas Drake was with her.

Duncan tried to peel Leilah off him. "What are *you* doing here?" He glared at his uncle.

Holly stood and faced her mother. "I caught Leilah breaking into our house."

"What?" Gwen's eyes swung from her daughter to Leilah.

I bent down scooping up my purse, the fallen hat and poppet. "She was carrying this." I held out the poppet.

"So, you're the one." Gwen took the poppet frowning at the girl.

Leilah coughed but managed to stand to her feet. "Yeah, so what? That's nothing compared to what Holly did to me. She almost killed me with magick!" Leilah glared and wobbled. Duncan put a hand out to steady her.

"Holly!" Gwen sounded shocked. "What did you do?"

"What did she do?" Leilah's voice was hoarse. "She filled up my lungs with water!" she managed and started to cough again.

"Impressive," Thomas Drake said.

I raised my eyebrows at Duncan. *What the hell is your uncle doing with my aunt?* I thought at him.

I have no idea. He sent his thoughts back.

Gwen grabbed Holly's arm. "Why would you do such a thing?"

"I lost control." Holly folded her hands and stared at the ground. "I admit it."

"Lost control?" Leilah rasped. "This isn't over— not by a long shot."

"Leilah, that's enough!" Thomas Drake snapped. He

stared her down, and Leilah's chin dropped to her chest.

What the hell? How could Thomas Drake get that kind of instant obedience from the girl? I heard the bell tower from the nearby church start to chime the hour—once, then twice. *Well, son of a bitch! He'd said to return to the manor within an hour and one of the magickal problems would be resolved.*

"I assume..." Gwen said to Thomas, "that you would prefer to keep the police out of this?"

"Yes, I would," he said.

"Alright." Gwen nodded in agreement.

"As her father, I will pay for any of the property damages she has caused, both tonight, and previously."

"Wait, Leilah Martin is your *daughter*?" I sputtered. Gwen didn't seem surprised, but both Holly and Duncan did. Holly narrowed her eyes as she considered the news.

Duncan frowned over at the girl— his cousin technically. "Are you serious?" he asked his uncle.

"She *is* my daughter," Thomas said defending his place as her father.

"I hate you," Leilah said to him... Or maybe to everyone.

Thomas took the poppet from Gwen's hand and studied it. "As to the poppets, and the attacks on the girls at the school... that stops. Tonight," he said. He held out the poppet, and the bindings seemed to fall away on their own. The twine turned to ash before it hit the ground.

Leilah crossed her arms defensively over her chest and glared at Thomas— her father. “Fine. Whatever. You’ve never given a damn about me anyway.”

“I’ve been watching you for some time,” Thomas said to Leilah. He handed back the poppet to Gwen and dipped his hands in his pants pockets as he studied the girl. “And I’m not happy with what I’ve seen. *You* caused the accident at the parade, didn’t you, Leilah?” While his expression was bland, his tone of voice was threatening.

Leilah cowered away from Thomas. As I watched the drama unfold, it dawned on me that I *had* seen him in the crowd right before the accident. My stomach turned over.

Holly glared at the girl in reaction to the news. “Megan broke her arm that day. A lot of people could have gotten hurt because of you!” Another strong wind came whistling around the back of the manor, and my cousin started towards Leilah who had started to gag again.

“Hey!” I stepped between the girls and gave Holly a hard shove away from Leilah. “Knock it off!”

“Holly Irene Bishop!” Gwen’s voice lashed out like a whip, and the wind died instantly. “If you can not control yourself, go inside the house right this minute!”

“Fine!” Holly gave one last glare at a shaking, but breathing, Leilah, and she went straight indoors. She slammed the door behind her. What was left of the glass fell on the patio.

"What do we do now?" I said to Gwen as Leilah started to cry.

Gwen glanced at Thomas, who gave a small nod to her. Apparently, he was content in letting her handle this. Gwen reached out and took Leilah by the chin. "As for you," she said, raising the girl's face up to hers. "If I even so much as *think* you might be up to your old tricks... your father will be the *least* of your worries."

Silent tears slid down Leilah's face. "Yes Ma'am," she whispered. Whatever she saw in Gwen's eyes must have made an impression.

"I'll take her home to her mother." Thomas held out his arm, and Leilah walked to his side. "Let me know what the damages are to the manor, and I'll have a check cut immediately to you."

"Thank you, Thomas." Gwen inclined her head in a regal nod.

Duncan shot me a look. I shrugged my shoulders. I was just as surprised as he was by the turn of events.

"Good night," Thomas said. He and his daughter walked away through the back yard and past a startled Mad Hatter Bran who had returned home. While Bran gaped at them, Thomas and Leilah disappeared around the side of the manor.

I heard car doors close and an engine start in the still night. In another moment, I heard their car drive off. Gwen dropped down in an Adirondack chair on the patio. "By the Goddess." She leaned her head back to stare up at the heavens.

"What in the hell is going on?" Bran demanded as he rushed to Gwen's side.

Gwen patted his arm. "It's alright, don't worry."

"Sparky, you just missed the big magickal showdown," I said.

"Why was Thomas Drake and that girl here?" Bran asked.

"That girl," Duncan said, "is apparently his daughter, my cousin, and the one who broke into your house."

Gwen held up the poppet. "She's also the one who's been hexing the girls on the squad."

"Well, for fuck's sake!" Bran tossed up his hands. "Has everyone gone mad?"

I snorted out a laugh as the irony of his statement sank in. Gwen started to laugh too, and Duncan joined in.

Bran seemed confused by our helpless laughter, then he remembered, and his eyes rolled up towards his oversized Mad Hatter top hat. "Ha. That's hilarious." He yanked the hat off his head and glared.

I caught movement out of the corner of my eye. The rose garden was visible from where I stood, and I saw the ghost of my grandmother sitting on the concrete bench. She seemed lit up from within, not unlike David Quinn's ghost had the night he'd helped Duncan and I locate Ivy.

Ro flashed me a smile, gave me a thumbs up, and her image faded away.

CHAPTER FIFTEEN

Duncan and Bran swept up the broken glass and covered up the smashed window with a piece of plastic tarp and duct tape. The rest of the family trickled back home shortly thereafter. Once the clean up was done, I headed inside to swap out my contacts for my glasses. Then I grabbed the shampoo, conditioner and old towels to wash out the colored hairspray.

I stood in a black camisole and my long, plaid pajama pants. My head was bent over the kitchen sink as I rinsed out the last of the conditioner. Duncan handed me a towel, and I wrapped my hair up in the towel— turban style.

I patted for my glasses on the counter and, finding them, I slipped them on. Great Aunt Faye, Bran and Ivy all came into focus. They sat, sipping coffee or tea around the breakfast bar, either in robes or their costumes. Gwen walked into the kitchen and handed me some cold cream and a washcloth. I ducked into the powder room, happily removing the makeup. I felt like

I'd lost a good pound off my face after I'd taken off the elaborate cosmetics. With a sigh, I rubbed the towel over my hair and began to work the tangles out with a brush. When I walked back in the kitchen, Great Aunt Faye was scrubbing the painted mustache off Duncan's face. Holly was still nowhere to be seen.

Ivy sat at the breakfast bar. "So to be clear, Leilah Martin, the JV cheerleader, is the one who made the poppets, cast the hexes *and* broke into the manor?" She swung her bare feet, still in her Glinda regalia.

"Correct," Gwen said.

"How was she able to get inside anyway?" I said. "I mean the house is *warded.* Even when Viviane's backpack had the poppet in it, she wasn't able to carry it in the house."

"During the preparations for Homecoming, Holly obviously invited Leilah inside the manor." Gwen explained.

"Wait, are we talking like movie vampire stuff?" I asked. "As in, once a vampire is *invited* in you can't keep them out?"

Gwen shook her head. "No. but I see how you'd come to that conclusion. When Holly invited her in, it basically rendered the wards ineffective to Leilah."

"How's that?" I asked.

"Mom, if you'd allow me?" Bran said taking over. "The wards are not like a force field. Instead they help to *turn away* and to repel negativity and evil intention making it harder for someone or something to get inside and do damage. However, if someone with negative intentions was formally invited inside the wards— it would make them uncomfortable, but not physically bar them. Classically, wards are designed to give the inhabitants of the house a warning that something is wrong."

"Like a magickal heads up?" I asked.

"Exactly." Bran nodded.

Ivy was practically bouncing in her seat. "So you guys came home and found Leilah, then Holly lost her temper, invoked the element of water and tried to *drown* Leilah while she stood on the back patio?"

"Yeah," I said sighing.

Apparently getting into the retelling of the tale, Ivy pointed at her mother. "Then you and Old Man Drake showed up after Autumn tackled Holly to get her to stop her magick against Leilah. And *he* is going to take care of the damages— and make sure the poppet problems stop because Leilah Martin is his *daughter*?

Duncan sat on a stool beside her. "That pretty much covers it," he said.

"And I *missed* it. Damn!" Ivy propped her elbow on the counter and dropped her chin in her hand.

Aunt Faye picked up her tea, shaking her head at Ivy. "This is a serious matter, young lady."

Ivy's head popped back up. "But I didn't even know Holly could lose her temper, let alone do something that awesomely advanced."

I grabbed a bottle of water out of the fridge and took

the remaining barstool next to Duncan. "It was *scary*," I said to Ivy. "There was nothing awesome about it."

"Where's Holly now?" Bran asked.

"She's in my room, resting," Gwen said.

"I wonder..." Ivy drummed her fingers on the countertop. "Do you figure she did that spell on the fly, or do you think she studied and had the elemental magick prepared?"

I felt a chill run down my back, and it was not from having damp hair. I didn't even want to contemplate whether or not Holly may have planned and/or practiced those types of magicks in advance. I tried to consider what Ivy said but was distracted by all the peach tulle. "Do me a favor and go change. I can't take you seriously while you are in that costume."

"Yeah, it's starting to bug me a little." Ivy scratched at the glitter on her face and hopped off the barstool. "Don't talk about anything good until I get back!" she said and raced up the stairs.

Bran drummed his fingers on the counter glaring at Gwen. "So the man dressed as *The Phantom of the Opera* at the Halloween Masquerade Ball was Thomas Drake?" Bran sounded scandalized. "Mom, you danced with him!"

I found Bran's tone a little offensive. "Hey, so did I," I pointed out.

"That was incredibly foolish," Bran snapped at me.

"Up yours," I shot back.

"Children..." Aunt Faye sighed at us both.

"Listen while Ivy's out of the room, there's something you all need to know..." I said. I psyched myself up and quickly told them everything. From my conversation with Drake on the terrace, to our talk during the dance, *and* how I'd screwed up.

Aunt Faye folded her hands on counter. "He knows about the pages, then."

Duncan rubbed my back in sympathy. "He's a manipulative old bastard. Don't beat yourself up."

"Yeah, but still. He told me if we returned to the manor within the hour that one of the problems we'd been dealing with would be taken care of," I said. "And he was right."

Gwen set her mug of tea down. "He came to me after you all had left and told me close to the same thing."

"So you came home to check," Bran said.

"Yes," Gwen said. "And he followed me back here to prove his words."

Duncan shook his head. "Do you think he set Leilah up?"

"You know... I have a hunch," I said to the family. "He reacted when I mentioned the attack on the girls and the poppets. I bet that's what made him realize it was Leilah."

Bran dropped a fist on the counter. "Now that he knows we have a part of the grimoire... I think he might be playing us, by trying to act altruistic."

Bran was right, Thomas Drake very well could be

playing us. The five of us sat around the breakfast bar. Everyone seemed lost in their own thoughts. It had been a wild night, and there was a lot to take in.

Gwen broke the silence. “I suppose we should discuss, as a family, what happened with Holly.”

“I am *so* not up for the magickal re-hash,” I said and yawned.

Aunt Faye frowned at me. “Autumn!”

I peered up at the clock in the kitchen. “Guys, it’s almost three o’clock. We’ve had the post-masquerade and Old Man Drake analysis. Can’t we save the Holly-almost-brought-about-the-apocalypse chat until *after* we all get a couple hours of sleep?”

“My dear,” Aunt Faye shook her head at me. “We really must work on that sarcasm of yours.”

“It’s her superpower.” Bran announced and yawned loudly. “But she’s right, let’s all regroup in the morning.”

To my surprise, the family agreed. So we called it a night. After kissing me goodnight, Duncan headed back to his place. Aunt Faye strolled off to her room saying she wanted to meditate on the turn of events with her crystal ball, while Gwen started turning off the lights. I dragged my tired ass up the stairs and shuffled towards my room. I wanted nothing more than my bed. I opened my door and frowned.

“Hi roomie!” Ivy was practically bouncing in excitement as she sat on my bed in her Harley Quinn character t-shirt and black flannel pajama bottoms.

I had forgotten about my temporary roommate. *Give me strength.* "I'm tired. Really want to go to sleep," I said and slapped off the overhead lights.

"Aw, really?" Ivy pouted. "I wanted to talk."

For a split second, I gave serious consideration to smothering her with the pillows, but, instead, I shooed Ivy off the full size bed, pulled back the comforter and climbed in. Nimble as a monkey, she climbed over me and got under the covers. I put my glasses in their case, plugged my phone in to recharge, clicked off the nightstand light, and blissfully closed my eyes.

Merlin popped open the bedroom door a moment later and joined Ivy and me. He walked up to the center of the bed, chose the tiny sliver of mattress between us, snuggled in happily and began to purr.

I ran my hand over Merlin's ears. "We can talk in the morning, Ivy. Let's try and get a few hours of sleep," I suggested. Exhausted, I started to feel myself drift off.

"Autumn," Ivy said.

I jolted awake. "What?"

"Do you think Holly will be okay after all of this? Will she be the same?"

I sighed. "You know more about magick than I do. So, you tell me." I rolled over onto my back and stared up at the ceiling.

Ivy, never one to respect personal space, tucked herself right up against me. She lay her head against my shoulder. "I don't know. She crossed the line and used her magick to harm another on purpose."

Merlin let out a soft meow, as if in agreement.

I automatically patted the cat's head. "Yeah, she did," I said. "But once she came back to herself, she also tried to repair the harm she caused." *God I was tired.* I covered my mouth to hide a yawn.

I heard a scraping sound behind me, and I glanced up. Even though my vision was out of focus, I could see the trio of botanical prints that I'd hung above my bed — had tilted. "Are those hanging crooked again?" I asked Ivy.

"Yeah," Ivy said yawning herself. "The two on the outside, the yarrow and lavender ones are crooked."

"I'll fix 'em in the morning," I said. "Go to sleep, Shorty."

Ivy patted my hip. "I'm so glad you're here."

"Me too," I said, and gave her hand a squeeze.

Merlin continued to purr and stretched a paw out over our joined hands. I smiled a little feeling that soft kitty paw and closed my eyes.

***

It was the smell of the roses that woke me. Strong and sweet, the scent enveloped me. I opened my eyes and looked blearily around my room. I reached for my glasses and put them on. Now that I could see clearly, I discovered November sunlight streaming through my window. A dozen little rainbows shimmered across the walls from the prisms that hung in my window. But nothing else seemed out of place. I checked the time, it wasn't quite 10:00 am.

Beside me, Ivy stirred. "Waz that smell?" she mumbled.

The scent of roses intensified. *Ro,* I realized. *Ro was trying to get my attention.* I cleared my throat, "Have I ever mentioned to you that our grandmother's ghost likes to visit me?"

Ivy sat straight up, her hair was wild and her eyes were huge. "Grandma Rose?"

"I've never seen her in the house though, only outside in the rose gardens." I leaned back against the pillows.

"So what's with the perfume smell?" Ivy asked.

"She usually does that to get my attention."

"Wait, what did you say?" Ivy cocked her head and looked at me.

"I *said*, she usually does that to get my atten—"

Ivy held up her hand. "Shut up!"

Surprised at the sharp tone, I did. Merlin's head popped up from the nest of blankets as Ivy closed her eyes, seemingly listening to something. I sat up and gave her a few moments, then reached out and patted her leg to get her attention. "Hey," I said.

"I can almost hear a woman's voice..." Ivy frowned.

I thought back to the night that the ghost of David Quinn had wanted my help so he could communicate with Duncan. "Give me your hand," I said to Ivy.

She held out her hand to me and as soon as we

grasped hands, the voice Ivy could 'almost' hear, was now crystal clear— as was the owner of the voice who had materialized in that beam of sunlight.

"There you are, my beautiful girls." Ro clapped her hands in delight and appeared very corporeal wearing her denim overalls, pink sweater and goofy gardening hat.

Ivy flinched and gasped. "Are you..." her voice trembled, but she recovered quickly. "You're my Grandma Rose."

Ro nodded her head. "I am so proud of you both."

"You've never appeared inside the house before," I managed.

"First time for everything," Ro said. "I don't have much time girls, so listen."

"Go ahead," I gestured to her with my free hand.

Ro took off the garden hat and held it in her hands. "This quest must be finished with three; as it was started with three. You must look in order to see."

"What does that mean?" Ivy asked.

"She rhymes. It's kind of a thing," I said to Ivy out of the corner of my mouth. To my grandmother's ghost I said, "begun with three, so the quest has to end with three. Got it."

"Three what?" Ivy asked.

"*Sub Rosa*," Ro said, fading.

"Hey, wait, don't go!" Ivy wailed.

Our grandmother's apparition held for a few more seconds. She blew us a kiss and disappeared.

I dropped Ivy's hand, snatched up my phone, and hit the notes app, I added this new information down before I could forget anything Ro had told us.

Ivy flopped back against the pillows and rubbed her hands over her face. "I did not imagine that!" she said.

"Nope, you did not." I set the phone down and patted Ivy's arm. "Welcome to *my* world."

"*Sub Rosa,* what's that mean, anyway?" Ivy bounced up, climbed off the bed— over a very annoyed Merlin — and started to look around my room.

"It's Latin. It means, *under the rose*, or a secret." I watched as Ivy sniffed around the room.

"The scent's fading." Ivy stalked towards my closet and, with a flourish, yanked open the doors. "Ah-ha!" She cried, seemingly surprised to see only clothes and shoes inside.

"Ivy," I tried hard not to laugh at her. "She's not in there, hiding."

"Well excuse the hell outta me!" Ivy flung her hands out dramatically. "I saw and communicated with a ghost thanks to you. I wanna check out the room. Maybe she left something behind."

I got out of bed, "I'm gonna go brush my teeth. If you find any ectoplasmic residue, be sure to let me know," I said straight faced.

Ivy froze. "Oh my god. Does that usually happen after a sighting?"

"No, I was teasing you," I said.

When I came back to the room, Ivy scampered

across the hall and came back in record time. She seemed disappointed that nothing other-worldly had occurred. "Nothing else happened while I was gone?"

"Nope. So far, so good—" I was cut off by a loud crash that came from right behind me. Merlin let out a screech and high tailed it out of my room.

"One of those old prints you had above the bed fell down," Ivy whispered. "And it *jumped* right off the wall."

Sure enough, the center picture was down. I rushed to see where the framed print had fallen. It was leaning against the wall behind my headboard. I hitched up my flannel pajama bottoms, climbed on the bed, and fished it out. The large, deep frame was broken, and the glass was cracked down the middle.

I carried the framed botanical drawing of a wild rose across the room. I knelt down on the rug and flipped the framed picture face down. "I hope the illustration didn't get damaged."

Ivy knelt down next to me. "Let me help." When Ivy touched the frame, the bedroom door slammed shut. All by itself.

I shifted my eyes to Ivy's. "Did you do that?" I asked her.

Ivy shook her head, no. "This ever happen to you before?" she whispered.

Suddenly, I got it. *Oh god, was it that simple?* "This is the rose illustration," I said. "Sub Rosa," I explained to Ivy. "Under the rose."

Ivy sniffed the air. "Hey, the smell of roses is back."

"Think our grandmother is trying to tell us something?" As soon as the words left my mouth, the overhead lights went on and off.

Ivy's eyes were wide. "I'm pretty sure that's a *yes*."

"Let's see," I said, grabbing a hold of the corners of the broken frame. I pulled with all my strength, but the frame only opened up a little farther. The two large pieces of glass slid free and landed on my lap.

"Don't move," Ivy said, before I could ask for help. "Did you get cut?"

"No," I said.

Ivy gently picked up the glass, setting the pieces aside. Ivy scooted closer. "Let me help you open up the frame."

"Okay, good." I nodded. "On three?"

"One." Ivy took ahold of the opposite side of the frame.

"Two." I took a deep breath.

"Three!" we said together and pulled as hard as we could. The thick wooden frame drew apart with a screech, and the matted print, backer board and something else, soft and rectangular, plopped onto the floor. I set my half of the frame down, and carefully picked up a thin, magazine-size bundle. It was wrapped in brown paper and tied with red string. As I turned it over, I saw that the package had been fastened with a decorative red wax seal.

"There's a rose embossed in the seal." I showed it to

Ivy, my eyes swelling with tears.

"Oh my Goddess," Ivy breathed. "Is that what I think it is?"

I tugged the string aside and broke the wax seal. When I did, a little blast of energy fluttered the hair back from my face. I stopped and looked at Ivy. Silently, she nodded at me to open it up the rest of the way. I gently tugged a corner off the bundle and saw parchment pages covered in beautiful writing and illustrations. "This *is* another section of the Blood Moon Grimoire," I said.

Ivy bit her lip. "It's not very big... maybe not even a half inch thick," Ivy ran her fingers over the part of the pages we'd discovered.

"The first part of the Blood Moon Grimoire wasn't that big either. But these pages do look to be in better condition than the first set." I said.

"They're beautiful," Ivy said with wonder.

"You know... those first pages were also tied up in red yarn." I turned the package over in my hands.

"I bet they were... since red string binds evil," Ivy said, still stroking the pages.

"Ah, okay. Maybe we *shouldn't* be touching this," I said recalling what Thomas Drake had told me about the pages being dangerous. I didn't want to take any chances with my cousin, so I pulled it out of her reach. As soon as I did, Ivy shuddered.

"Whoa. I feel a little dizzy," Ivy said brushing at her hair. "Does it bother you to touch the pages?"

"No, actually, I don't feel a thing. No visions this time either." To be safe, I tugged the brown paper wrapping back into place and gently set the pages aside on the area rug.

Ivy picked up the botanical drawing our great-grandmother had done. "So part of the grimoire was hidden behind that rose illustration all this time?" She flipped over the large print, and I saw, for the first time, all of the magickal information that had been concealed behind the matting.

"Which means that my father *did* take a part of the grimoire with him when he left William's Ford," I realized. *Maybe he wasn't such a coward after all...*

Ivy rubbed her hand down my arm. "It was ingenious, really. He found a way to hide the pages in plain sight."

"Dad had those hanging in his office at home for as long as I can remember." I blew out a breath, and my bangs fluttered. "After he died, I inherited the botanical illustrations, so I brought them with me."

Ivy grinned. "So part of the grimoire has literally been *under the rose* for over twenty years! Until you and I found them!"

I had to laugh. "You know, I do feel a little Nancy Drew right now..."

Ivy pumped a fist in the air. "Go us!" She hopped to her feet and tried the door. It opened easily. "*Mom!*" she shouted at the top of her lungs. "Come see what we found!"

CHAPTER SIXTEEN

I had to admit, it did feel a little anti-climatic finding the second set of grimoire pages like that. As we gathered around the dining room table that afternoon, Ivy regaled Duncan and the family with the details of communicating with our grandmother's ghost and finding the pages. I sat back and let her tell the tale—Ivy was the center of attention for the moment, and she was loving it. Holly sat off in the corner of the room, sulking.

The two remaining prints had been checked, but they held nothing other than the glass, the illustrations, and the matting. Aunt Faye and Gwen had laid a large piece of white silk down on the table and placed the newest set of grimoire pages and the paper they'd been wrapped in on top of those. Silk, Aunt Faye explained to me, muffled psychic vibrations. Bran had the antique pages spread out on the dining room table, and Duncan was carefully photographing them with Ivy's digital camera.

I thought about the red wax seal. "Gwen do you think that your mother was the one to seal up the pages? There is a rose stamped in the wax."

"I would imagine so. She used to have a rose stamp and sealing wax," Gwen said.

"Rose always loved the flower she was named after," Aunt Faye said.

"Yeah, I noticed that," Ivy grinned at her mother and Aunt Faye. "I'm never gonna react to the smell of roses the same way again."

"I've experienced that when I was with Autumn. But I wish I could have seen or spoken to her again." Gwen said tucking her arm around Ivy's shoulders.

"She was in the rose garden last night," I said, watching the family all whip their heads to stare at me. "I forgot to tell everyone." I shrugged. "Things have been a little chaotic."

"Go on," Gwen said.

"Anyway," I continued. "I didn't notice her until everything was over— that's when I saw her. It was right after Bran showed up and fussed at us all."

"I do *not* fuss," Bran said.

"Yes you do," Ivy and I said in unison.

Gwen tried to maintain a serious expression. "What was she doing? I'm fascinated by her presence last night and now this morning. Especially considering what happened."

"She was sitting on the little concrete bench in the rose garden," I told Gwen. "She appeared more ghostly than I'd ever seen her before."

"Meaning?" Aunt Faye took her gaze off the pages she'd been studying and raised her eyebrows at me.

"Meaning, she seemed like she was all lit up—almost transparent," I explained. "She smiled at me, and then gave me the thumbs up."

Gwen threw back her head and laughed. "That sounds like my mother."

Aunt Faye knocked on the table to get our attention. "Has your grandmother's ghost ever given you information about the grimoire before today?"

"She has," I said. "But I've had a hard time figuring out what Ro was telling me. I've kept notes about it in a journal and mostly in an app on my phone."

Bran stopped rearranging the pages. "That's clever."

"Why do you refer to your grandmother as *Ro*?" Aunt Faye asked.

"Because the first time I saw her, I thought she was a real person, and she introduced herself to me as Ro."

Gwen picked up the old brown packing paper. "I am still trying to wrap my mind around the idea of Arthur hiding the pages under the botanical drawing."

"Rose helped him conceal the pages before she died," Aunt Faye announced.

"Really, do you think so?" I asked her. For once, I hoped someone would tell me that my father had done *something* noble.

"I don't think. I *know.*" Aunt Faye said. "When I first touched the wrappings, I had a vision of the past. Rose meant to keep the pages in the manor, but when she died, Arthur took them with him."

"Seems like he took a lot of things," Ivy said, then cringed. "I'm sorry," she said to me.

"It's okay." I waved away any apologies. "We know he did, that's how I ended up with the scrying mirror that belonged to our grandmother." I stared at those pages, and said what I was thinking. "Those grimoire pages were hidden in plain sight under one of a trio of prints in our house in New Hampshire for over twenty years. My mother would have sold off these antique botanical prints if not for my father leaving them to me in his will. When I brought them along with me, I'd thought they were simply a cool old set of botanical drawings. I never knew my great-grandmother was the artist— until Gwen told me this fall."

Duncan set the camera aside and put an arm around my shoulders. "Have you considered that maybe your father intuitively *knew* what tools you would need in the future? You're a Seer— and he made sure you had the scrying mirror. He entrusted the pages to you for safe keeping."

"I admit that I'd hoped that we'd find a letter from him behind the other prints..." I leaned into Duncan. "I don't know, it's probably dumb. But I hoped there would be something to explain what happened."

"It's not dumb," Duncan said.

"I want to see if these pages react to your touch the way the first set does." Bran pulled off the cotton gloves he'd been using.

"What, right now?" I asked.

"Yes," Bran said, pulling me over to stand next to him.

"Don't yank me around," I glared at Bran.

"Then don't act like a child," Bran said pleasantly.

I tugged my arm away from him. "You want another punch in the nose, *bro*?"

"Children," Gwen warned us.

"The pages didn't change when Ivy and I were upstairs." I stalled. The whole family was staring at me, and I felt really uncomfortable.

"How would you know?" Ivy said. "They were mostly wrapped up. We wouldn't have been able to see any changes."

"Well, if I do this... no making-the-pages-come-to-life shaming!" I scowled at Bran.

Bran rolled his eyes at me and set his phone to record a video. "Stop stalling."

"Ooh good idea!" Ivy said and got her phone out to record also.

Duncan nudged me closer to the table. "Go ahead, I want to see what happens."

I shot a glance at Gwen and Great Aunt Faye. One was curious and hopeful, while the other kept their expression regal and bland. Two guesses as to which Witch was which. Holly walked closer to the table, her arms folded over her chest, but she remained silent.

"Okay, here it goes," I said, laying my hands on the

outside edges of the two closest pages that featured illustrations. With no wrapping paper to get in the way this time, I felt as before when I'd had direct contact with the first section of pages— a warmth that started in my hands. Energy traveled up my arms in a little rush, and the pages started to look brighter. Slowly, the illustrations began to shift and change. While the family gasped watching the transformation of the illustrations on the parchment pages, I felt my arms start to tremble.

"You okay?" Duncan asked, laying his hand on my shoulder.

Everything changed. The pages lit up with a bright golden light. One by one, I could see the edges of the pages on the table start to flutter.

"Duncan," Gwen said, "put your hands on top of hers and touch the pages too."

Duncan reached around me with his chest up against my back. He laid his hands over mine, and his fingertips touched the pages. I felt him jump in surprise.

"Are you alright?" Gwen asked with a frown.

"Yeah," Duncan said slowly. "It's like a magnetic type of energy. There is a pull and a rush of warmth. I wonder—"

Before he could finish his sentence, the pages began to flow together, one on top of the other they shuffled like a big deck of cards. They slithered around and stacked themselves neatly. The pages pushed against the two that Duncan and I had our hands on. Without a word, we lifted our hands as one, and the pages slid and arranged themselves into one neat stack.

"Holy shit," I managed.

Duncan stepped back from me, reached over and pulled on the cotton gloves Bran had discarded. "I want to see something." He carefully ruffled through the pages. "It's almost as if they put themselves back in an order they preferred." Gently, he set the stack of grimoire pages back on the silk.

"Can I try and touch the pages?" Ivy asked.

"By the edges only," Bran and I said together.

Ivy made a face at us. "History nerds."

"I'm serious, Ivy," I said. I watched as she took a deep breath and set her fingertips on the edges of the pages. Nothing otherworldly happened except that Ivy swayed a little.

Duncan reached out to steady her as she snatched her hands back. "You okay?" he asked.

"Whoa," Ivy put a hand to her head. "Head rush."

Holly, who'd been silent until now, reached towards the pages with a tentative hand. "Let me see..." Her fingertips barely grazed the pages. They slid neatly away from her and closer to where Ivy, Duncan and I stood. Holly squeaked jumping back.

I narrowed my eyes at Ivy.

"I did *not* do that!" Ivy scowled at me.

Gwen patted her arm. "I know you didn't, honey. I would have felt the energy surge if you had."

"If I didn't know better," I gave a half-laugh, "I'd think the pages were alive or something."

“And they don’t like me,” Holly pouted.

“That’s a good thing,” Bran said to her.

Duncan picked up the pages, placing them in the tissue, and then the archival box Bran had ready. “I’ll ask my mother about the reactions the pages cause and how they *behave*, I suppose, when I see her tonight. We are going to dinner, and I can bring her up to speed on the newest discovery.”

“That’s good,” Gwen said. “Now we need to store these somewhere safe. Bran, I’d like you to load the images up on a new flash drive, and I will see that it is stored in a separate location.”

“Like a safe deposit box,” Aunt Faye suggested.

“That’s where we stored the first flash drive,” Gwen said with a smile.

***

Within a week, the family seemed to settle back into whatever passed for normal. The Halloween— Samhain — decorations came down, and the mantle in the family room had been shifted to creamy colored pumpkins and a golden brown floral display for Thanksgiving.

Fall break was over, I was back in class, and knee deep in my studies at the Museum. I was assigned a rotation working in the archives, and it gave me access to many older books and journals in the museum’s collection. Whenever I had the chance, I carefully went through the books, and while I didn’t find any information about the town's *magickal* history, I did learn more about the families who had immigrated here along with the Bishops.

Marie Rousseau held an open house for the official grand opening of her tattoo parlor, and Duncan and I had fun attending that. The shop had a gift section in the front half, and the tattoo area was in the back. The ceiling of the shop had been painted a dark purple with little golden stars. Twisty branches hovered from the ceiling on clear fishing line, and Spanish moss dripped down from the branches along with Mardi Gras beads.

Beautiful decorated bottles of bath salts, potions and waters were arranged on shelves, and I even saw little voodoo dolls tucked here and there. The whole shop had a clever New Orleans vibe, and I knew that Marie would do well with her business. Ivy spent a good hour at the open house going thru the album that held photos of Marie's tattoo designs. While Cypress and Holly carried on a quiet conversation, Ivy had tried to talk me into getting a large black crescent moon tattooed on my right shoulder with the same Celtic knot design like Gwen and my father's. I told her I would wait until she turned eighteen next month, and we'd do it together.

Cypress had discreetly filled me in on the recent developments up at the high school. The injured cheerleaders were recovering, and Leilah was now very subdued. She didn't seem to be causing any more problems for the squad. Also, Cypress informed me, with no small amount of glee, that Leilah was now absolutely terrified of Holly.

With every passing day, Ivy seemed to be more her old self, but Holly had become even more sullen and withdrawn. I felt sorry that she was struggling, and was biding my time there. Part of me wanted to rap her head against a wall and tell her to snap out of it, while another part of me didn't want to cross her.

I would remember what she'd done to Leilah with her magick for a long, long time. I never told anyone... but what I'd seen her do had given me nightmares. Gwen and Aunt Faye had been working with Holly making sure she had a tighter control on her temper and her magick, but those were private lessons, and they did not discuss them with the rest of us. I thought that might have been for the best.

Bran and Officer Lexie were an item now, and whenever Bran's bedroom door was closed, I stayed away from that part of the house. We'd never discussed my bursting in on them, and I avoided him as much as possible. This wasn't hard, as he typically ignored me whenever I was around. I didn't think he was still holding a grudge about me punching him in the nose—part of me knew it went deeper than that. He was having to live with me, the child our father chose over him.

I guess it all came down to my realizing that my older brother not only felt hurt by my mere presence, but that he also didn't want me as a sister. He felt rejected by our father, and I, in turn, felt rejected by my brother. I hoped that, in time, we'd work it out. Either that or I'd simply punch him again. Maybe not the most mature response on my part, but imagining it sure made me smile.

Rebecca Drake-Quinn had come over to view the photographs of the second set of grimoire pages. She wasn't happy that the family wouldn't tell her where they were storing the actual pages, but she graciously accepted the decision, especially after Duncan pointed out the farther away from Thomas the pages were, the better.

Gwen and Rebecca seemed to be on their way to becoming friends again, and I decided to wait until winter break to continue my search in the manor, in case the whole *Sub Rosa* clue still applied to the floral emblems that were worked into the architecture of the house.

The family was slowly working its way back to being whole, and by mid–November, things were going pretty well. Great Aunt Faye showed no signs of ever planning to leave, but the old girl had kept her promise and had been working with me on psychic abilities. I had learned that technically, I was a 'sensitive'— not a Medium. A sensitive, Aunt Faye informed me, could see and interact with ghosts that were stuck in the physical realm. While a Medium acted as a bridge or a messenger for spirits that were on the other side of the veil.

Apparently, I could, in fact, be both snarky and

'sensitive' all at the same time.

I stood at the kitchen stove and put the finishing touches on supper. It was a cold gloomy day, and I wore old jeans, a university sweatshirt and mismatched thick fuzzy socks. The family was mostly at home, but Gwen was still out and on a holiday shopping trip to St. Louis with Rebecca. She had called earlier and told me to save her some supper since she wouldn't be home until later.

I stirred the big cast iron pot I had simmering on the stove and listened to Ivy. She sat at the island and chattered about her plans for Thanksgiving with her father and his family. Holly sat at the end of the counter in a pink hoodie and jeans studying from a big book of spells. She still seemed to be moping. Great Aunt Faye came cruising in wearing killer black pumps, gray slacks and a burgundy, silk kimono. The old girl had nimbly climbed on a tall barstool and was holding court at the island with the twins.

"Bran's home," Aunt Faye announced. A second later, I heard the garage door open.

Bran came in through the potting room, his navy wool coat was damp. "It's really getting nasty out there. It's going back and forth between freezing rain and sleet." He shook the damp from his coat and hung it to dry on the hooks in the potting room.

Holly went to look out one of the kitchen windows. As if on cue, the sleet started making little *pinging* sounds as it bounced off the windows of the manor.

"The storm's come in earlier than they predicted."

"We have more company coming," Aunt Faye announced.

A couple of seconds later, I heard another car out front, and when I glanced out the windows above the kitchen sink, I saw Duncan pull up in his blue truck. He hopped out of the cab and angled the brim down on his ball cap. He ran towards the front porch while the sleet dumped down.

"Ivy, would you go open the door for Duncan?" Aunt Faye asked. From her perch on the barstool, Aunt Faye couldn't have seen out the window.

"Sure." Ivy headed through the family room towards the foyer.

I raised an eyebrow at Aunt Faye, "Impressive," I said at her announcement of Duncan's arrival. In return, she patted her silver hair and smiled at me.

"The roads are going to be bad. I texted mom and told her to stay in the city for the night and not to risk the drive home," Bran said.

"Good idea," I nodded at him and went back to finishing up supper.

"Whatever it is you are cooking smells good enough to make the trip worthwhile," Duncan said as he walked into the kitchen wearing boots, jeans and a heavy work coat. He gave me a kiss and went to hang his outerwear next to Bran's.

"White chicken chili." I told him. "A little something I *conjured* up."

The timer went off on the oven. I grabbed a mitt and pulled a batch of corn bread muffins out. I flipped the muffin tin over and the muffins rolled out on a rack to cool.

"Holly and Ivy, would you get the bowls and plates out and stack them up on the counter?" I asked.

"Gotcha," Ivy said and began to set up.

As I went to rinse out the empty muffin pan, I caught movement in the window above the sink. I stopped and looked. *What was that?* I shrugged, figuring it must have been my own reflection in the window. Then I froze and stared. The reflection was moving. With a feeling of dread coming over me, I held my breath and watched.

I saw a hand reach out and position a white, long stem rose on a wooden surface... As the rose stem was set into place, it finished an arrangement. The final rose had created an upright pentagram.

I came back to present time with a snap. I jumped back from what I had 'seen' in that window, and the muffin tin clattered down into the sink.

"Did you burn your fingers?" Duncan reached out for me as I stood there breathing hard. I swung my gaze past him. In the family room, Ivy was ragging on Bran about his new longer hair while he built a fire in the fireplace. Holly sat on the couch staring off into space.

The girls and Bran were preoccupied, so I said, "I *saw* something."

"What did you see, child?" Aunt Faye asked.

I quietly told them what I had seen in the vision. "That's the second time I've had this particular vision. Once at the masquerade ball and then today. I suppose I have roses on the brain right now..." I shook my head with an effort. I smiled and handed Duncan a metal box grater. "It's probably nothing," I said to them and asked Duncan to grate up some Monterey Jack cheese to top the chili.

Ivy slid back in the kitchen on her thick striped socks. "Can I do anything to help?"

"Sure." I pointed at two avocados and asked her to dice them up in little pieces.

Ivy pushed up the sleeves of her black sweater, "I'm on it."

"I'm not a big fan of avocados." Aunt Faye frowned at the offending produce.

"Don't worry," I smiled at her. "You'll like it."

A short time later, the six of us all sat in front of the family room fireplace with bowls of white chili. I smiled at Aunt Faye's careful tasting of the avocados mixed in her chili.

"This is wonderful," she said after a moment.

"I've never had white chicken chili. It's great," Duncan said as he enthusiastically dug into the bowl.

"Told you." I smirked at him.

Bran cleared his throat. "This *is* very good," he said looking directly at me.

"Thank you," I said, trying to be polite.

Aunt Faye sighed and slapped her bowl down on the

family room coffee table. "How much longer are you two going to act like this?"

"Like what?" Bran and I said together.

"How long are you going to hold a grudge?" Aunt Faye asked Bran pleasantly.

Bran narrowed his eyes. "Until she apologizes for punching me in the face."

"You're going to have a long wait," I said around a mouthful of chili.

"I've held my peace on this topic," Aunt Faye began, "...until now." She glared at the pair of us. "Your family has worked to repair the rift caused by recent events, but you two are still divided. That's not a strong position to be in. Until you both come to terms with the fact that you *are* siblings, and set aside your differences, our enemies will have an advantage over us all."

The room fell silent. I thought about what my great-aunt had said, and I realized that she was right. Merlin strolled in and sat beside the fireplace. He started to groom his paws and stared disapprovingly at me. *Jeez, shamed by a cat and an old Witch.*

"I agree. This conflict is a weakness," Bran said. "It can and will be used against us if we allow it to continue."

"Fine." I set my bowl down on the coffee table. "I'm sorry I punched you in the nose."

"I am sorry for not handling it better," Bran said, almost sounding sincere. "All I can say was that I believed that you *not* knowing I was your brother would keep you safer."

"How's that?"

"I knew that discovering the truth about our father would make you emotionally vulnerable," Bran said. "You were only beginning to come to grips with your magickal talents. Being a full time student, learning magick, and building a new life here with us is a lot to take on. I wanted you to be at full strength and not conflicted over this."

"Okay, I can *almost* see that," I said to him and pointed to the twins. "But you're forgetting that you and I aren't the only ones who were hurt or made vulnerable by that secret."

"I am not now, nor was I ever, *vulnerable*." Bran argued.

"Rejection makes you vulnerable. It hurts, Bran," I said making direct eye contact with my brother. "Whether that rejection is by a parent or by a sibling, it really doesn't matter. It still hurts."

Bran studied me as intently as I did him. "Point taken," he said. "No matter who our biological parents are, whether we are siblings or cousins, we are *family*. We all share in the legacy of magick."

"I guess we all better work on it," Ivy said. "And Holly needs to stop sulking."

"Hey!" Holly glared at her twin.

"I agree," I nudged Holly who sat beside me on the couch. "Blondie, you really need to knock this off. So, you're not perfect... No one is."

"Holly," Duncan said, "You've learned a hard lesson." Holly met his eyes and seemed to be actually listening, so he continued. "Keep in mind that the mark of an adept Witch is one who learns from their mistakes, does not repeat them, and then goes forward."

"I have learned," Holly whispered. "And I am trying to move forward."

"You'll get there," Duncan said confidently.

I leaned against him. "Thanks for helping her," I said.

"No problem," he said.

The family was quiet for a time as we all turned our focus on the meal. After we finished, Duncan had added a few more logs to the fire, and Bran was checking his cell phone. "Anybody want dessert? I made brownies," I said coming back from taking the dishes to the kitchen.

Aunt Faye stiffened in her chair. Before anyone could answer about dessert, she spoke. "Listen to me, you must all pull together now," she said her voice breaking.

"That's a little out of left field…" I said to her.

Aunt Faye ignored me. Her eyes were clear, and she seemed to be looking past us, not at us. "More now than ever before, *you must be strong*," she said.

I shuddered. Aunt Faye seemed to snap back to herself, but the look on her face had my heart beating faster. She had *seen* something.

Before I could ask her what she'd meant, there was a knock on the front door. "I'll get it." I went to the main foyer, opened the door and found Officer Lexie standing in the sleet. "Lexie, come on in."

Lexie stepped in, took her uniform hat off and held it in her hands. "Autumn, is the family all here?" she asked.

"Yes." I frowned at Lexie, who was standing there stiff and so official. *Oh god. Official. She was here in an official capacity.* I thought back to the vision I'd had in the kitchen a few hours ago and the words Aunt Faye had just spoken. My heart started to beat harder in my chest as I silently ushered Lexie into the family room.

"Lexie? What's happened?" Bran said and stood.

"Can we all sit down?" Lexie asked.

I made myself go sit on the couch next to Duncan and the girls. I gripped Duncan's hand. *This is going to be bad.* I sent the thought to him. Aunt Faye was pale and held herself very still. She met my eyes and nodded at me slightly. I saw a tear run down her cheek.

Bran sat back down and waited.

"Bran, Autumn, girls…" Lexie looked at all of us. "I have very bad news. I am sorry to inform you that your mother, Gwen Bishop, has been in a car accident. She was taken to County Hospital. Unfortunately she didn't make it."

"No!" the girls said in unison.

"The roads," Aunt Faye stated. "The roads were icy from the sleet." Merlin leapt up on Aunt Faye's lap, and she wrapped her arms around the cat for comfort.

"That can't be right," Bran said, his voice sounding hollow. "I'd texted mom a couple hours ago and told her to stay in the city..."

"Are you sure? Maybe it's a mistake?" Holly asked.

"I was at the accident scene." Lexie said quietly.

Dead. Aunt Gwen was *dead. Now? After what we'd been through? How could this happen when we were just beginning to come back together?*

The twins started to sob. I blindly reached out, and they both fell into my arms. Duncan wrapped his arms around all of us, holding on as we all cried together. "I'm so sorry," I whispered to the girls. I pressed kisses to each of their heads.

I knew Lexie had delivered the news as quickly as possible on purpose. When my father had died, and the police came to inform us, they'd said close to the same. Lexie went to Bran. She hunkered down in front of his chair and laid her hands on Bran's knees.

"I truly am sorry for your loss," Lexie said.

Bran's chest heaved once, and tears welled up in his eyes. Lexie held out her arms, and he leaned into her embrace.

They held each other. I clutched onto the girls, and Duncan held me.

Outside the sleet came down and beat against the windows. The wind howled around the manor, almost as if it was grieving with the family. Maybe it was.

EPILOGUE

The November sky was a hard and brilliant blue. A cold wind blew, stripping any remaining leaves from icy tree branches. While scarves and heavy coats rippled in the wind, I sat with my cousins, Great Aunt Faye, and my brother at the side of Gwen's grave. I studied the large crowd that had gathered for my aunt's funeral. I saw all of the coven members, their families, Holly and Ivy's father and his family, and many other people from the community. Gwen Bishop had been respected and loved.

An awning had been erected blocking some of the bitterly cold wind, but not all of it. They had ushered the immediate family in to sit in five metal chairs at the graveside. First, Aunt Faye, then Bran. Holly, Ivy were third and fourth, and lastly— me. Lexie stood behind Bran, and Marie and Cypress Rousseau were right behind the girls. Duncan and his mother stood behind me. I was grateful for Rebecca's kindness and Duncan's hand on my shoulder.

I tried to focus on the flowers, and not the casket. The sympathy arrangements that had been placed along side of the coffin were filled with brilliant and bright autumn flowers. Their vivid colors seemed defiant somehow, and I knew that Gwen would have approved.

To my relief, very few people had worn mourning black to the funeral. Instead, I had seen lots of white and plenty of bright colors. I tugged my long, blue skirt down over the top of my suede dress boots and fastened the top button on my purple wool coat in defense against the cold that seemed determined to blow down my neck. I felt Ivy shift beside me, and I squeezed her gloved hand.

She turned her head to look at me, and her dark sunglasses concealed her eyes but not her grief. She held Holly's hand too, and they leaned into each other. Holly's brilliant hair shone against the pale blue winter wool, while Ivy sat shivering in her long burgundy coat. Bran sat in his dark blue wool trench coat staring directly ahead, his eyes never leaving the casket. Aunt Faye was stoic. Her hair was in an elegant twist that even the bitter wind couldn't unravel. She wore a black and white Houndstooth cape over a long white woolen dress. A crescent shaped pin of garnets sparkled on her cloak.

The officiant, a Priestess, Bran had informed me, concluded the ceremony. "Merry Meet. Merry Part. And Merry Meet again," she said.

The group echoed the words back.

The funeral director handed each of the five of us a white rose. We were to step forward one by one and place a long stemmed flower on the lid of the coffin now that the ceremony was completed.

Seeing Aunt Faye, Bran, and the girls do so was brutally hard. I watched as they arranged the flowers one by one into the shape of an upright pentagram. My stomach roiled. It made me recall the vision I'd had at the Ball and again on the day of Gwen's car accident.

I went last. I tried to be strong, but a sob escaped anyway. "Merry Part, Gwen," I said, and carefully placed the rose with the others so the star shape was completed.

The Priestess came forward to shake all of our hands, and the funeral director started to usher us slowly away from the graveside. We were quietly escorted to the funeral home's limousine to be driven back to the manor. However, before we could leave, the five of us ended up standing in a line accepting a few last condolences. People seemed determined for one last handshake or a parting hug no matter how cold it was.

Marie Rousseau handled the people who remained, subtly shifting folks away. She stood tall and strong, her red coat was a bright splash of color against the dreary, icy cemetery. I heard her invite the twins' father and stepmother back to the manor for food now that the ceremony was complete. I waited until she was free, and I went and hugged her hard.

"Thank you for helping us," I said. My voice cracked with emotion. I held on while she squeezed me tight.

"Girl, no worries. I got your back." Marie said. "I'll head to the manor and get things started."

As Marie and Cypress left, Duncan came to stand with me and put an arm around my shoulders. He'd been an unshaking source of support for me over the past few days. I was beyond grateful for him being at my side. The familiar little zip of energy when we touched was still there, but muffled somewhat from the sadness of the day.

I turned to shake hands with a member from the museum board, and as I murmured my thanks to him for coming, I saw a lone figure walking towards the gravesite. It was a man wearing a long grey overcoat. Sunglasses shielded his face, and a hat was tipped down over his brow.

As Holly and Ivy climbed into the limo, I watched the elegant man, who carried a single, long-stemmed red rose, stop and stand at the side of my aunt's open grave with his head down. Suddenly, I felt my hair stand up on end. *It was Thomas Drake.*

"Stay with my family," I said to Duncan, marching back through the cemetery.

"Autumn, wait," Duncan said, his voice pitched low.

"I mean it," I said from over my shoulder. "Keep them all safe."

My knee length, black boots crunched softly as I moved quickly down the frozen gravel path. As I walked towards Thomas Drake, I heard a crow calling from somewhere close by. Thomas angled his head up as he too focused on the crow that had landed on the top of a nearby oak tree. I wasn't sure what amazed me more... the man's audacity to come to the funeral, or that I managed not to make a scene the moment I recognized him.

"You are not welcome here." I said, my anger making me brave as I faced him from the opposite side of the casket.

Thomas removed his sunglasses. To my shock, I could see that he was grieving. "I came to pay my respects," he said and tucked his sunglasses into his breast pocket. "Your aunt was a brave and wise woman."

"It's a little late to be remorseful you son of a bitch," I kept my voice down. I had no illusions that we'd have more than a few moments to speak. "It's your curse that started this. All of the deaths, the accidents... *you* caused them with your dark magick."

Thomas looked me straight in the eye. "I did not curse your family."

"Liar!" I snarled.

"I have *never* lied to you," Thomas' voice was soft, but his eyes were intense. "I tried to warn you the Blood Moon Grimoire is powerful. The more pieces you assemble, the more dangerous it becomes. Clearly you have found more pages. You must return them all to me for your own safety."

"So you're telling me you want the grimoire pages back so you can *protect* everyone?" I scoffed at him. "That's real noble of you."

Thomas reached across the casket and gripped my coat sleeve. "I did not curse your family twenty years ago, that was the destructive purpose of the grimoire."

"Let go of me right now— or I will knock you on your ass," I said between my teeth.

A funeral home employee stepped up, "Is there a problem here?" he asked.

"No." Thomas focused on him, and the man's face went blank. "Leave us," Thomas said. The man turned and walked away without another word.

"You stand over my aunt's casket, do magick on innocent bystanders and expect me to believe you?" I said.

"There is always a price to be paid for those who do not understand or respect the grimoire's power." He gripped my sleeve tighter, apparently, to make his point. "Julian's exposure to the leather bindings was enough to send him into madness."

I yanked my arm back and considered. *So, they had the fourth piece the bindings.* "You talk like the book is alive," I said.

"It is sentient. Haven't you noticed that the pages change?"

Oh god. So far Duncan and I had been the only ones

who could make the pages come to life. That meant Thomas could as well. My thoughts were interrupted when I noticed that more crows had flown in and landed in the surrounding trees.

"How you have managed to not be tainted by the book is the real mystery," he said. "And it's one we must solve." Thomas gently laid the red rose on the casket. He brushed his gloved fingers over the casket lid and stepped back. "Let me work with you and your family. Only together can we bind the power of the Blood Moon Grimoire once and for all."

"Thomas Drake." Great Aunt Faye, the last person I had expected to appear, stepped up. She put her arm around my waist and stood with me. Looking feisty and tough, she stared the man down.

"Aunt Faye, I—"

"You've been brave enough," Aunt Faye cut me off, but gave me an approving nod. She focused her full attention onto Thomas. "Today is not the day for topics such as these."

"You know this must be settled and soon." Thomas scowled at us. He took a breath to argue, but before any sound came out, I felt Aunt Faye draw up an amazing amount of magickal energy.

Oh shit. I wanted to duck for cover, but I was at the center of that storm. With no where to go, I could only stand by her side. I made a split second decision and tucked my left arm around her waist firmly linking us together. I opened myself up energetically and lent Aunt

Faye whatever magick she needed.

Somehow, I managed to stay steady when her energy lashed out.

Thomas Drake was knocked back two full steps. He staggered but caught himself on a nearby tombstone. He stared in shock at my great-aunt.

"As the head of the Bishop family, I am the one to say when that time will be." Aunt Faye inclined her head regally. "Rest assured Thomas, *I* will speak with you when my family is ready and not one minute before."

Thomas Drake nodded at that, tipped his hat in deference to my great-aunt, turned and walked silently away from the grave.

"Come with me now, dear." Aunt Faye tugged me away from the gravesite, and we started walking towards the limousine still linked with our arms around each others waist.

The noise of our footsteps on the gravel path seemed overly loud after what had happened. "That was some pretty impressive magick you just threw down..." I shivered in reaction from that and from the cold. "You are one scary old lady, you know that?" I gave her waist a gentle squeeze.

"Don't you forget it." She squeezed me right back.

Even with the sadness of the day, I couldn't help but smile a little. "I love you. You old Witch."

"And I love you. Don't worry now, we will get through this, together."

Somehow, hearing her say that— I believed it. While dozens of crows circled and called above us, we walked through the icy graveyard towards the waiting limousine and our family.

The End

Legacy of Magick: Book Three
Coming January 2016

30558375R00172

Made in the USA
San Bernardino, CA
16 February 2016